Blue Silk Stalkings

Amanda Rittenhouse Mystery #6

Blue Silk Stalkings

Amanda Rittenhouse Mystery #6

KATE MERRILL

SAPPHIRE BOOKS

SALINAS, CALIFORNIA

This and other Sapphire Books titles can be found at
www.sapphirebooks.com

Acknowledgements

Special thanks to Chris and the wonderful team at Sapphire Books, my amazing editor, Tara Young, who always goes the extra mile, and all the readers who have followed Diana and Amanda Rittenhouse for eleven years to this, their final adventure.

Dedication

To THE MOUNTAINS of WESTERN NORTH
CAROLINA.
They inspired my books, including this one,
which includes scenes in Asheville and its River Arts
District.
They inspired Thomas Wolfe and F. Scott Fitzgerald.

SEPTEMBER 26, 2024
HURRICANE HELENE
stormed through these beloved mountains.
So much was destroyed.

May the vitality and resilience of the people of WNC
serve to restore their unique utopia
and make it better than before. In the meantime…
those magical mountains are forever memorialized
in literature, song, the visual arts,
and the hearts of all who love them.

Chapter One

Till death do us part...

It was that magic golden time in late afternoon when the sun is low and the shadows are long and nature seems to hold her breath before sighing into sunset. Fewer than one hundred rented folding chairs were set up in the yard, divided equally in rows of eight to either side of a grassy aisle. It was an intimate gathering for a wedding, but every chair was filled. The venue was set up midway between Carl Fisher's elegant house that seemed to grow from the land and Ron Dunifon's large, rustic barn where both men had their art studios. All chairs faced west to where the ceremony would be held on the crest of a gently elevated hillside overlooking fields, forests, and the distant rolling mountains. The grooms had lovingly planned it that way, so that afterward the guests could behold one of Carl's beloved sunsets.

"I can't believe it's really happening," Amanda Rittenhouse said as she took Sara Orlando's hand.

"I know, we've waited almost two years for this," Sara replied.

A chill hung in the late October air. Amanda wore a long-sleeved silk blouse, but Sara's arms were bare but for a shawl draped over her shoulders. Amanda appreciated the warmth radiating from Sara's skin and moved a little closer. The low light glistened on Sara's long, silken black hair and cast her classic features and chiseled cheekbones into sharp relief. When Sara turned to smile at Amanda, her full lips, emerald eyes, and porcelain complexion were illuminated in a moment of epiphany, as they had been seven years ago, when Amanda first laid eyes on her. Amanda had just moved to North Carolina from Sarasota, Florida, and she and Sara were both exhibiting at Metrolina, an arts and antiques expo in Charlotte. They had both been twenty-eight, and since then, time had flown by in a whirlwind of passionate chaos. Amanda wished to slow down time and solidify it into something permanent.

A hush fell on the audience, and heads turned as four men in dark suits exited the barn and moved to a makeshift stage erected near a stand of rhododendrons. Two carried violins, one a viola, and the fourth approached a cello already set up onstage. As the quartet settled, Amanda recognized several familiar faces in the audience from when she had visited Asheville once before. Sara and she had been going through a rough patch then, and Amanda, a professional sculptor, was considering relocating to the mountains. Fortunately, they had patched up their differences during that fateful visit, but not before enduring some life-threatening mayhem and several embarrassing moments. Amanda recognized Gina, the woman responsible for those embarrassing moments, and plotted how to avoid her after this event.

At that moment, Sara lifted Amanda's hand and kissed Amanda's "friendship with benefits" ring. "How are you holding up, babe?" Sara whispered. "Could this be any more romantic?" Amanda's ring was silver with inlaid turquoise. Sara had given it to her hidden in a blueberry muffin for Amanda's thirtieth birthday.

Amanda reached across Sara's lap and captured Sara's left hand. She kissed Sara's silver ring inlaid with ruby, which Amanda had given her in a cranberry muffin on Sara's thirtieth.

"I'm so happy for them," Amanda said. "Lord knows, Carl and Ron deserve to make it official, after all these years." Carl was seventy-five, a nationally renowned potter. Ron, twenty years younger than Carl, was a practical nurse and aspiring painter who had loved and cared for Carl for over two decades. Those cynical souls who thought Ron was after Carl's vast wealth were badly mistaken. Amanda had never seen a more devoted couple.

A thin cloud passed over the sun, and the quartet began playing a solemn, measured tune Amanda remembered from her high school graduation.

"That's Pachelbel's Canon in D," Sara informed her. "I remember it from an old movie called *Ordinary People*. The film's about teen suicide, really great."

Really? Leave it to Sara, a connoisseur of classic films, to recall the title. Leave it to Sara the shrink to appreciate the subject matter.

Just as the sun broke through the cloud, everyone turned toward the house. Carl and Ron stepped out onto the deck and began the long stroll down the grassy aisle. Arm in arm, they moved like a grandfather lion king and a long-legged giraffe. They wore dark tuxedos. Carl's bright blue shirt enhanced his sparkling blue eyes and set off his luxuriant mane of snow white hair. Ron's pink shirt and black bow tie worked well with his pale complexion, dark hair, and eyes. They were grand.

"Look, Carl's not limping," Sara said.

"He looks younger than I remember," Amanda agreed. The ceremony had been delayed due to Carl's health issues, including heart surgery. Whatever procedures had been done appeared to be working because Carl, who reminded Amanda of her beloved Grandpa Whitaker, looked more vigorous than ever.

As the couple reached the altar, a buxom, middle-aged woman bustled from the barn and approached them. The short-haired blonde, likely the officiant, was grinning ear to ear.

"My God, Mandy! Do you recognize her?" Sara exclaimed.

"Our good friend Chief Toni Hall! She must be a lay minister, as well as a police officer." Toni was also a cat-loving lesbian. Amanda and Sara had a checkered relationship with the woman since Toni had almost arrested Amanda for theft. In the end, they'd all become good pals.

Toni held up her plump hands, the quartet stopped playing, and the audience silenced as the service began. Amanda was determined not to cry, as she always did at weddings. Sara, who had carefully honed a stoic couch-side manner for her patients, would not shed a tear. To distract herself from the beautiful heartfelt vows being spoken at the altar, Amanda concentrated on her personal romantic dilemma and gripped Sara's hand. Yet by the time Carl and Ron exchanged rings, Amanda was in an emotional state.

The ring was burning a hole in her pocket. Not literally, of course. No, Grandma Vivian's family heirloom engagement diamond was actually hidden away in Amanda's travel suitcase, wrapped in tissue in a compact in her makeup bag. Grandma's ring was a sacred trust. The ring had been stolen last year after Grandma's murder but eventually recovered. Grandma's will stated that the ring should "go to either

Amanda or her brother, Robby. Whoever married first shall have the option of keeping it or giving it to his or her spouse."

At the time, Amanda had dared not hope for marriage. Over the years, Sara had made her views on gay marriage clear: "Who needs a marriage license to prove they love each other?" Lately, however, Amanda sensed a softening in Sara's position as several friends of theirs had tied the knot. Lately, the need to propose had become a nagging obsession for Amanda, a way to solidify their lives into permanence, into a "till death do us part" kind of commitment. Problem was, Amanda didn't know how, when, or where to pop the question. Indeed, she was terrified that Sara would laugh—or, God forbid, say no.

"I now pronounce you legally married!" Chief Toni whooped with glee. "Go on and kiss, you guys!"

Suddenly, everyone was standing, laughing, clapping, and hollering as tears welled up and poured from Amanda's eyes. Sara dragged Amanda to her feet and hugged her.

"Awesome, right?" Sara crowed.

Amanda gazed at her loved one. "Hey, are you okay?"

Miracle of miracles, Sara was crying.

Chapter Two

A secret transaction...

Amanda and Sara drifted with the crowd onto the large wooden deck, where a free bar was doing a swift business, serving everything from champagne to complex mixed drinks. Through the plate glass windows, Sara saw servers setting up a buffet-style feast just inside the house. Embarrassed by her emotional display after the wedding, she walked a few steps ahead of Amanda, discreetly drying her eyes on the hem of her shawl. Then she glanced up at the distant mountains. They looked like waves children had cut from black construction paper and then pasted them onto a pastel, poster paint sky.

"It's getting chilly out here," she told Mandy. "Grab us some drinks, and I'll run upstairs and get your sweater."

"Sounds like a plan." Mandy gave Sara's arm a little squeeze, then hurried off in search of a rum and tonic. Sara knew Mandy would choose red wine for her because they'd be eating Italian, Carl's favorite.

Thinking of Carl, Sara worried. How would she ever get him alone, so they could complete their secret transaction? He and Ron were the center of attention, as they should be, but somehow, she'd have to snag a private moment of his time.

Inching her way past the waiters busy in the big, modern kitchen, Sara inhaled the tantalizing aromas of bubbling tomato sauce and hot garlic bread, and her stomach growled. They hadn't eaten since breakfast in their condo in Davidson, miles away and hours ago, and she was starving. Glancing under the kitchen table, she saw that Barney's bed was empty. Likely Carl's ancient bloodhound had been locked away in the first-floor master bedroom, where he was probably salivating over the delicious smells wafting through the house. Poor thing. Maybe later Sara could sneak him a yummy piece of sausage.

When she finally made it to the grand entrance foyer, Sara was startled by a hand on her shoulder.

"Sara Orlando, is that really you?"

Sara figured the tall, elderly woman who'd surprised her had just emerged from the hall powder room. The woman still wore her long silver hair in a braid, and her dress, a woolen sheath that had seen better days, smelled vaguely of mothballs.

"Gladys Uplander, it's great to see you!"

"Huh, I bet you thought I wouldn't have the nerve to show up," Gladys said in the deep, Alabama accent that reminded Sara of Tallulah Bankhead.

No, Sara had not expected to see the merry widow at the wedding because when Mandy and Sara had visited before, Gladys had been engaged to marry Carl. When Carl proclaimed his sexual preference for Ron, it had seriously upset Gladys's apple cart.

Gladys continued, "Oh, don't worry, Carl and I resolved our differences, and we've remained friends. But I can't talk now. We'll catch up later. Now I better see to the mess those young caterers are making in the kitchen."

With that, Gladys bustled off and away. Apparently, she still felt a proprietary obligation to organize Carl's life. Sara chuckled and hurried to the spiral staircase leading to the second floor. As she climbed, she wondered if it had been a good idea to accept Carl's invitation to spend the night. Sara was apprehensive that Gina Molerno had also been invited to stay over. After all, they were all from the Charlotte area, and it was a long drive home. She knew Carl was very fond of Gina. She had been one of his art students, and Carl had been Gina's mentor.

Last time, Mandy and Gina had come to Asheville without Sara. When Sara finally arrived to patch up her differences with Mandy, she had found the two women in bed together. Both swore that nothing sexual had happened, that they had simply collapsed onto the bed in a drunken stupor and innocently fallen asleep. Sara had totally believed them after hearing the full story. Still, she was jealous and hurt and had suffered several agonizing moments of uncertainty. Now, in spite of Mandy telling Sara that Gina was fun and funny and that they could all be good friends, Sara had no desire to spend time with the woman. On the other hand, maybe Gladys was right: Let bygones be bygones.

Earlier that afternoon, Ron had assigned Sara and Mandy that same upstairs bedroom with that same queen-sized bed. Sara rushed into the room and quickly found Mandy's pretty white sweater coat and slung it over her arm. She also dug into her purse and retrieved the wad of hundred-dollar bills. She didn't know how much her secret purchase would cost. It wouldn't be cheap, but it would be worth every penny. But only if Mandy said yes.

Sighing, Sara glanced at her reflection in the mirror above the antique dresser. Her eyes were slightly red from her crying jag at the wedding, but her mascara hadn't run. All in all, she looked as presentable as a woman could hope to look when set on a perilous journey that would define her happiness, or lack thereof, for the rest of her life. Being a psychiatrist didn't help. When it came to personal mental stability, she was hopeless. *Physician, heal thyself!*

Sara slipped the money into the roomy pocket of her flowing dress trousers and started down the staircase. Everything was her fault because she'd given mixed signals to Mandy. How many times had Sara declared that marriage was unnecessary, only to turn around and claim she wanted commitment? The month they met, same-sex marriage became the law of the land. The very day *Obergefell v. Hodges* was decided, Sara's exact words to Mandy had been: "Those crazy folks who are into relationship commitment? To each his own, but I don't buy it."

Then the following summer, when they'd met a happily married lesbian couple at Cape Hatteras, Mandy had been enthralled, but Sara had again said gay marriage was silly. Now Sara feared she had disparaged the idea so many times that she would sound like a hypocrite, or at least seem insincere, if she changed her mind. But the desire to marry Mandy had crept up on her gradually, like sinking into a warm, soothing bath. Now the desire was drowning her. She couldn't breathe until Mandy accepted her. But how and when should she ask?

Sara was so distracted by the dilemma that when she reached the bottom of the stairs and stepped into the foyer, she clumsily bumped into Carl Fisher, who was rushing from the master bedroom.

"Whoops, sorry!" she sputtered as Carl stabilized from the collision. He got his balance and gave her a big hug. She kissed his cheek. "Oh, congratulations, Carl! The wedding was absolutely beautiful, and I'm so happy for you both!"

"Me too, Sara. Better late than never."

Carl had changed from his tux to comfy corduroy trousers and an old green pullover sweater and looked more like himself. "I tried to get Ron to change, too, but he wanted to stay fancy till the guests go. He's holding court right now at the dinner buffet. Me, I just fed old Barney and wish they'd all go home, so I can take my husband to bed." Carl hesitated and then held Sara at arm's length. "Oh, not *you*, Sara. I don't want you to leave. In fact, we'd like to keep you and Amanda nearby permanently. Where is she, by the way?"

"I suspect she's holding a drink for me and thinks I've abandoned her."

"Perfect!" Carl dragged her down the hall toward the master suite. "I've got what you wanted, and I think it's magnificent. We'll conclude our business, and you'll be back with your lady in a jiffy."

He guided her into the bedroom and closed the door. The room was as she remembered: two walls of shelves displayed Carl's stoneware pottery, a set of sofas grouped on a well-used oriental carpet, and Barney curled up on a quilt near the bed. The bloodhound smiled and wagged and thumped his tail. Sara knelt and patted him, while Carl brought a small, blue silk box from his dresser.

She was still on her knees when Carl ceremoniously handed her the box. He held out his free hand to her.

"Get up now, girl. You're not fixing to propose to me, are you?"

Sara laughed and stood, her hands trembling as she accepted the treasure. Carl was a mover and shaker in the River Arts District, where he had exhibited for many years. The community included a renowned jeweler, whose work Sara had admired when they'd last visited, so she had persuaded Carl to commission the ring she would offer Mandy. She was almost afraid to look…

Holding her breath, Sara opened the lid. Nestled in its white silk slot, the narrow silver ring displayed the concentric circles of the infinity symbol. Inside one circle was round turquoise for Mandy, in the other, a ruby for Sara. The design was delicate and graceful. When she slipped it on her finger, it was lightweight and not at all bulky. It was perfect.

Her eyes misted for the second time that day. "Oh, thank you, Carl. The artist truly brought my concept to life." She tucked the ring away and put the box in her pocket. At the same time, she brought out the cash. "How much do I owe you?"

Carl wanted her to accept the ring as a gift, but Sara refused. "It has to come from me, you know that, right?" He finally agreed and accepted her money. "I only hope Mandy accepts it," she murmured.

Carl squared his shoulders and crossed his arms, pinning Sara with his sapphire eyes. "Amanda would be crazy not to accept you, and in my experience, Amanda is perfectly sane. In a few months, Ron and I will be attending *your* wedding."

From your mouth to God's ear, Sara prayed.

Chapter Three

Not the jealous type...

Where the hell was Sara? Amanda shivered. Balancing her rum and tonic in one hand and Sara's wine in the other, it was impossible to hug herself and warm up. And where was Carl? Poor Ron had been glad-handing and hosting the crowd on his own all through the happy hour, and it didn't seem fair. Amanda's smile felt frozen as she attempted chitchat with strangers, and she felt stranded, even worse than attending an art opening. Like many creative souls, she was an introvert at heart, while Sara was always the life of the party. Together, they seemed to balance each other out in the big bad world.

※ ※ ※ ※

Sara and Carl left the bedroom together and rushed toward the kitchen. Guests were already drifting inside, seeking warmth and food, their voices and laughter escalating as the alcohol did its work and they lost their inhibitions.

"Ron's gonna kill me!" Carl moaned.

"Mandy's gonna kill me first," Sara said, picking up her pace. Carl would easily spot Ron, whose great height made his head visible above any crowd, but Mandy would be hiding in some quiet corner wondering why it took Sara so long to bring a damned sweater. She would not be a happy camper.

⚘⚘⚘⚘⚘

Amanda finally spotted Carl elbowing his way to Ron, and moments later, the newlyweds embraced. She hoped Sara was close behind, and she started moving toward the glass sliders opening into the house. Suddenly, two arms slipped around Amanda's waist from behind, pulling her backward.

"Where do you think you're going, Amanda Rittenhouse? You can't get away from me that easy!"

Amanda's breath caught in her throat, and she almost dropped the drinks as her whole body tensed. She'd recognize that low, gravelly cigarette voice anywhere. There was no escape, so she awkwardly squirmed around to face the woman. Before she knew what was happening, the woman took the drinks from her hands and set them on a nearby table. Seconds later, she was in Gina's arms, smelling her familiar, tangy perfume and feeling the press of Gina's big breasts against her ribcage. The sensation was upsetting but undeniably sexy.

⚘⚘⚘⚘⚘

Sara saw Mandy walking in her direction, across the deck toward the kitchen. The sight took her breath away. Mandy looked beautiful tonight in the blue silk shirt that precisely matched her eyes. Her short, duck-soft blond hair glowed in the warm light from the tiki torches ringing the deck, while her tall, athletic body moved gracefully with each stride. Yet Sara sensed the tension as Mandy scanned the crowd, looking for her.

She seemed lost, as she often did at such events. She also looked irritated. Sara knew she was in trouble.

At the same time, Sara saw someone quickly approach Mandy from behind. The stalker seemed intent with a mischievous glint in her smoky gray eyes and a naughty twist to her lips. Suddenly, the shorter woman wrapped her arms around Mandy, pulling Mandy against her. A look of panic crossed Mandy's face as the woman snatched the drinks from Mandy's hands and set them aside. Somehow, Mandy got maneuvered around and ended up in the stranger's arms. The embrace did not look platonic. *What the fuck?*

Shoving aside two guys blocking her way, Sara inched closer and then tapped Mandy's shoulder. "Hey, babe, am I interrupting something?" As Mandy struggled free, her eyes as round as Delft Blue saucers, Sara recognized Gina Molerno.

"Hi there, Sara." Gina flashed a wicked smile. "I was wondering when you'd show up. I was just enjoying a moment of quality time with your lady. Hope you don't mind." Gina extended her small hand like a peace offering.

Naturally, Sara shook it. The multiple rings on Gina's fingers bit a bit too firmly against Sara's flesh. "No problem, Gina. You know I'm not the jealous type."

This was true, up to a point. Sara had come to terms with Gina's flirting long ago and understood it was relatively harmless. She studied Gina more closely. Sara and Gina were about the same height, but Gina was at least fifteen years older than she. Gina still wore her short black hair in a retro punk cut, gelled and peaked like a cactus. Her amazing smoky gray eyes were almost violet, her mouth was wide and sensual, her figure as voluptuous as a Playboy bunny. But the years had taken a toll with deeper lines etched into her pale complexion. Aside from that, she had not changed.

Sara smiled at Mandy, whose irritation seemed to have dissipated in a flush of embarrassment, and she seemed at a loss for words.

"Hey, Gina, aren't you going to introduce me?"

Sara had been aware of a very tall woman standing a few paces behind Gina. Until that moment, her face had been in shadow, but when she came close and turned toward them, Sara was struck by several things at once: The woman was at least six feet tall and powerfully built. Her long, wild red hair was in a ponytail, but the damp evening air threatened to kink it free of its bounds. Her eyes were green, amused, and seemed to carry the weight of the world in their depths. She was somewhat older than Gina, but to Sara, infinitely more attractive—the type one might call "handsome," rather than "pretty."

Gina introduced her. "Sorry. This is Red Calendar, my partner."

≈ ≈ ≈ ≈

Amanda was stunned. She had heard so much about Red from Gina. She knew that Gina and Red had been off-again, on-again lovers for decades. Indeed, Gina had been in one of her many rebounds from Red when Gina attempted a fling with Amanda. Carl had told her that Red was the love of Gina's life.

Amanda also knew that Red was a detective with the Charlotte police and that Gina's brother, Rick Molerno, was Red's longtime partner on the force. Finally, Amanda knew that the daily risks Red faced on the job, coupled with Red's refusal to quit police work, were the cause of their many breakups.

"Wow, are you guys back together now?" Amanda blurted out.

"Together almost a year." Red laughed and took Gina's hand.

"We're together *for now*," Gina amended. "But last summer, Red almost got herself killed, so I almost split then."

Was Gina kidding? Amanda couldn't tell. She was so lost in speculation, she hardly noticed as Sara helped her slip into the warm sweater. Amanda rarely had to look up to any woman, but she did so as she studied Red.

"You almost got killed?" Amanda asked.

Before Red could answer, Sara handed her the rum and tonic, picked up her wine, and wrapped her arm around Amanda's waist.

"It sounds like Red has quite a story to tell," Sara said, "but I'm cold and hungry, and I say we move this party inside."

Chapter Four

The dark side...

They loaded their platters with Italian cuisine, then moved across the foyer to a small study, which offered some privacy. Like Amanda and Sara, Gina and Red didn't seem to know many of the guests. Were they "fifth wheels" or four squares seeking a round hole? Or was Amanda's tortured analogy a byproduct of her general anxiety: worry about proposing to Sara, surrounded by strangers, and a close encounter with Gina? Whatever. She welcomed some peace and quiet.

The room was comforting with gently burning logs in a stone fireplace and classical guitar music drifting in from hidden speakers. Two hunter green sofas faced each other beside the fire with a square mission oak coffee table between them, and shelves bulging with books lined the walls. Amanda and Sara sat on one sofa, Gina and Red on the other, and for a few awkward moments, they stared at one another.

"It was a beautiful ceremony," Red said, breaking the ice. After everyone echoed that sentiment, Red dipped into the deep pocket of her dark, pirate-like cape and brought out a bottle of Jack Daniels. "Now I don't know if you girls drink this stuff, but it's my poison of choice, and I thought we'd need it tonight."

"Amen!" Amanda quickly agreed. Sara wouldn't go for whiskey, but Amanda wasn't picky. Red was already pouring for herself and Gina.

Sara eyed the bottle. "Are you two driving back to Charlotte tonight?"

Gina laughed. "Nope, Red's an officer of the law, so she doesn't drink and drive, not too far, at any rate. Besides, she got us a room at the Biltmore."

"No way!" Amanda exclaimed. "Is this a special occasion?" She'd heard that a night at the magnificent Biltmore Estate cost eight hundred bucks.

"Every night with Gina is a special occasion," Red said.

Amanda saw Sara's subtle eye roll and knew what she was thinking. Such an extravagance was over the top because surely a city police officer didn't make that kind of money. Either Red was badly smitten, or she was planning to propose to Gina. Then again, Amanda had a one-track mind.

She took another fast swallow of rum, picked up her fork, and took a huge bite of baked lasagna. The perfectly melded flavors of ricotta, parmesan, and ground beef calmed the butterflies in her stomach. Taking Amanda's cue, Sara dug into antipasto from a charcuterie wreath and licked her lips. Red ate chicken cacciatore, and Gina had something called pumpkin risotto. Amanda didn't know much about these gourmet dishes, but she knew her way around Italian desserts and planned to save room for the raspberry tiramisu she'd seen on the buffet table. Far as she was concerned, the best part of eating was it limited the need for conversation.

The others managed to talk between mouthfuls. Sara asked Gina how her career as a painter was coming, and she told them she was now exhibiting, along with Ron, in Carl's coveted space in the River Arts District. This caused Amanda a pang of envy.

She'd had an opportunity to show her sculpture there, but she'd let the chance pass her by. Sara asked if Gina was still teaching Sara's twin brother, Marc, who painted abstracts as a hobby. But Marc had dropped out of Gina's class and moved on to more rewarding pursuits, like chasing gorgeous women, his top priority in life.

Gina and Red were curious about Sara's work as a psychiatrist. She told them she worked for the city of Charlotte as a counselor to at-risk people, mostly teenagers, parolees, and people with debilitating addictions. It wasn't glamorous, it didn't pay for extravagant nights at the Biltmore, but Sara loved it. Amanda knew it was a "calling" for Sara, not a job. Amanda was surprised and pleased to hear Sara talking about her work because she rarely opened up about it, especially to strangers.

The effort seemed to have exhausted Sara, however, because she soon excused herself, saying she was going for more wine and a rum and tonic refill for Amanda. The moment Sara left, two pairs of eyes focused on Amanda, and Gina began the interrogation.

"So, Mandy, the last time we met, you'd just completed that monumental sculpture of a bird in flight for Wells Fargo. We met at its unveiling at the bank, remember?"

"Yes, and the next day, you drove me to Asheville, and I met Carl and Ron."

"What an adventure, right?" Gina winked.

More like a roller coaster flying off the track. "Past history. Let's not rehash it, okay?"

Gina shrugged. "So what are you working on now? Any big new commissions?"

"Afraid not. I'm living on bread and butter, my

small sculptures." Several local galleries were selling Amanda's affordable little welded pieces: flowers, funny animals, and sailboats. She badly needed another major commission, like the two she'd landed at fifty thousand apiece since she'd moved to North Carolina. She was struggling to pay her half of the rent for their condo in Davidson, even though Amanda's mom owned the condo and rented it to them cheap. She'd have to earn more money if she ever hoped to buy a house with Sara, if they got that far.

"Well," Gina continued, "the offer still stands. You can share space here in Asheville with Ron and me. We'd love to have you."

"Thanks, Gina," she answered quietly. Amanda would consider it. She had to.

꙰꙰꙰꙰꙰

Sara stole a half bottle of red wine for herself and mixed a carafe of rum and tonics for Mandy. She added an assortment of dessert goodies to the tray and headed back to the study. She figured they'd need the drinks before the night was over to keep up with Gina and Red. Although Red seemed to be pacing her consumption. Likely Red was the designated driver. As she walked, Sara realized she was exhausted from talking about her work at the clinic, yet their new friends hadn't pressed her for gory details, which she appreciated. In fact, their first meeting seemed to be going quite well. Maybe Mandy was right, and they'd see them again socially. Gina was Gina, an outrageous force of nature, but Red was an enigma, and Sara was determined to draw her out.

She entered the study during a lull in conversation

and slid the tray onto the coffee table amid grunts of approval. She refreshed Mandy's drink and filled her own wine glass. She took a seat, a sip, and then pinned Red with her eyes.

"Out on the deck, you said you had a story," Sara began. "I'd like to hear it."

Red took off her cape and leaned forward, elbows propped on her knees. "Gina makes too much of it. I'm here, I'm okay, and we're celebrating now."

"She almost got herself killed last summer!" Gina grabbed Red's arm and hung on tight. "She won't talk about it, but I will. It all started when Red got together with four old friends at a high school reunion, and they tried to re-create what they'd called the True Love Club, when they were teenagers. So these idiot adult women decided to join a dating site online and got themselves hooked up with a serial killer!"

"It wasn't my idea," Red muttered. "I just went along because I knew how dangerous it could be. I wanted to monitor it and keep my friends out of trouble."

"Yeah, Red claims she got involved in the line of duty." Gina scoffed. "She'd just attended a conference on cybercrime and figured she was an expert."

"I shouldn't have let it happen." Red stared into her whiskey glass. "I was supposed to be the responsible one."

"But it didn't work out that way, did it?" Gina interrupted. She balled her fist and hit Red's knee. "One of her friends was murdered, one was almost raped, another brutally attacked and hospitalized for months, and Red. She was…"

"Shut up!" Red roared as she pulled away from Gina. "They get the general idea, so can you please put a lid on it?"

Sara abruptly stood and picked up the dessert tray. She walked around the table and offered it to Red and Gina. "Yes, let's not dwell on the dark side. This is Carl and Ron's big day, so let's just stay in their light."

Sara knew where the argument was heading. She saw it every day in the office—victims of violence avoiding their trauma and stricken by guilt, loved ones lashing out at the victims because they'd almost lost them. It could be a lethal combination for any relationship. Parents and children, spouses and lovers—all blame shaming. It had to stop.

Miraculously, Gina quieted, and Red relaxed. They both took a classic cream-filled cannoli sprinkled with powdered sugar. Returning to her seat, Sara chose a cranberry biscotti, and Mandy dug into the raspberry tiramisu.

For a beat, all was calm. But then Sara couldn't resist asking, "Have you had counseling, Red?" She knew the Charlotte-Mecklenburg Police Department provided it.

Red snorted. "Been there, done that."

Luckily, Sara's question hadn't prompted another outburst. She suspected Red would be a stubborn patient—the strong, silent type who figured she could handle anything. Sara had counseled a few retired cops in the past and found it challenging. Still, she had one more thing she needed to ask.

"I often treat victims of cyberbullying, and it's awful. I've studied the phenomenon relating to mental health, but I know next to nothing about how law enforcement gets involved. Can we compare notes? If the need arises?"

Red grinned. "I could do that."

Gina frowned. "I'd rather get together again for fun, not that stuff."

"Me too," Mandy echoed. "I'd like to see you guys again."

Sara smiled at Mandy, who had kept quiet throughout the last exchange. It seemed Mandy had finally gotten over her lingering embarrassment with Gina.

Soon, Red stretched, yawned, and stood to her impressive height. She pulled on her cape. "I've enjoyed getting to know you, but I'm beat." She offered Gina her hand, and Gina also stood.

Gina wiggled her shoulders seductively. "Yeah, we've got an elegant suite waiting for us with a big ole king-sized bed. We gotta get our money's worth, right?"

Everyone laughed. The evening was drawing to a close. In the distance, Sara heard other guests leaving, saying goodbye to Carl and Ron. She sighed and was glad the night was ending. After all, she and Mandy had a big ole bed waiting, too, and Sara was more than ready to use it.

Chapter Five

Heading home...

The perfect opportunity never presented itself. At breakfast, the newlyweds were giddy with joy. Carl did happy dances with a reluctant Barney, while Ron sang opera and flipped pancakes so high off the griddle they hit the floor, pleasing Barney. Amanda couldn't see hiding Grandma's diamond in a pancake, nor proposing with an audience, so after breakfast, many hugs, and good wishes, she and Sara said goodbye, leaving the guys to pack for their honeymoon in Europe.

Next stop, the River Arts District, so Amanda could show Sara the wonderful arts and crafts she'd seen there. She especially wanted to see Gina and Ron's space. "What do you think?" she asked as Sara studied Ron's paintings of abandoned barns, waterfalls, and mountain landscapes.

"I like Gina's work better." Sara turned to the large, splashy abstracts, where the colors and shapes seemed three dimensional, too alive to be contained on a canvas.

"Right, I like Gina's work better, too. But do you think *I* should show *my* work here?" It was a touchy subject. The River Arts District required exhibitors to manage their own spaces, to design and install their displays, and ring up their own sales—in other words, artists were supposed to live locally. Gina was able to bend the rules only because Ron covered for her. Amanda thought it was asking a lot of him.

Sara smiled. "It's your decision, Mandy, entirely up to you."

This was one of Sara's traits Amanda both loved and hated. Sara never interfered with a personal decision, but in being so understanding, she often forced Amanda to make tough choices on her own. In this case, Amanda needed the money and would definitely profit from the endless flow of wealthy, discerning tourists flocking through the area. But she and Sara both had loving, supportive families in the Charlotte area, Sara loved her job, and neither wanted to move. Amanda decided to shelve the idea, again.

They enjoyed a late lunch of egg salad sandwiches and sinful éclairs at a trendy café in the complex, where Amanda decided it was goofy to present an heirloom diamond in a chocolate pastry. Indeed, by the time they merged onto Route 40 east, heading home, she realized it had been Carl and Ron's romantic weekend, not theirs. For now, the ring would stay hidden in her compact.

※ ※ ※ ※

Sara drove her red Miata sports convertible through the twists and turns outside Asheville. She marveled at the riotous colors, autumn leaves aflame on the receding mountain ranges on either side of the highway. Mandy also seemed transfixed as they sat close, arms touching in the cramped front seat. Mandy thought the season was sad, with the life force leaving the trees and nature hibernating. It was Sara's favorite time of year, melancholy but magical, the crown jewel in the natural cycle.

She especially liked it now, driving east with the setting sun behind her like a golden spotlight casting deep shadows in the valleys and burning the slopes and crests with yellow, orange, and red flames. It was the perfect ending to the whirlwind weekend, but she was glad to be going home.

Truth was, Sara was emotionally exhausted after so much laughter, tears of joy, and the intensity of meeting new people. But she now possessed Amanda's engagement ring, a huge relief. Before they left, Carl had taken her aside and quietly asked when she intended to propose. Sara had no answer because the moment had to be perfect, if there was such a thing.

She was plotting that perfect moment as she drove, imagining scenarios when the time would be right. They loved Thai food, and a dish called Sea of Love was their favorite, but she couldn't see hiding Mandy's ring amongst calamari, shrimp, and scallops. In fact, the food ploy no longer appealed at all. It was fine to give a friendship ring in a muffin, but an engagement ring? No way.

"A penny for your thoughts?" Sara asked Mandy, who had been uncharacteristically quiet since they left.

"They'll cost you a quarter," Mandy said, snuggling closer.

"I'll pay, babe." Sara gazed out at the blue mist rising like a scrim across the receding foothills.

Mandy yawned and stretched out her hands to the warmth of the heater vents. "Well, the weekend was awesome, but I'm tired, you know? I can't wait to curl up with a drink, maybe a movie, then hit the sack."

"Are you hungry?"

"Nope."

After agreeing on scrambled eggs, Mandy closed her eyes and fell asleep.

Unfortunately, Sara had to work the next morning, which meant she'd be out the door while Mandy was still in bed. Why hadn't she asked for Monday off? Could she get away with calling in sick? By the time she drove into their condominium complex, it was completely dark outside, and Sara's thoughts were dark, as well. Mandy was still asleep and didn't stir until Sara slowed on the approach to their two designated parking spaces. Sara saw Mandy's aging white cargo van, Moby Dyke, in its usual spot, but when she made a sharp right turn to slide in beside Moby, she abruptly hit the brakes. "What the fuck?"

Mandy slid forward, almost hitting the dash. "What's happening?" she cried.

"Some jackass took my spot!" Sara glared at an old white classic Jeep hogging her space. It happened, especially on weekends, when guests of other residents figured they could get away with parking poaching.

Mandy blinked and rubbed her eyes. "I've never seen that car before."

"I should call the cops and have it towed." But Sara never did. "Oh, what the hell? I'll drop you off with the bags, then drive around till I find a space. See you soon, I hope."

❧❧❧❧

Amanda's long legs were asleep and cramping as she stepped from the sports car. She stomped a few times, fetched the bags from the trunk, and then stepped out of the way when Sara peeled off. She chuckled. Amanda was more philosophical about parking issues than Sara, but then, she didn't have to fight for spaces in the city, as Sara did each day. Also, she was fascinated by the Jeep. She'd always wanted one, thought they were cool and butch. Peeking inside the vehicle, she saw a few tears in the seats, some rust here and there, and a row of little yellow rubber duckies on the dashboard. What was that about?

As she proceeded down the sidewalk and climbed the three stairs to their front door, Amanda was struck by how quiet the community was on a Sunday night after a weekend of play, before a week of work. She saw the blue flicker of television sets through several windows, and the only sounds were Sara's car circling the lot and the gentle lap of waves against the seawall on the other side of the building. It was eerie.

Davidson Landing included row upon row of three-tiered condos, several hundred souls living in close proximity in the upscale development on the shores of Lake Norman. It was close to the interstate, an easy commute to Charlotte, and the small town of Davidson boasted a prestigious college. It was popular with young professionals, especially those who loved water, like Amanda. So usually the joint was jumping, but not tonight.

She set the bags down, fished her keys from her purse, and opened the door to a dark hallway. A hint of the vegetable soup they'd eaten Friday night still lingered in the air. When she flipped the light switch, the graceful, modern interior was illuminated fore to aft. The white walls were hung with old art and music posters, some dating back to Amanda's college days, and the hardwood floors were strewn with the colorful, geometric-patterned rugs Sara favored.

Amanda moved the bags inside and looked around. They'd lived here several years, but it still didn't feel like home. Yes, it included Amanda's posters and Sara's collection of carved Santos from her native Puerto Rico, but it was too perfect, too *Architectural Digest* for Amanda. She'd spent her childhood in a drafty, two-hundred-year-old farmhouse in rural Pennsylvania, which suited her much better.

She figured the odd sense of loneliness would evaporate as soon as Sara stepped in the door. She dropped the bags in their bedroom, gazed longingly at the bed, then moved on to the great room, which included the kitchen. As she walked, the feeling of unease intensified, and she felt ridiculously vulnerable. They had neglected to close the drapes when they left, and she felt exposed to the large dark panes of window glass.

She jumped when the entry door opened, then closed.

"I'm here, babe!" Sara called out.

"I'm in the kitchen!" Amanda turned her back to the spooky double sliders leading to the patio and was relieved to see Sara walking briskly toward her, a welcome smile on her face.

Then suddenly, Sara's eyes stretched wide open in fear, and her smile dissolved. "Behind you, Mandy!" she screamed.

Amanda froze in place, terrified to turn around as Sara dropped her purse and ran to the counter. She lifted a carving knife from its wooden block. "Someone's on our patio!" Sara shrieked.

Finally, Amanda's adrenaline kicked in, and she spun around. Her legs almost buckled, her heart beat inside her ribcage, but she saw it, too. The figure was tall, shrouded in a black coat, face dark as the night as it pounded two large fists against the glass.

Chapter Six

The intruder...

Call the cops!" Sara moved toward the patio door, the knife swinging back and forth in her hand.

"Watch where you wave that thing! You'll hurt yourself!" Amanda was frantic, digging into her pocket for her phone, only to remember it was in her purse in the bedroom. Shit! Adrenaline was still chugging through her veins, demanding fight or flight, but as the intruder continued to pound the glass, flight was winning out.

"Call the cops!" Sara shouted more forcefully.

In that suspended moment, as Amanda wrestled with indecision, she realized the person outside was also shouting, but the words were muffled through the soundproof glass.

"No fucking cops!" the person pleaded. "It's me—Lori."

Sara stopped moving and stared at Amanda, a question in her eyes. Amanda's jangled brain registered that the voice was female and familiar.

Sara was first to make the connection. "Lori Taylor, your cousin?"

Amanda tried to put the puzzle pieces together. Impossible. Couldn't be. She hadn't seen her teenaged cousin for two years, and there was no good reason for her to be here now, so far from home.

"Let me in, for fuck's sake. I'm freezing!" the muffled voice continued.

"What do you think?" Sara put the knife down on the counter.

"It sounds like Lori…"

They simultaneously sprang to action. Amanda bent over and removed the safety rod that prevented the door from sliding, while Sara turned on the patio light and, in a leap of faith, opened up for the stranger. The young woman blew in on a gust of cold air, dressed in a swirl of gray trench coat stinking of cigarettes. Her short, reddish Afro and large silver hoop earrings stuck out from under a neon pink ball cap, and her amazing amber eyes seemed haughty and amused in a cocoa brown face.

"You guys didn't recognize me?" Lori's deep, seductive voice was unmistakable.

Speechless, Amanda opened her arms, and Lori rushed in for a hug. The girl seemed to have grown several inches and was almost as tall as Amanda but thin as a cinnamon stick.

Sara frowned and crossed her arms. "Do your parents know you're here?"

"I've been waiting outside for hours, freezing my tits off," Lori said, evading the question. "I got your address from Mom's Christmas card list, you know? Sorry I parked in one of your spots, hope that's okay."

"That's your Jeep? It's awesome!" Amanda couldn't hide her enthusiasm.

"Dope, right?" Lori grinned.

Sara kept her distance. "You could've waited in your car, and how the hell did you get onto our patio?"

Amanda knew Sara was playing her obligatory

role as the adult in the room, but Amanda sensed Sara's delight. Two years ago, when they all met for the first time, Sara had been enchanted by Lori, and the feeling was mutual. Even though Amanda was a blood relative, Lori had hero-worshipped Sara, and that dynamic seemed unchanged.

Lori glanced shyly at Sara. "Well, the heater's broken in my car. Besides, from where I parked, I couldn't watch your front door. So I counted from the end of the building and figured yours was the fourth unit, and then I zipped 'round back and flew over the wall."

Sara finally laughed. "Like Superwoman? Lucky we live on the first floor."

Lori shucked off her coat and tossed it onto a barstool. "I'll get my bags later," she said. "Any carbs in the house? I'm famished."

Sara glanced sideways at Amanda, which translated: *OMG! Is Lori planning to stay here?*

But Amanda was more focused on the request at hand. "We have leftover soup and some sandwich stuff."

"Perfect!" Lori cried.

Lori electrified the kitchen. She wore black skinny jeans and an oversize sweatshirt decorated with pink hearts and the words *Anime & Ramen*. Amanda didn't get it. She did get that Lori was high on nervous energy and couldn't settle. Clearly something was bothering her.

Amanda took the saucepan of soup from the fridge and set it on a burner at low. She returned to the fridge and rummaged for bread, lunchmeat, and cheese. In the meantime, she could almost hear the gears grinding in Sara's head as Sara tried to analyze

Lori's motivation. From the corner of her eye, she watched Sara guide Lori into a chair.

"So do your parents know you're here?" Sara repeated.

"Not really," Lori muttered and stared at her hands.

"You need to call them." Sara was firm. "I'm sure they're worried."

Lori shrugged. "I doubt it. Not yet, anyway."

Amanda was surprised by Lori's dismissive tone. Judd Taylor, who was Lori's dad and Amanda's first cousin, was gentle and understanding. In the past, Lori's relationship with Judd had been close and loving. Lori's relationship with Ella, her mom, and with Jana, her younger sister, had also seemed great.

The Taylor family itself, however, had been a huge shock to Amanda's family. When Amanda's Grandma Vivian died, her will had revealed that when Viv was no older than Lori, Viv had a passionate love affair with a young African American, and they had a son together. Baby Andrew had been a mixed-race scandal in the small Southern town of Mount Airy, better known today as "Mayberry," home of Andy Griffith. Back then, both sets of the teenagers' parents thought it best to separate the couple, to raise Andrew at home, and send Viv away.

Andrew had died in Vietnam, but he'd fathered a son, Judd, who was Amanda's cousin. Grandma Vivian never forgot her lost family. In her will, she bequeathed one hundred acres in Mount Airy to Judd, Amanda, and Amanda's brother, Robby. That valuable land had instigated murder and mayhem. Luckily, the new, diverse family had survived the chaos and now embraced one another.

"My parents think I'm staying over with a friend," Lori told Sara as Amanda set the table.

"Well, that's a lie, isn't it? Take out your phone and call them right now, or I'll call for you," Sara promised.

Sara and Lori glared at each other during this standoff, while Amanda put out the food, so everyone could help herself. She knew Sara would win this argument, but at the same time, Amanda was still fixated on the Jeep. Mount Airy was almost an hour and a half away, due north on the interstate. Lori had driven the route once before, but it was complicated, especially at night.

"Was your drive here okay?" Amanda asked.

Lori looked guilty as she ladled soup into her bowl. "Well, I didn't get stopped by a trooper, thank God," she muttered.

"Would that be a problem? After all, you have a license," Amanda pressed.

"I do, yeah, but it's kinda suspended. Stupid."

Amanda was horrified. "Jesus, Lori, how did you lose your license?"

The girl gnawed her lower lip and refused to meet her gaze. "DUI. It was just the one time, I swear. I really am a good driver."

Sara angrily took out her phone. "Stupid is an understatement, Lori. You are up shit creek without a paddle. Do you realize what would have happened if you'd been stopped? Kiss your ambitions to go into law enforcement goodbye. You or me, Lori? I have your mom's number on speed dial."

Lori's mom, Ella, was a high school teacher and guidance counselor. Sara and Ella frequently compared notes about helping troubled teens, so naturally, Sara had Ella's number on speed dial. Amanda also knew kids could seek legal "emancipation" from parental control once they turned sixteen. She hoped Lori had no such thing in mind. Yes, Lori was the daughter of mixed-race parents, and she was an out lesbian, which could be hard in a small town, even now. But Amanda suspected something even more disturbing was afflicting her cousin.

Sara walked out of earshot and made the call. Even from the kitchen, Amanda could hear Ella's voice raised in panic from the Mount Airy side of the conversation, while Sara remained calm. Lori's hands shook so much, she lowered her spoon and stared at Amanda in misery.

Amanda slid into the chair beside Lori and took her hands. "Hey, what's going on with you?"

"OMG, I am so shook!" Lori pulled her hands away, dug her phone from the back pocket of her skinny jeans, and laid it face-down on the table. "Remember Lilly?" Lori waited for Amanda's response.

Amanda recalled Lori's plump, shy girlfriend with a buzz cut and tattooed arms. "Sure, you guys used to date, right?"

"Yeah, but I broke up with her a few months back, and she freaked. Lilly ghosted me, told everyone in our squad I slept around, like I had a massive body count, but it was bullshit. She went all emo and started sharing naked photos of me. I am so fucked!"

Lori was hyperventilating, blinking double-time to hold back tears. Amanda got the gist of what Lori had just told her, but Sara was better at deciphering Gen Z speak. She wished Sara would hurry up and finish her call because Amanda needed help.

Sara must have sensed the drama coming from

the kitchen because she hung up with Ella and rushed over. She took one look at Lori's face and said, "What's wrong?"

Amanda was at a loss. "Revenge porn?"

Lori moaned. "My ex, Lilly. It's all over the internet—Instagram, Snapchat, TikTok, Tumblr, even fucking Facebook before they took it down. I can't take it, Sara. I can't live there anymore."

Lori's beautiful face was contorted in anguish. Her shoulders sagged as her body melted into the chair.

"Let me see," Sara demanded, holding out her hand.

Lori flipped her phone over so they could see and brought up a text. The nude woman in the photo was clearly Lori. She lay on her back in a bed of rich blue sheets. Her head was thrown back on a pillow in an expression of ecstasy, her small breasts peaked like chocolate ice cream cones, and her hands disappeared between her legs as she squeezed a pillow between her knees. It was both the most erotic and degrading thing Amanda had ever seen.

Even Sara seemed stunned. "Are there more like this?" She gasped.

"Could be." Lori bowed her head in shame. "Like I said, I'm fucked."

Chapter Seven

A conundrum...

Lori refused to talk about it. After they ate, she said she was bonked and wanted to catch winks, so Sara showed her to the guest bedroom. After offering a shy smile and saying thank you, Lori entered the room and closed the door.

"I can't believe Lori would be that stupid!" Sara moaned as Mandy hurriedly closed the drapes across the double doors leading from their bedroom to the patio.

"I don't like it that our door opens to the patio," Mandy said. "It makes me nervous, you know?"

Sara figured they were both on edge, also exhausted. She closed the door to their bedroom, something she never did when they were alone in the house. Too tired for a shower, she peeled off her clothes and fetched her nightgown from under the pillow. She sensed Mandy watching her strip, her gaze lingering on Sara's breasts, but then Mandy yawned and said, "Do you think her parents know about the pictures?"

"Would *you* show that filth to *your* parents?"

"Not a chance," Mandy said before disappearing into the bathroom.

Sara listened to Mandy brush her teeth, wash her face, and then flush the toilet. Sara's parents, Juan and Sofia, were old-school conservatives and would have grounded Sara for life had she pulled a stunt like Lori's.

But Lori's dad was a part-time deputy sheriff, and her mom was a guidance counselor. Surely Judd and Ella could help, but would they be sympathetic? Sara didn't know. She did know from experience that kids with understanding parents were less likely to admit their stupid mistakes because they were supposed to know better. It was a conundrum.

"Your turn!" Mandy called as she emerged from the bathroom wearing one of the oversize T-shirts she preferred to sleep in. Before Sara could make a move, Mandy continued, "Did Ella agree that Lori could stay with us?"

"Well, she was furious, of course, and had no idea Lori was here, but she also said Lori had been moody and depressed lately and that a vacation might do her good."

"Are you serious?" Mandy flopped down on the bed. "What about school?"

"Lori graduates next spring and took her SATs earlier this month. Ella just got Lori's results, and she scored above 1400, which puts her in the top ten percent of all kids taking the test. Apparently, her school gives top ranking seniors some leeway. They can skip days to visit colleges, work from home, and even take tests online, so Ella figured a few days off won't hurt her."

"So my cousin is brilliant, but stupid," Mandy said as she stared at the ceiling.

"Seems that way." Sara moved toward the bathroom, but Mandy blocked her with a bare foot.

"Remember Lori saying how she wants to go into law enforcement like her dad? She wants to join the fucking FBI, for Christ's sake! You realize those pictures will haunt her forever, right? They could prevent her from getting a security clearance and ruin her career."

"They could." Sara sadly agreed as she slipped past Mandy and made her way into the bathroom. "Let's worry about that later, okay? Like Scarlett said, 'Tomorrow is another day.'"

❧❧❧❧

Amanda woke up disoriented. She and Sara had fallen asleep after little more than a good night kiss, spooned together in exhaustion, and now Sara's place in bed was cold and empty. Amanda heard water running in the shower, and the events of their tumultuous weekend came rushing back to her in living color.

She jumped out of bed, pulled on panties and jeans, and then tiptoed to the bedroom door. Opening it just a crack, she heard the faint clatter of pots and pans and soft music coming from the kitchen. Lori was up and about. Amanda couldn't believe it! Too curious to wait around for her turn in the shower, she put on some thick socks and stepped onto the cold tiles of the foyer. As she moved closer, she smelled bacon and eggs.

Lori turned and smiled. "Hey, cuz, do you guys always sleep this late?"

The big rooster clock on the kitchen wall said nine o'clock. "Oh, God." Amanda gasped. "Sara will be late for work."

Lori shrugged and beckoned her into the room. "No prob, I made scrambled eggs."

Yeah, the scrambled eggs Sara was gonna make for me last night, before you showed up. Amanda slumped into a chair at the kitchen table and stared at Lori. The girl looked much younger this morning without makeup, her reddish curls crumpled from the pillow.

She wore old gray sweats with Queen Latifah on the shirt and fuzzy pink slippers, just like Sara's.

"Want coffee?" Without waiting for an answer, Lori poured Amanda's cup full.

Amanda helped herself to cream and sugar. "When did you get up?"

"How long do I get to stay here?" Lori countered.

Amanda had no idea.

"Too long!" Sara appeared, letting out one of her famous Liberty Bell laughs. She entered the room, her long black hair still damp from the shower.

"How long is too long?" Lori persisted.

Amanda stood and gave Sara a hug. "You'll be late for work," she whispered.

"Nope, I called in sick, babe." Sara gave Amanda a quick peck on the cheek, and then they sat at their usual places at the table. "What else could I do?" She gave Lori a dark look. "I'll take off from work through next weekend. I had leave days coming to me. Then, on Sunday, young lady, your father will arrive to take you home."

Lori seemed elated. "A whole week? That's lit, for real, but why is Dad coming?"

"You didn't expect him to let you drive back illegally, did you?" Sara frowned. "He's hitching a ride from Mount Airy with a friend who lives in Charlotte, then he'll drive you home in your Jeep."

"But why can't I—"

"Stop!" Sara cut Lori off. "Don't say another word. Feed us, and then we'll talk."

They ate in silence but for a set of iTunes streaming from Lori's phone, some kind of trance music. Bright sunlight poured in through the patio doors, and Lake Norman was that deep, brilliant blue seen only in winter. Amanda felt sorry for Lori. She was about to receive one of Sara's lectures.

Sure enough, Sara finished her second cup of coffee, wiped her lips with a napkin, and then pinned Lori with her analyst stare. "Now I'm sure you haven't told your parents about the photos, but does Jana know?"

"No way! My sister's only fourteen, she'd freak!"

"Why did you let Lilly take those shots? Didn't you worry that she'd post them?"

Lori blushed to her roots. "Not really. We were tight, you know? I trusted her. Besides, it's not like she used her phone or anything, she used her camera."

Even Amanda knew that was a lame excuse. Digital images on a camera could easily be uploaded to a phone. Did Lori actually believe those porn shots would remain in Lilly's private collection?

Sara certainly didn't buy it. She snorted. "Give me a break. Have you talked to Lilly since all this happened?"

Lori averted her eyes and pushed some eggs around on her plate. "At first I wanted to kill her, you know? But then I saw AJ, and he said someone stole Lilly's camera. I believed him."

"Who's AJ?" Amanda asked.

"Lilly's clueless twelve-year-old brother."

"So you think someone other than Lilly uploaded them?" Sara was relentless.

Lori rolled her eyes but still refused to look at them.

Sara took a deep breath. "Let me tell you, Lori, it doesn't matter who did it. Even if you're under eighteen, posing, passing, forwarding, or sharing nude pictures of a minor—like you—is illegal in North Carolina. You and any other kid who did this might have to hire a lawyer, go to trial, and if convicted, maybe go to jail for those offenses. Are you hearing me? They could even put you on the sex offenders' registry for life."

Lori finally looked at them, her amber eyes stretched wide with fear, and her blush drained away until she was dangerously pale. It seemed she had no words and looked like she was about to upchuck her breakfast. Even Amanda was shocked. She knew adults got into serious trouble for sharing child porn, but kids? It seemed harsh. "But what if the teenagers were just joking around?" Amanda asked Sara. "Are you saying a kid like AJ could be convicted?"

"He could." Sara was firm.

"Can you help me?" Lori pleaded in a tiny voice.

"Not me," Sara replied. "But I know someone who can…"

Chapter Eight

A bad idea...

While Lori cleaned up the dishes, Amanda led Sara into the privacy of their bedroom. "I know what you're thinking, but are you sure we should drag Red into this mess? We only met her two days ago."

"Yeah, I hate the idea, but from what Red told us, she's had personal experience with an online stalker, and she's become something of an expert on cybercrime. If anyone can help Lori, she can."

"She's a cop, Sara. Do you want her to throw Lori and her friends in jail?"

Sara sat on the edge of their bed, seemingly lost in thought. "I think Red could talk to Lori informally, off the record, and not get officially involved. Hopefully, she could give Lori some tips on how to keep these photos from going truly viral, maybe put an end to the feeding frenzy."

In Amanda's opinion, it was too late; that horse had already left the barn. She sat beside Sara and took her hand. "I feel guilty," she confessed. "I think we should tell Judd and Ella what's happening. They have a right to know."

"I agree. In fact, as a counselor, and because Lori is a minor, I have a duty to tell the parents. But I'd like to give it a day or two. Let Lori talk to Red first, then when we tattle, Lori won't feel completely betrayed."

It seemed like a bad idea. The whole concept of asking Red for a favor before they'd even become friends gave Amanda the willies. "But I don't even have Red's number," she whined as she flopped back and lay on the bed.

"But you have Gina's, right?" Sara winked. "So call your old girlfriend, and she'll put us in touch with Red. Isn't that the best approach?" Sara lay down beside Amanda and hooked a leg over Amanda's knees, pinning her to the spot.

"But what if they're still on vacation? For all we know, they're still at the Biltmore."

"No more excuses, babe." Sara gave her a peck on the cheek and then released her. "Take out your phone and make the call. I know I can count on you."

As it turned out, Gina and Red were still in Asheville. They had stayed an extra night at a cheaper hotel and were about to leave for Charlotte. They'd be following the same route as Amanda and Sara had taken the day before. After a few embarrassing moments chatting with Gina, who always managed to flirt, Gina put her phone on speaker, and Red came on the line. Without going into detail about Lori's dilemma, Amanda asked if Red would be willing to speak to Lori. Much to Amanda's surprise and delight, Red agreed and even offered to meet with Lori that very night. Once Amanda explained that they lived in Davidson, right off the interstate, they all realized it would be an easy stopover for Red and Gina. And since they'd be arriving right at suppertime, Amanda invited them to dinner.

"You did *what?*" Sara was blindsided. "What should we feed them?"

It was a well-established fact that Amanda was

hopeless in the kitchen, while Sara was an excellent chef. "You'll think of something, honey," Amanda teased. "I know I can count on you."

Lori was understandably nervous about meeting a cop, but she was also intrigued by the fact that Red was a lesbian. Other than Amanda and Sara, Lori had no adult gay friends. Not that Lori was looking for role models, Amanda wryly thought. However, she needed to get Lori out from underfoot so Sara could agonize about dinner, and she asked Lori if they could take a ride in Lori's Jeep.

"Fire, Mandy! Let's do it!"

"Can I drive?" Amanda didn't want to beg, but she did want the driver's seat. When Lori hesitated, Amanda said, "Because I know the territory, I'll show you around the lake."

"Rad, we'll go ducking along the way."

It was an amazing adventure. Turned out "Jeep ducking" meant leaving little rubber duckies on other Jeeps to surprise the owners, kind of an inside joke, a random act of kindness among Jeep fans designed to put a smile on someone's face.

Amanda loved it. All along the way, they pulled up beside parked Jeeps in parking lots and even driveways to leave duckies on someone's car. They drove in and out of neighborhoods fronting the lake, discovering coves and communities Amanda had never seen before and finding far more Jeeps than she expected. When they went into a shop for an ice cream cone, they came out to find a new ducky buddy on Lori's hood.

"This is fun!" Amanda cried. "Sara and I should get out and about more often."

"You guys don't drive around just for the hell of it?"

"Not really," Amanda sadly admitted. It seemed they never had time to play like teenagers. In the future, they should make time.

As the sun dropped lower above the lake and commuter traffic picked up, Lori's conversation turned to her hopes and dreams. She still wanted to join the FBI and wondered if she needed to complete college to get that job. She asked if there was a police training academy in Charlotte and if Red would have the answers to those questions. Amanda suspected Red would be more concerned about Lori's more immediate, potentially criminal problems than Lori's future.

Amanda hoped Red would be gentle with Lori and not make a bad situation worse. Sara was confident that throwing them together was a good idea, but Amanda sensed that Red was a tough lady who would not suffer fools. She was not a nurturing counselor like Sara.

As they neared the condo, Amanda's worries escalated, and Lori began gnawing her fingernails. When they arrived, Amanda saw that Sara had reclaimed her parking space, so that Moby Dyke had her red Miata bedmate back. Which meant that Amanda had no choice but to circle the lot. Driving around the complex, she watched a familiar green Nissan Frontier pickup with a cargo top steal the space Amanda had her eyes on. It was the vehicle Gina used to haul her art. Sure enough, Red climbed stiffly from the driver's seat and stretched her tall body, while Gina wiggled out on the passenger side and joined Red. They glanced apprehensively at each other and then walked slowly in the direction of Amanda and Sara's condo.

Lori pointed at the couple. "Is that them?"

"Yep." Suddenly, Amanda was extremely nervous.

"Shit," Lori mumbled.

What would the evening bring—success or disaster?

They would soon find out.

Chapter Nine

A dinner party...

Sara paced back and forth in the kitchen, adjusting the place settings, folding napkins, and glancing at the containers of Thai food lined up on the counter. Did Red and Gina even like Asian food? Which selections would they have made? Well, she'd done her best and chosen a bit of everything—hot, mild, vegan, and, of course, Mandy's and her favorite: Sea of Love. But there would be no proposal tonight nor any time in the near future.

It wasn't supposed to be this way.

And where the hell were Mandy and Lori? She'd expected them home an hour ago. Feeling nervous and abandoned, she walked to the patio sliders and leaned her hot forehead against the cold glass. The lake outside was restless and black, matching her mood. Mist gave halos to the lamp posts marching along the deserted boardwalk. Weird. Usually, she was the gregarious one, always up for a dinner party, but she really didn't want to greet these guests alone. She was already second-guessing her decision to involve Red in Lori's drama and kicking herself for not calling Lori's parents. She longed to shift the whole hot mess onto their plates, not hers.

Too late now because the doorbell rang. Mandy wouldn't bother, she'd just walk right in, so now Sara was well and truly on her own. Shit! She tucked her long black hair behind her ears, smoothed her sweater with sweaty palms, adjusted her smile, took a deep breath, walked through the hall, and opened the door.

They stood side-by-side in the porch light: Red towering in her dark cape, Gina squirming with nervous energy, while two sets of eyes—green and gray—seemed as apprehensive as Sara felt. Figuring they were all relative strangers and anxious to please, Sara opened her arms, gave each woman a stiff hug, and then invited them in.

Together they proceeded down the hall to the great room, the guests professing interest in the posters, the décor, and of course the brooding lake beyond the windows. When they entered the kitchen, Gina thrust a bottle of white wine into Sara's hands.

"Hope this works with dinner," she said. "I didn't know what to choose."

Sara studied the prestigious Biltmore label. "Whoa, you guys really splurged! Thank you, it's perfect." She pointed at the counter. "Do you like Thai?"

"Perfect." Red grinned and shrugged off her cape.

Gina wriggled out of a vintage red leather bomber jacket and handed it to Sara. As Sara moved back to the hall closet to hang up their coats, she felt their gazes boring into her back and wondered if she could manage to keep up the small talk until Mandy deigned to show herself. Luckily, the front door flew open, and the tardy ones blew in from the cold.

"Glad you could make it, babe," Sara muttered as she pulled Mandy close and gave her an angry kiss.

Lori hung back a few paces, seemingly overcome by an uncharacteristic shyness as Sara took their jackets and busied herself hanging them up.

❧❧❧❧

Amanda tasted Sara's bitter kiss and knew she was in the doghouse, but she also knew Sara's mood wouldn't last. When Amanda heard Gina and Red laughing in the kitchen, she strode right in, arms open wide. Gina needed no formal invitation and rushed in for a big, bosomy hug, while Red looked on in amused indulgence. In the meantime, Sara guided Lori into the circle and introduced her.

Gina looked Lori up and down, seemingly unsurprised by the fact that Amanda's cousin was African American, and then pulled the surprised teen into a Gina embrace. "Oh, so *you're* the bad girl I've been hearing about."

Red intervened and shook Lori's hand. "Never mind, Lori," she said in a deep, reassuring voice. "You and I will discuss all that stuff after dinner, but for now, let's just enjoy ourselves."

Amanda felt grateful to Red as Lori visibly relaxed. Even Sara thawed, recognizing another voice of reason in the room, and Amanda began to believe the evening would actually be a success. After cocktails, which broke the ice for everyone but Lori, who was only allowed a Diet Pepsi, Sara lit candles and everyone served themselves. After that, the dinner unfurled as easy as a rainbow flag.

The adults told funny stories about Carl and Ron's wedding, which seemed to fascinate Lori, who had never attended a same-sex ceremony. Red entertained with police humor, describing goofy traffic stops like one where a wealthy middle-aged lawyer drove into a stop sign because the young hooker on his lap bit him. The lawyer wasn't injured, but his Mercedes was trashed. Sara told bizarre tales of couples in counseling who should never have been together, while Amanda detailed her clumsy mishaps in her sculpture welding studio involving minor burns, stubbed toes, and general chaos. Gina punctuated each story with risqué punchlines that made everyone blush.

As the food disappeared and the candles melted into puddles, Lori remained quiet and wide-eyed, taking it all in. Amanda suspected the girl had never seen so many adult lesbians together in comfortable community. If Lori was looking for role models, she had plenty to choose from here. Amanda excluded herself from the mix because so far her relationship with Lori had been less like a mentor, but more like a buddy, a pal, another kid up for an adventure. Amanda was okay with this. She liked playing with her cousin.

Amanda also noticed that Lori's hero-worship seemed to be shifting from Sara the shrink to Red the cop. Lori hung on Red's every word, shyly asking questions about police procedure and how Red had climbed to the rank of a senior detective in what Lori perceived as a man's world. While Red patiently answered each question, Amanda wondered if Sara had noticed Lori switching allegiances. Did Sara mind? Amanda doubted Sara would care. Besides, Sara would always be Amanda's superhero.

As an hour ticked by on the rooster clock and the meal ended, Lori began to fidget and with good reason. Because instead of being invited to help with the cleanup, Sara stood and said, "Lori, it's time for you and me to have our little chat with Red."

Red also stood. "No, Sara, I'd prefer to speak with Lori alone if you don't mind."

Sara hesitated but soon relented. "No problem.

You can use the study near the front door and have your privacy."

"Thank you, ma'am." Red grinned. "Let's go, kid."

Red strode forward, with a droop-shouldered Lori lagging behind like a naughty student heading to the principal's office. Amanda felt for her. *Been there, done that.* She wouldn't want to be in Lori's shoes.

Chapter Ten

A right to privacy...

Sara sent Mandy and Gina to the great room with coffees, while she stayed in the kitchen to fill the dishwasher and gather her thoughts. The dinner had gone well, better than expected. She enjoyed their new friends and hoped that once Lori's problems were resolved, they'd continue to see Red and Gina socially because since their former best friends, Maya and Shar, had moved to Washington, D.C., Sara and Mandy had been a two-woman show. This wasn't a bad thing. They hadn't become an "old married couple," far from it. The passion was still there, stronger than ever, as their lives blended and they'd come to know each other's blemishes and imperfections. She smiled, thinking about the custom engagement ring now hidden at the back of the drawer beneath her undies. If Mandy said yes, they'd have plenty of time to become that old married couple.

She joined them in the great room, carrying her own mug of coffee and a plate of almond cookies. Surprisingly, Mandy was sprawled on the couch, while Gina had kicked back, legs up, in the recliner chair. Sara had expected Gina to be cozied up to Mandy, doing her flirting thing, but perhaps the long weekend had finally exhausted the older woman. The spiked peaks of Gina's short black hair had flattened, and Sara saw gray roots. Her red lipstick was eaten away, and the age lines in her pale face made her seem endearingly vulnerable as she yawned and discussed art with Mandy.

Sara showed them the cookies, then set the plate on the coffee table between them. With her free hand, she lifted Mandy's legs, sat beside her, and then rearranged those long legs across her lap. Mandy acknowledged her presence by squeezing Sara's hand on her thigh before returning to a lazy discussion of female artists who had managed to achieve superstar fame in a culture previously dominated by men. Neither woman wanted a cookie.

Sara tuned it all out. She took a swallow of coffee, put down her mug, leaned back onto the headrest, and closed her eyes. She listened intently for any snatch of conversation coming from the den, but Red had closed the door, so all Sara heard was a muffled buzz, like dialog from a faraway, muted TV.

❧❧❧❧

Amanda realized that Sara was asleep. Her beautiful face had fallen sidewise on the headrest, facing Amanda. Sara's soft, full lips were slightly parted, and she looked as she did every morning on her pillow. The sight overwhelmed Amanda with tenderness, and she thought about Grandma Viv's diamond ring, still hidden in an empty compact in her travel makeup bag, which was now buried at the back of Amanda's closet. The ring would remain buried undiscovered until the right moment for a proposal presented itself.

Gina's discussion was stalling out between yawns because, let's face it, there weren't all that many female artists who had truly made it to the big-time. It was a depressing thought, and Amanda wanted a cookie, but if she moved her legs off Sara's lap, she'd awaken her lover.

As Gina droned on and Amanda stared at her sleeping beauty, suddenly, the slack muscles in Sara's face contracted, and her green eyes popped open. Then Amanda heard it, too—the bursts of laughter coming from the den. She lifted her legs, sat up straight, and her companion came to life as the study door opened and brisk footsteps echoed across the tiled floor.

Red arrived first, Lori right behind her. Both women were smiling. Amanda took it as a good sign. "Hey, we have coffee!" she called.

"Praise the Lord!" Red rolled her eyes as Lori headed for the kitchen, but Red grabbed Lori's arm, stopping her. "Go on and get your coffee, but then take it to your room and get the stuff I asked for, okay?"

"Yes, ma'am." Lori did as she was told and then disappeared into the guest bedroom.

"She's a good girl who made a bad mistake," Red said as she settled into the second recliner with a steaming mug. "We had a very productive talk."

Amanda sat forward, as did the others, all eyes on Red as she kept them in suspense, sipping her coffee.

"Well?" Sara demanded impatiently.

"Well, first we looked at some X-rated pictures of Ms. Taylor..." Red paused, while Amanda bit her tongue. "Lori is quite photogenic, but luckily, she's not necessarily recognizable in all the shots."

Red explained that by going through a range of social media on Lori's phone, they had found only a half dozen compromising photos. "Fortunately, Lori's face was hidden in all but one of the pictures, and since she has no distinguishing features like scars, birthmarks, or tattoos, you can't prove it's her."

"Plausible deniability?" Amanda asked.

"Exactly." Red smiled. "Of course, that one damning image of Lori on the bed, her head thrown back, and the pillow between her legs is still out there for all to see and recognize, so it doesn't take a genius to deduce whose body it is in those others."

Sara groaned, and Amanda sighed. She felt horrible about her young cousin's plight.

"I wish I'd seen them," Gina said with a seductive pout. "How come I miss out on all the fun?"

Everyone ignored her.

"So what can we do?" Sara pressed.

"I have some ideas..." Red said that after a cursory glance at the various media where the photos had cropped up a week ago, it appeared that many of the chains had been broken by deletions. "So some kids did the right thing."

They learned that there were six self-destructing messaging apps kids often used on their phones: Snapchat, WhatsApp, Telegram, Wickr, CoverMe, and Bleep. To varying degrees, these apps might have erased the offending material, but it wasn't guaranteed.

"Charlotte police have a computer forensics department. They can analyze Lori's laptop and phone to trace where this filth has traveled. They can also extract the names and online addresses of all Lori's contacts."

"How can that help?" Amanda asked.

Red spread her hands, palms out. "I'm no expert, but I think they'll use facial and image recognition apps to discover where Lori's pictures are still popping up and then burn the chain. From what I've seen so far, the frequency of them appearing is slowing with each passing day, and that's a good sign."

Amanda was concerned about the police having access to Lori's friends. "Don't Lori's contacts have a right to privacy? What about the First Amendment?"

"Forget it," Sara said angrily, surprising Amanda. "I see kids' lives ruined by this shit every day. Perverts who pass it on have no rights!"

Red nodded. "When criminal conduct is involved, no one has a right to privacy. That's been true since September 11, 2001. You have no idea how closely Uncle Sam is watching you, Amanda."

Amanda generally scorned conspiracy theories, but this sounded bad. "How will you use the contacts?"

Now even Red seemed uncomfortable. She took two cookies and ate them slowly before answering. "I know a way to scare the shit out of the clueless assholes forwarding Lori's image, but I'm not sure it's strictly legal. If I run it past my boss, he'll likely say no." Red brought something up on her phone and passed it around.

When it was Amanda's turn, she read the text:

N.C.G.S. 14-190.17A, a North Carolina statute dealing with child pornography. The law stated that any individual (including minors under eighteen) can be charged with third-degree sexual exploitation of a minor if they possess material containing a visual representation of a minor engaged in sexual activity. It was charged as a Class A felony and punishable with five to twenty months in prison and inclusion in the Sex Offender Registry for life.

Amanda realized the penalty was much as Sara had described the night before, but Amanda failed to understand how Red planned to use the statute to Lori's advantage.

"So what?" Amanda said when she'd finished

reading.

Red licked her lips and brushed a cookie crumb from her blouse. "What if every one of Lori's friends got that statute sent to their phones on official police stationery with an implication that they were personally being investigated?"

"Jeez, that's harsh!" Amada exclaimed. "Every kid would suddenly become deaf, dumb, and blind, and Lori's pictures would disappear from the ether."

"Most pictures, probably," Red agreed. "But if some smartass decided to take a screen shot of an image and transferred it offline, it could still hang around like an IED and explode at a future date."

Sara frowned. "But sending the statute would eliminate most of the problem, I think. It is radical, though, Red, and I'm sure your department won't approve it."

"You'd get in trouble, honey," Gina whined. "And I won't allow it."

Red held up two fingers in the universal peace sign. "I'd need Lori's parents' approval, but what if they agreed? Her dad is a deputy. Perhaps the memo could originate from the Surry County Sheriff's Office in Lori's hometown of Mount Airy. Would that work?"

Amanda glanced at Sara. "Lori's parents don't even know about all this shit, and you'd have to ask Judd."

"What do you want to ask Daddy?" Lori walked into the room and eyed the cookies.

"We talked about this, Lori," Red said and held out her hand. In turn, Lori gave Red the laptop she had tucked under her arm.

Red snapped her fingers. "Now give me your phone."

When Lori fished the cellphone from her pocket and handed it over, she acted like she was cutting the lifeline to her entire existence.

Amanda understood. To a teenager, losing a phone was sudden death. "When does Lori get her stuff back?"

"Tomorrow!" Lori brightened. "Red invited me to come down to the headquarters in Charlotte tomorrow afternoon. I can meet some of her colleagues, get the grand tour of the office, and get my stuff back!"

"Nice, but how do you plan to get there?" Sara growled. "You don't have a driver's license."

Amanda saw that Lori's amber eyes were pleading with her. Lori wanted her cousin, her ducking buddy, her pal to intervene on her behalf. "I'll take her." Amanda exhaled with a sigh. "But only after she calls her parents."

Chapter Eleven

Starstruck...

Tuesday dawned cold and gray, mirroring the mood at the breakfast table. Sara served pancakes and sausages, hoping to lift Lori's spirits, while Mandy performed comic routines to entertain the girl. At the moment, Mandy was on the freezing patio prancing around in a Santa Claus hat anchoring a white dishtowel beard. She wore only a bathrobe, and her feet were bare, so soon she danced back into the kitchen.

"Ho, ho, ho...Who's been naughty, and who's been nice?"

Sara thought it was a loaded question. Lori just shrugged.

"So I smell snow in the air!" Mandy grinned, trying to read her audience.

"Is she for real?" Lori finally smiled.

"She's too early for Christmas or snow." Sara laughed. "Settle down and eat, babe."

Sara realized that Lori was at a loss without her phone, and she suspected Lori's talk with her parents last night had been an embarrassing ordeal. Yet she'd done it. As soon as Red and Gina left, Lori had locked herself in the guest bedroom, where there was a landline, and made the call. Sara knew this because shortly after Lori disappeared, Mandy got an irate call from Judd. Lori's parents had been furious about the pornographic pictures. Ella had been in tears, and Judd had threatened to come fetch Lori first thing in the morning. Yet somehow, Mandy had managed to talk him down, to give Lori a few more days. Mandy had told Judd about Red's offer to try an intervention and begged him to give Red that chance. Because Judd was also a law enforcement officer, Sara figured he felt some professional jealousy   , and as a father, he must have been hurt because Lori hadn't come to him first.

"Dad wants Red to call him," Lori mumbled through a mouthful of pancake. It was perhaps the third full sentence she'd spoken all morning.

"That shouldn't be a problem," Sara said.

"Yeah, I'm sure Red will do that." Mandy nodded. "We'll ask her this afternoon."

Sara smiled at the cousins. Mandy had an easy way with kids. She knew how to be a friend. She was fun, funny, and non-judgmental, and Sara loved her for it. Sara wished she had that talent. Perhaps because of her role as a psychiatric counselor, she was unable to let her guard down with teenagers. Too often, she was the bad cop. That in mind, she made a snap decision.

"I'm not going with you today," she told them. "I'll just hang here and do a few video appointments if that's all right."

Lori seemed incredulous. "Don't you want to see the police station?"

"I've seen it plenty of times." Indeed, Sara had endured many unpleasant hours with her clients in that building. "So you guys go without me." She winked at Mandy. "Take the Jeep."

❧ ❧ ❧ ❧

Just after lunch, Red texted that she was ready for them. Amanda and Lori bundled up in layers and got the Jeep on the road. In spite of the heater not working, anticipation warmed up the bumpy cab, and the atmosphere was much more convivial than it had been at the breakfast table. Lori asked to borrow Amanda's phone.

"No sexting," Amanda teased.

Lori groaned and snatched Amanda's Android. Her fingers flew over the keyboard as they drove south toward Uptown. Amanda could see Lori was Googling, not messaging.

"This is dope, Mandy!" Lori held up the screen. "To become a cop, you only need to be a citizen of the United States, twenty years old, be a high school graduate or have your GED, and be of good character."

"Oh, yeah? Do you qualify on that last requirement?"

Lori frowned. "It also says you can't have a felony or misdemeanor conviction, no DUIs for the last five years, no marijuana within one year…"

"So are you screwed?"

"My DUI will disappear in four years, so I'll have to wait a little while. Nobody knows about my occasional use of marijuana," Lori said, "but I'm worried about the felony shit. What if Red can't fix it?"

Amanda swallowed hard. She hoped like hell that Red could fix it. "Keep the faith, baby." What else could she say? When Lori fell silent, Amanda continued, "And what about the FBI? You need college for that."

Again Lori did not respond, but her thumbs kept bumping the keyboard as Amanda paid closer attention to her driving. She didn't know her way around Charlotte. The only other time she'd been in this part of town was when she and Sara attended a funeral at the courthouse for "Brownie" Bruinstein, an awesome liberal lady chief prosecutor who had been murdered. It was not a happy experience.

"Where's Shopton Road?" Lori asked.

"No idea. Why?"

"The Charlotte Police Academy's there, and they do basic law enforcement training. It takes about sixteen weeks to complete. What do you think? Can I live with you and Sara?"

"I think first things first. You know you're going to college. Your parents wouldn't have it any other way. So we're talking years in the future."

Lori frowned. She powered down the phone and slipped it into Amanda's pocket. Amanda got it. When she was Lori's age, she couldn't wait to have it all. She'd run away from home at age eighteen, the biggest mistake of her life.

"Look, here we are!" Amanda pointed at the soaring white building at 601 East Trade Street. The Charlotte Police Department seemed to fill the entire block. It was punctuated by long black tiers of vertical windows with an arched atrium entrance running the height of the entire building. She saw groups of officers with dark blue uniforms mulling about and a line of white patrol cars, mostly Dodge Chargers and Ford Tauruses, with long blue horizontal stripes on the sides bearing the police logo.

Lori sat up rigid and straight, future ambitions momentarily forgotten, as she beheld the spectacle. "Guess I'm not in Mayberry anymore."

Amanda followed the signs to visitor parking

and prayed she wouldn't get lost. They parked without incident, entered the lobby, passed through security, and were welcomed by a receptionist who gave them ID passes and told them Detective Calendar's office was on the second floor. As they walked toward the elevators, they paused before an imposing portrait of a striking African American man, his uniform jacket laden with medals and ribbons. The plaque said he was Chief Johnny Jennings.

Lori stared at the portrait. "Yo, Mandy, check it out. That's me in twenty years."

Amanda didn't doubt that Lori would someday rank in some branch of service, unless her impatience and raging hormones got in the way. As they rode the elevator, Amanda texted Red to let her know they had arrived and were greeted by Red herself when they stepped out. Red's grip was firm and business-like when she shook their hands. She wasn't a huggy kind of woman, at least not on the job. Red wore a tailored blue pantsuit, a crisp white shirt, and spit-polished black shoes. Amanda saw a gold badge holder clipped to her waistband, and she appeared to be wearing a concealed shoulder holster under her jacket. It was a turn-on. Except for her red hair, she reminded Amanda of Amy Aquino, the actress who played Grace Billets on the TV series *Bosch*.

"Good afternoon, Detective," Amanda said with a wry smile.

"Good afternoon, ladies. Come this way, please."

Red led them off to the right, while explaining that the second floor was the hub of the city's law enforcement, with all major units quartered on both sides of a long hallway. She pointed to the end where her former partner, Gina's brother Rick, worked in homicide, and then continued on to the Sexual Assault Unit where Red had worked for most of her long career. Red was now assigned to the Cold Case Unit in the same wing.

Red's colleague, a woman named Sergeant Darling, was waiting to meet them. The petite blonde was perched on the edge of what was obviously Red's desk. They all said hello, introductions were made, and then Darling excused herself to the other side of the large airy room.

Red watched Darling as she sat at a window desk with an impressive view of the old City Hall and the Police Memorial. "That used to be my desk," Red grumbled, looking at the blank wall where she was currently situated. "Now I have no view at all."

"Don't you enjoy working cold cases?" Amanda wondered.

"Yes, I do. But it wasn't my choice. I was injured on the job, and it wasn't the first time. I suspect they thought I was trigger-happy or getting too old or whatever—so they transferred me to this desk job." Red smiled wistfully. "Gina approves, however. She never would have taken me back if she thought I was risking my life on a daily basis."

Amanda nodded. Gina had told her as much the first time they'd met in Asheville. Yet the conversation seemed to sour the moment, and Red turned to Lori. "Time for us to get down to business, Ms. Taylor."

As Red led Lori away to some undisclosed location, another officer strode into the room. Homicide Detective Rick Molerno was still tall, dark, and handsome with buzz-cut hair and a crooked grin. Unlike Red, Rick had a rumpled look, and he was the huggy type. When he pulled Amanda and Lori into an embrace, Lori looked downright starstruck by it all.

Red said, "Keep Mandy company, will you, Rick, while Lori and I do our thing?" She ushered Lori out of the room but then called back over her shoulder, "But don't drink the coffee. It tastes like cat piss."

Chapter Twelve

It could happen to you...

Rick Molerno made himself at home, taking Red's chair at the desk and gesturing that Amanda should sit across from him in the visitor's seat.

Amanda really needed a caffeine fix. "Is the coffee really that bad?"

"Yep, it's like Red said—cat piss." He nodded toward a mousey, middle-aged woman tiptoeing around the room peeking over people's shoulders. "That's Gladys, the brewer of cat piss and gossip extraordinaire. Keep your thoughts hidden from Gladys, or eighteen hundred cops will know your secrets by the end of the day."

Gladys bustled over and jabbed a long finger into Rick's shoulder. "Like *you* have secrets, Molerno? Huh, your life is one big yawn." She winked at Amanda and then tiptoed away.

Next Rick pointed at the petite blond sergeant. "Don't let Darling's name fool you. That woman has a fist of steel and an iron heart."

Darling spun around in her chair, showing Rick her back and plugging in earbuds.

Rick grinned. "They pretend to ignore me, but they lust after my body, Mandy. You know how it is, rooster in the henhouse."

A young, uniformed Latina shouted, "Shut your mouth and go back to homicide, Molerno, or they'll be investigating *your* murder."

Amanda tuned out the office banter and thought about her complex and evolving relationship with Rick. A few days after Amanda and Sara met for the first time, Rick had arrested Sara on suspicion of murder, making him a bitter enemy. Then two years later, Rick had turned up at an art event featuring the unveiling of Amanda's commissioned sculpture in the company of Marc Orlando, Sara's brother. The two men explained that Marc was now taking painting classes from Gina Molerno, Rick's sister, and an uneasy friendship was born. The next day, Amanda had taken that fateful trip to Asheville with Gina, and Gina had described an almost incestuous love triangle: Rick was Red's longtime police partner, Rick was Gina's brother, and Red was Gina's lover. Reading between the lines, the divided loyalties had taken an awful toll on Red and Gina's relationship. It was complicated.

"Did you hear me, Mandy?" Rick interrupted her trip down memory lane. "That whole internet dating mess almost got Red killed. I sure hope your cousin Lori isn't mixed up with a psycho like that."

"Sorry, Rick, I was in a fog." She hated herself for missing the story Red had avoided talking about the night of the wedding.

"Like I was saying, Red actually dated that sicko serial killer, and she ended up killing him."

Amanda snapped to full attention. "God, that's terrible, I had no idea! But honestly, Lori's situation is nothing like that. She and her stupid friends got caught up in teenage revenge porn. It's pathetic, but it's not sinister."

"That's what you think." He leaned forward on his elbows, dark eyes burning, so close she could smell the bite of his aftershave. "These five middle-aged women who experimented with a dating app were all highly intelligent professionals, but they were targeted. Anyone can get hooked by these online predators. It could happen to you."

Ridiculous as that seemed, Rick's words sent a chill up her spine. The man was deadly serious, and it frightened her. "I'll be careful," she promised in a small voice.

"Careful of what?" Lori's voice carried across the room. She walked toward them, her repossessed laptop under her arm and Red right behind her. "I got my stuff back, Mandy."

"And I spoke to Lori's dad," Red said. "I think we've come to an understanding."

"That's good," Amanda stuttered. She was still shaken by Rick's talk of murder and his ominous warning. The worry must have shown on her face.

"What's wrong?" Red asked. "Has my reprobate partner been scaring you with his blood and guts stories?"

Rick pouted. "Why would I do that? I did try to hit on Mandy, but she wasn't interested."

Lori burst out laughing. "Not in this life, bruh. Mandy has better taste, plus, she's taken."

Amanda didn't expect to get an update on Lori's situation with Rick present, so she stood and prepared to leave. With a little luck, they'd just miss the rush hour traffic. She said goodbye to Rick, waved to the other officers, and was moving toward the exit when Lori blocked her progress.

"Wait! Red has invited us to visit the crime lab with her before we go. It's right here in the building, so it won't take long, and I really want to see it."

Red smiled. "Lori's set on a career in law enforcement, so it would be a learning opportunity for her."

"Pretty please?" Lori thrust out her lower lip, pleading like a six-year-old. She looked as plaintive as an orphaned waif, but Amanda knew she was stubborn as a mule in mud, so naturally, she relented.

"Let's be quick about it, though," she said as they followed Red's long strides into the corridor, took the elevator down to a sub floor, and made so many turns through identical hallways that Amanda felt like a mouse in a maze. She heard laughter and voices raised in anger behind closed doors, imagined the many dramas playing out in this building, and noticed a few curious stares as people wondered what two outsiders were doing in this inner sanctum. Lost as she was, she decided to grin and bear it.

"Red's working a cold rape/murder case," Lori explained along the way. "She gave an old evidence bag to a doctor in the lab to analyze for DNA. Guess what's in the bag?"

"What?" Amanda figured it was something juicy or gross to excite Lori.

"Lacy panties from the fourteen-year-old victim, soaked in her blood and his splooge." Lori grinned.

Amanda got the picture and was actually interested as Red told them the sample would be cross-checked with the FDDU, the Federal DNA Database Unit, and the NDIS, the National DNA Index System, established in July 2013.

"My crime took place in 1995, before we had the indexes, so unless my perp got nailed for something else in the past nine years, his DNA won't be in the system. It's a long shot," Red finished as they stopped outside a set of doors leading to the crime lab. "And before we go in, I should warn you, we'll be meeting with Dr. Nicole Moss. She's been with us less than a year. She's tops in her field, but she's also moody and rather abrupt. Don't take offense if she's rude, it's just her way."

"Will she mind strangers tagging along?" Lori asked.

Red pressed a button on a wall-mounted intercom unit, spoke her name and badge number, and they were buzzed in. "Hell yes, she'll mind, but Dr. Moss will be curious about you two because, according to Gladys and the gossip mill, Nicole Moss is a closeted lesbian."

"No way! Is she a dyke?" Lori asked.

"I doubt she would describe herself that way." Red winked.

Amanda didn't care. She was more disturbed by why Dr. Moss would be curious about them. Did she have a scarlet "L" printed on her forehead?

They progressed through a wide concourse with a glassed-off series of rooms on the left where people in white coats worked at tables, with sci-fi-looking machines that resembled the sterile laboratories of Amanda's imagination. But they headed to one of the offices on the right with Dr. Nicole Moss's name on the door. Red tapped once, and then they all entered.

The striking woman behind the desk did not bother to stand. She appeared to be about Amanda's age with long brunette hair pulled into a tight ponytail. Trendy blue-rimmed glasses blurred the color of her eyes, which proved to be a milky azure when she removed the glasses to glare at them. Her slim, yet voluptuous figure was obvious under her white lab coat, and oddly, she wore thin latex gloves as she worked at a laptop.

If it hadn't been for her stony expression, a sharper, more pronounced bone structure in her face, and a twitchy attitude, she would have reminded Amanda of Sara. Perhaps this was due to the intelligence sparking in her eyes. Aside from that, Dr. Moss was ice to Sara's fire.

Red introduced them, and without being invited to do so, she sat at the chair across from Dr. Moss. Red indicated that Amanda and Lori should sit on the sofa against a far wall, which they did.

Dr. Moss pointed at Lori and said, "You are Ms. Taylor, and what's the other woman's name?"

"Amanda Rittenhouse," Amanda answered.

"Really?"

Did the doctor think she was lying? "Have we met?" Amanda asked.

"Of course not." Dr. Moss was dismissive as she turned her attention to Red.

They watched as the doctor ceremoniously placed a sealed brown paper bag on the desk. Amanda assumed it contained the soiled panties, and as the professionals talked about DNA extraction, dissecting microscopes, and something called polymerase chain reaction, Amanda was lulled by the doctor's monotonous, robotic voice. Even Lori seemed bored. It also became obvious that Red's cold case was not solved; the rapist/ murderer's DNA was not in the system. Red had to be disappointed.

As the meeting drew to a close, Dr. Moss told Red that she had a troublesome teenaged nephew named Jayden. It seemed the boy had gotten hooked on his mom's prescription meds. He was raiding his friends' medicine cabinets, stealing money to buy street drugs, and Dr. Moss wanted the name of a good children's counselor. Naturally, Red recommended Sara and began singing her praises.

Lori suddenly said, "Hey, Dr. Moss, maybe you've met Sara Orlando. She's a psychiatrist with the city of Charlotte, and she's visited this building many times."

The doctor's eyes began to blink with disturbing rapidity. "No, I do not know Dr. Orlando. Why should I? Just because we're both women with a PhD. behind our names does not mean we're in some intimate club."

Her response seemed unnecessarily testy to Amanda. Was this the prickly personality Red had warned them about?

But Lori seemed determined to get a rise from the ice lady. "My cousin Amanda here is Sara's partner. They've been together for seven years."

What the hell? Was Lori trying to yank Dr. Moss out of the closet in this bizarre way? Amanda did not appreciate being outed for Lori's amusement. Later, she'd strangle the kid.

Red gave Lori a dark look, while Dr. Moss seemed completely flustered.

"Well then," the doctor said, "I'm very happy for Amanda and Sara. I think we're done here."

Chapter Thirteen

Different generations...

W hat got into you, Lori? Why the fuck would you tell Dr. Moss about Sara and me?" Amanda was seething as she fought the rush hour traffic looping around the city. It was stop, go, hurry up, and pray each time they changed lanes. Lori seemed oblivious to the cars playing Russian roulette as she fiddled with her phone.

"Why not tell her? The doctor was a total Karen, right? She deserved a goose up the backside."

"What does that even mean?"

"A *Karen*—like, she's rude. She's the kind who sends her drink back at a restaurant just because there's not enough ice."

Amanda didn't disagree. "But you have no right to expose other people's personal lives without their permission."

Lori sighed. "Tell me about it. It's not like I posted your nude photo on the web."

Amanda's anger boiled into the red zone. She'd almost risk a car crash for the pleasure of reaching over and smacking Lori. The comparison was so unfair, but she did some deep breathing and got her temper under control by maintaining stony silence as the setting sun glanced off the dashboard, blinding her. She jerked the visor down and squinted through the windshield.

Lori noticed the silence. It was an intimidation

trick Amanda had learned from her mother. Eventually, Lori turned her phone face-down on her lap. "Look, I'm sorry, okay? I just don't get why people your age keep everything secret."

People my age? She was twenty years older than Lori, but that didn't make her ancient, did it? It was true that she and Sara seldom showed physical affection in public, and it made her uncomfortable when other people did. Straight or gay, she hated it when couples hung all over each other like monkeys in heat. What were they trying to prove?

"I never see you guys kissing, you know?" Lori was relentless. "Pretty much everyone's down with being gay these days. Times have changed."

"Not as much as you think." Amanda gripped the steering wheel. As a solitary artist working on her own, being "out" was not an issue. But for Sara, Red, and even Dr. Moss, being open about their sexual identities could cause huge problems, even now. Working with vulnerable teens or fellow officers, homophobia was still alive and well, and eventually, Lori would learn it the hard way.

"You read sapphic novels, right?" Lori continued. "They're practically mainstream, and those authors don't hold back."

"No, they don't," Amanda mumbled. She had read all the classics, loved Katherine V. Forrest, Clair McNab, and many of the suspense novelists following in their footsteps, but recently, she'd read a book dubbed "romantic suspense," which proved to be eighty percent graphic sex and twenty percent suspense. The experience made her want to puke, like she'd swallowed several hundred pages of pornography.

"What are you thinking?" Lori demanded.

"That maybe we are from different generations."
Amanda wasn't a prude, far from it, but she was
outwardly reserved, like her mother. Diana was
considered a proper lady, but anyone who knew her
saw the passion lying just below the surface of her calm
exterior. Sara, in private, was much less conservative
than Amanda and often took the lead in sexual
encounters that made Amanda blush. It was a secret
that few of their friends would believe.

"Can we change the subject?" Amanda asked as
the traffic opened up on the outskirts of Charlotte and
the cold winter fields and forests sped by on either side
of the highway, bringing a measure of peace.

"Yeah, let's talk about supper. I'm hungry. Do
you think Sara made us something good?"

❧❧❧❧

Sara had browned the ground beef, yellow pepper,
and chopped onions. She'd added the chili powder,
tomato paste, kidney beans, and diced tomatoes, so
she gave it a stir and set it to simmer. The cornbread
muffins were ready to pop in the oven, and she had all
the ingredients for a super salad, so she was good to go.

Mandy had texted an hour ago as they left the
city, so she waited and nursed a glass of dry wine.
She'd closed her laptop an hour ago, having discovered
that the clinic had effectively covered for her and
rescheduled her appointments for the week. Was she
that easily dispensable? Should she have gone with
Mandy and Lori? No, to both questions. She smiled,
sipped, and finished the last two chapters of her
Jonathan Kellerman novel, deciding a day of peace was
good for the soul.

But then her cellphone chimed, and the name

Diana Rittenhouse pulsed on the caller ID. She adored talking to Mandy's mom, so she answered with a cheerful greeting.

"I hope I'm not disturbing you at work," Diana said.

"Nope, I'm off all week."

Diana was obviously surprised, reminding Sara that she should take more downtime so that she and Mandy could be more than passing strangers. She told Diana about Lori's unexpected visit, but not about Lori's troubling situation.

"My niece has been there three whole days and nobody bothered to tell me? You must know I'm dying to see her, or did you plan to keep her all to yourselves?"

Diana immediately extended a dinner invitation to the lake house for what she called an impromptu family feast. "Tomorrow's supposed to be sunny and warm. I'll try to get the whole gang together, then maybe Matthew can take you all out on the pontoon boat."

It sounded like heaven, so Sara said yes. She didn't know what kind of mood Mandy and Lori would be in after their session with Red, but she did know a day with Mandy's family was good for the soul—better, even, than solitude.

⁂

Amanda was shocked that Lori downed three bowls of Sara's famous chili, especially during what Amanda considered to be disturbing dinner conversation. According to Lori, Red and Judd had come up with a strategy to "disappear" all the compromising photos. The technicians in the CMPD computer forensics unit had isolated and zapped most, if not all, of the pictures, and Judd had agreed to initiate a version of the North Carolina statute citing the penalties for possessing child pornography from the Surry County sheriff's website. Judd would send the frightening letter to Lori's contacts without specifically naming Lori as the victim. The letter would imply that the kids on the receiving end could potentially be investigated for the offense.

"It'll scare them shitless," Lori said through a mouthful of cornbread. "And I'll be in the clear— except Dad says I'm grounded for a month."

"Only a month?" Sara raised an eyebrow.

"Aw, he'll change his mind. Daddy's a pussy when it comes to discipline. I'll be free in a week."

Amanda thought Judd should confiscate Lori's phone and put a tracker on her Jeep. Maybe Amanda was just exhausted by the whole ordeal, but she thought Lori was getting off too easily. She worried that someday, somehow, that snake would rise from the dust and bite her on the butt.

Lori was wired, and Sara was rested from a day of leisure, so that only Amanda fell asleep during *Desert Hearts*, a movie from 1986, made two years before Amanda was born. It was, in her opinion, the best lesbian film ever made. Lori had never seen it and was rooting for cowgirl Cay to seduce the uptight professor Vivian. They woke Amanda up in time for the last romantic scene at the train station.

Lori was also pumped by the dinner invitation from her Aunt Diana and couldn't wait to spend time with her new extended family.

"Is that okay with you, Mandy?" Sara asked.

"Yup." Amanda yawned and headed for bed while the credits were still rolling.

Chapter Fourteen

Blue silk stockings...

Sara found Amanda collapsed on the bed, fully dressed. "My little party pooper," Sara whispered in her ear. "Rough day, was it?"

"You have no idea. I chatted with Rick Molerno, saw Red in her sexy work outfit, complete with gun and badge, and met an uptight lesbian doctor."

"Sounds like a good day to me, babe. Should I be jealous?"

"Not a chance," Amanda said, just before Sara silenced her with a kiss. When the kiss ended, Amanda added, "Besides, I already have my lesbian doctor, and she's not the least bit uptight."

Sara cupped Amanda's left breast. "Hold that thought," she purred, before heading to the shower.

Amanda sank deeper into the pillow and exhaled. Why was she so tired? Yes, her quiet little artist's life had been upended for four days, from the wedding in Asheville until this moment, but surely it shouldn't sap her like this. She felt uneasy and glanced at the drapes, which were safely closed against the treacheries of the night. She seemed oddly disconnected from the woman she'd been Saturday morning. Why? Because she hadn't checked her emails or visited Facebook, where her friends always posted calming, happy shots of dogs and cats and awesome sunsets? She needed a fix of normal, so she picked up her phone and opened her email.

She read a newsy note from her brother, Robby, in Philly, then opened one from her friend Maya, who said that she and her partner, Shar, were coming home from D.C. on Thursday, and could they all get together for dinner? This idea lifted her sky-high, and she couldn't wait to tell Sara. After deleting the usual string of ads and come-ons, she hesitated over a header titled "Call for Regional Artist Submissions." Did the submissions involve cash prizes? Amanda opened the message.

The bizarre image dropped her mood from the sky to the basement. The two Barbie dolls were naked, their legs painted blue up to their thighs, like they were wearing blue silk stockings. They were positioned flat on their backs, with their legs straight up in the air, butt to butt, and their arms flat at their sides. Both necks were twisted so they faced away from the camera; one doll had long black hair, and the other's blond locks had been hacked off so short she appeared almost bald. The photo was not a submission to a regional art show. It was not art. It was like a still frame from a horror flick, and it required no imagination to understand that the dolls were intended to represent Amanda and Sara.

Amanda threw the phone to the foot of the bed as tears leaked from her eyes. Sara found her gasping to catch her breath.

"God, what's wrong?" Sara cried as she held Amanda in arms still wet from the shower. "You look like you've seen a ghost!"

❧ ❧ ❧ ❧

Hours later, as they lay in bed unable to sleep, Sara said, "It's just a sick joke." It was the umpteenth time she'd said this. Was she trying to convince Amanda or herself?

"It doesn't feel like a joke. I think posing dolls is creepier than using live models—like Stephen King's clown or Annabelle or Chucky." At first, Amanda had considered not showing Sara the image, but Sara had snatched the phone and looked for herself. Sara's eyes had first widened with surprise, but then her dark brows dipped in a frown, and her lips compressed in anger.

"Shouldn't we delete it?" Amanda asked.

Sara studied the heading. "Wait, let me get the sender's details." She tapped the text and got an address: RACommis@gmail.com. "Well, that seems to make sense since the header asks for a regional art submission."

"It's a scam. No art commission would send that shit."

"Should we send a reply and find out if the address is for real?"

"No! A response might complete the connection and open me up for hacking. Isn't that what happens?" Amanda wasn't a tech wizard, but she knew basic precautions, like *don't open an email you don't recognize.* Too late. She'd already emancipated that can of worms.

"Okay," Sara agreed. "Block it by reporting it as spam and then unsubscribe. That way, this asshole can't contact you again, but you'll have the image in your spam folder if you ever want to retrieve it again."

"Why would I retrieve it?"

"To show Red? So her computer team can trace it?"

Amanda groaned. She'd never admit her rookie mistake to Red, especially after all Red had just done for Lori. She'd die of shame or embarrassment. "I'm never telling Red!" Amanda exclaimed.

"I understand." Sara reached up and turned off the bed light. She gathered Amanda into her arms and stroked the tension in her back. "You need to sleep, babe."

"Who would want to hurt me like this?"

"No one. It's random. You don't have enemies, Mandy. Please try to forget it. I'm sure it's a fluke, and it won't happen again."

Sara drifted off right away. Or was she faking, hoping that her regular breathing and warm body would lull Amanda into dreamland? That wasn't happening. Tired as she was, the whirlwind events of the past few days kept zig-zagging around in her brain: the wedding party, the chaos at the police station, and the terrifying dolls kept waltzing through her subconscious. Worst of all? The memory of Rick Molerno leaning forward on his elbows, the bite of his aftershave, and his words: "It could happen to you, Mandy."

⁂

Sara sat alone at the breakfast table, sipping coffee. She wasn't surprised that at nine o'clock Lori was still asleep because it seemed teenagers never got enough. She was relieved that Mandy had finally succumbed to sleep at four in the morning after a horrible series of nightmares. Talking about the provocative email clearly upset her, so Sara had downplayed it, trying to comfort Mandy with tenderness, not words.

Was it a fluke? Sara hoped so, but she wasn't sure. The use of dolls to terrorize was classic, almost comical, but it was nonetheless unnerving since the

Barbies were clearly intended to be Mandy and her. But why? It was true Mandy didn't have enemies. She was a loving, easygoing soul who worked alone and chose diplomacy over confrontation—for the most part.

Indeed, Sara was the much more likely target of psychotic wrath. It came with her job. Every day, she worked with unstable adults and children, many of whom likely wished her harm. Every doctor in her clinic had a file for threatening mail, some of them death threats, and Sara was no exception. She made unpopular decisions: a parolee's freedom revoked, an unwanted assignment to a mental health facility, removing a child from abusive parents. Recently, Sara had received several credible threats and knew precisely which patients were sending them.

Whatever. It made her blood boil to see Mandy harassed in this way, but what could she do about it? Sara sighed, took another sip of coffee, and watched bars of light playing across the table. She felt the warmth on her back from the sun streaming through the patio doors and made a decision. Picking up her phone, she did what she had wanted to do the night before.

She had memorized the email address of Mandy's tormentor: RACommis@gmail.com. Using an old address she had abandoned at AOL, one that did not include Sara's name, initials, or any other personal identifier, she typed in the tormentor's address and the simple header, "Stop," and then pressed SEND. She immediately got an NDR, non-delivery report, saying that her message had failed because the address had not been found. Shit! Whoever sent the picture to Mandy was a clever little bitch. Likely this person had created a new address for the sole purpose of contacting Mandy and then quickly canceled the account.

Sara stretched, stood, and walked to the patio doors to gaze out at the lake. The clear blue water and cloudless sky, punctuated by a half dozen lazily drifting seagulls, were obscenely at odds with Sara's dark mood. As she returned to the table to check her own emails, her gut told her that the sicko bothering Mandy was a woman, not a man. Had to be. Everything about the dolls, the silk stockings, and twisted humor was feminine and juvenile. Was the sender a girl?

She went back to the table, scrolled through her regular mail, and found the usual boring memos regarding budget, appointment cancellations, and upcoming meetings. Among them was something from her dear friend Maya Hunter. Mandy had mentioned that Maya and Shar were visiting toward the end of the week and wanted to get together. When she excitedly opened the message, Sara's heart raced. She dropped the phone and spilled her coffee.

Dear God in heaven! The Barbies were back! Again the two dolls were naked. This time, they were standing front to front, with their little mounds of plastic breasts and scrawny hips pressed together, bound at the waist into this position by an actual blue silk stocking. Their arms were pointed straight up in the air and tied together at their wrists by a blue rubber band. Their faces, now twisted to face the camera, had been blanked out with flesh-colored paint. The erased faces were most horrifying of all, like ghosts in bondage.

Gasping for breath, Sara stood and staggered to the counter, where she tore off a hunk of paper towel to clean up the coffee mess. The stalker was a whole lot harder to wipe away. She eased into her chair and gingerly picked up the phone to inspect the sender's address: MayaHunts/860@gmail.com. Of course, she had opened it because this *was* Maya's address. She'd seen it a hundred times. To double-check, she opened her contacts and brought up Maya's name. There it was: MayaHunts#860@gmail.com. Fuck! The imposter had inserted a slash instead of Maya's pound key. She'd been suckered.

She was a pathetic fool. From the degree of sophistication, Sara guessed this creep was not a girl, but a very clever woman. She already knew the outcome should she attempt to reply to the sender— she'd get an NDR notice, and the address would have been removed from service. So she did what Mandy had done—marked it as spam and   unsubscribed. Now Sara understood how Mandy felt. No way would Sara go running to Red for help. She was too proud to ask and reveal what an utter idiot she had been. But as Sara's mother had warned her: *Pride goeth before a fall.*

But, by God, she would handle this herself. Sara had some cyber tracing resources at the clinic, which she could discreetly access, including several apps that could maybe root out the sender's identity. If these failed, she'd seek more help. In the meantime, she would not tell Mandy, at least not yet. And she'd never, ever tell Lori what had happened. Because today they were going to Diana's for a family celebration, and Sara wasn't about to spoil it.

Chapter Fifteen

Coming home...

Sara's Miata sat only two, the Jeep's backseat was cramped, so they took Amanda's Moby Dyke to the lake. It was early afternoon, just after brunch, with plenty of daylight left for a boat ride. Lori couldn't hide her enthusiasm. She talked nonstop as they drove north on the interstate and turned west at Exit 36, Mooresville.

Sara seemed unnaturally subdued. Amanda figured she was sleep-deprived, having endured Amanda's distress all night. Certainly, Amanda felt hungover and paid careful attention to the road as she half-listened to Lori and allowed her thoughts to wander. She guided her brain away from internet monsters and thought about pleasant things, like her wonderful family and beautiful Lake Norman. After Sara, these were the anchors of her new life.

Her life had unfurled in three stages: *Before Running* was her idyllic childhood in rural Pennsylvania, which ended abruptly with her parents' divorce, when she ran away from home. *After Running* came her decade in Sarasota, Florida, when she discovered her love of art and a passion for Rachel, a much older woman who became her mentor and lover, and then broke her heart. *Returning,* she arrived in North Carolina with her tail between her legs and reunited with her estranged mother, who had just married

Matthew Troutman, whom everyone but Mom called Trout. She discovered that Trout was a kind and loving stepfather with a welcoming new family. Finally, of course, she had fallen in love with Sara, making these past seven years the best ever. If she convinced Sara to marry her, the rest would be perfect.

Lake Norman had been a bonus. North Carolina's "inland sea" had five hundred twenty miles of jagged shoreline, with the Troutmans' magical home at the end of a private peninsula. For Amanda, who adored boats and water, it was heaven.

"Are we almost there?" Lori was like a kid on a too-long journey to a vacation destination.

"Not long now," Sara said as they passed two original landmarks on River Highway that preceded the fast-food chains, shopping malls, and other suburban debris that came with rampant development. Trout hated the so-called progress, saying the old way of life was "slipping away faster than a minnow through a dip net." Mom, a Realtor, secretly loved it because the folks flocking here from all over the nation needed to buy homes. The first landmark was Fat Daddy's, a great seafood restaurant with NASCARs on the roof. The second was Trout's Place, a combination mini-mart, gas station, and auto repair shop. Trout had built the place and managed it for forty years. He also rented an abandoned repair shop to Amanda for next to nothing. It was her studio, where she welded her metal sculpture and spent her days while Sara was at the clinic. The arrangement was ideal. Not only did Amanda get to see her family on a regular basis, including many impromptu dinners, but she also got free snacks from the mini-mart.

Amanda turned left and drove down a winding

road with leafless hardwoods and green pines partially concealing the older cottages and new McMansions on both sides. Through the trees, sparkling like a winking blue eye, they caught sight of the lake.

"I recognize this!" Lori exclaimed. "I was here two years ago, but only for a few hours."

This was true. Lori Taylor and her family had met the Troutman family only briefly. Everyone got along famously, but it was an odd situation, considering neither family had known these close relatives existed for most of their lives.

Turning onto the Troutmans' lane was like coming home. As Amanda approached the sprawling cedar shake ranch house at the end of the peninsula, sure enough, the screen door to the porch slammed, and Trout stepped out to greet them, arms open wide, as he had a hundred times before. He was sixty-seven now, semi-retired, and revisiting his hobby of painting watercolor landscapes. Today he wore a classic blue and brown plaid flannel shirt and well-worn jeans on his strong, six-foot frame. His thick brown hair was mostly gray, and his warm brown eyes were framed by webs of laughter lines. He was a striking man, and Amanda could see why Mom fell for him, opposite as they were. Trout was easygoing Southern charm, while Mom was the epitome of Yankee reserve.

"My favorite girls!" he said, gathering Amanda and Sara into his long arms, while Lori hung back, suddenly shy. "You too, Lori. I haven't seen you in a coon's age." Somehow, he managed to drag Lori into the hug, as well.

Right on cue, Ursie, Trout's ancient Doberman, padded into the love fest. Amanda figured the Troutmans' beloved dog was at least fourteen years old, but she was hanging in. Ursie walked stiffly up to Amanda, whined, and then shoved her gray muzzle into Amanda's palm.

Amanda broke loose from the embrace and knelt down to cuddle Ursie. "How are you doing old girl?" she cooed.

"Her arthritis is acting up, her eyesight and hearing aren't what they used to be, but she'll still run after the blue heron when the spirit moves her," Trout said.

"Good for you, girl!" Amanda scratched behind Ursie's ears, and Ursie wagged her stubby tail.

"You say we're your favorite girls, Trout, but you got nothing but girls, right?" Lori teased.

"Right, I have my own harem," he agreed as he led them up the steps and into the screened porch. "Ginny's here today with the kids, so at least I've got baby Thomas to supplement the Y chromosomes."

Amanda laughed. "Trev couldn't make it?"

"Nope, he's busy at Buffalo Guys."

Trev was Ginny's husband, who owned a bar and grill at the top of the lake. Lori was right. Trout was blessed with a family of women. Along with Mom, Amanda, and Sara, he had his daughter, Ginny, and Ginny's thirteen-year-old daughter, Lissa. Ginny's toddler son, Thomas, and Trev were the only other males. Trout said he preferred the company of women, so it was all good.

"Who's cooking dinner?" Sara asked as they entered the house through the laundry room.

"Don't worry, Diana's not cooking." Trout chuckled. "I put two pot roasts into crock pots this morning, so no one's messing in the kitchen but me."

Even Lori laughed. She already knew that Amanda

couldn't cook worth a tinker's damn because she'd inherited her mother's clueless-in-the-kitchen genes. Amanda had smelled the rich aroma of simmering beef and onions the moment they'd entered the house, and suddenly, she was starving.

"When do we eat?" Lori asked as Trout hustled them through the old-fashioned kitchen.

"Not until after the boat ride. All that fresh air and rolling waves will get your juices flowing," Trout said as he ushered them into the great room, where Mom, Ginny, and Lissa were playing Scrabble at the big all-purpose picnic table, which was the heart of the house, while Thomas galloped around the comfortable leather furniture, skidding on the oriental rugs and hardwood floors.

"My juices are already flowing, Daddy!" Ginny exclaimed as she jumped up and hugged Amanda first.

Ginny was Amanda's "lost soul's mate," as Ginny called them. They were exactly the same age, both had run away at eighteen, and both now regretted their misspent youths. But Ginny had short, black razor-cut hair and a silver stud in her left nostril. She was graceful and petite, with big boobs and an attitude to match, while Amanda was tall, Nordic, flattish-chested, and slightly clumsy.

"When do I get my hug?" Sara winked and blew Ginny a flirtatious kiss.

"Bring it in, girl!" Ginny and Sara embraced and kissed on the lips, before collapsing in laughter. They played well together: Sara spunk and Ginny punk. They high-fived each other as Diana looked on in wry amusement.

Amanda was the spitting image of her mother—blonde, blue-eyed, tall, athletic, and yes, somewhat reserved. In her teen years, Amanda had hated their similarities, but now she was honored when someone compared them. She was grateful to be the daughter of someone as brilliant and kind as Diana Rittenhouse.

"Yeah, Grandpa, when can we eat?" Lissa pouted. "You say I'm getting too skinny, so why don't you feed me?"

Lissa had wild, curly red hair, a pale, freckled face, and big glasses with green frames to match her eyes. Amanda had known her since she was a little kid when she was chubby, wore braces on her teeth, and drove everybody crazy with her precocious questions. Now she was slim, almost as tall as Ginny, and still drove everybody crazy with her questions.

"We'll eat after the boat ride," Trout repeated. "So get your butts in gear, we're leaving now."

Amanda's heart was full. She loved that her family knew about her and Sara. Sometimes she suspected they loved Sara more than they loved her, and that made her even happier. They all milled about. Trout kissed Mom on the head before leaving to prep the boat. Mom set up her laptop to work since she'd decided to skip the outing. Lori collected blankets to take along, Sara cleared the game off the table, Ginny dug a Scrabble tile from Thomas's mouth, and Amanda's tension evaporated. She was a million miles away from cyber threats, revenge porn, and blue silk stockings.

Chapter Sixteen

Home are the sailors...

Mandy took over the captain's helm as soon as the pontoon boat left the dock, and Sara was delighted to see her relaxed and laughing. The wind whipped her short blond hair and stung her cheeks rosy, and she was beautiful. It seemed Mandy was never happier than when messing with boats. Lori, Lissa, and Thomas were in the bow seats, where they got bounced the most and often got   splashed. They were clowning and squealing like kids on a carnival ride, and Sara hoped Lissa kept a close eye on Thomas as he leaned out over the waves like an animated figurehead. No one would enjoy rescuing him from the frigid water.

Sara had expected Lori to sit in the stern seats with her, Ginny, and Trout. Had Lori chosen to be with Lissa because she reminded her of Jana, Lori's younger sister? Lori was on the cusp of adulthood, with her smoking, trash talk, and general rebelliousness, but she also had one foot in childhood. Perhaps playing with the kids today was a much-needed respite from the world of revenge porn and internet bullies. Lori deserved a break.

Sara leaned back on the headrest, closed her eyes, and enjoyed the sun's warmth on her face, while the rest of her body shivered in spite of the blanket wrapped around her shoulders. Who went on a joyride in an open boat in November? The hardy Troutmans, that's who.

"I should've brought my fishing rod," Trout said

"I should've brought my swimsuit," Ginny said.

"You should both have your heads examined," Sara said, getting the last word. It was a joy to watch the father/daughter routine. Clearly they adored each other. Sara had a similar relationship with her dad, only they had bonded over gardening, not water sports.

"Too bad Ursie couldn't come," Ginny said.

Trout shook his head. "Yeah, but the old gal isn't up to it anymore. She's lost her sea legs."

Sara agreed it was sad. Ursie had come down to the dock but hadn't attempted to jump aboard. After watching them chug away, she had wandered up into the yard and then padded down the road, out of sight. Sara hoped Ursie got some good sniffs along her journey or maybe a chance to chase the heron.

She opened her eyes and gazed at Mandy, who was intently watching the waves and steering with them to reduce the drag and avoid splashing. Mandy looked so happy and carefree that Sara felt a sudden jab of guilt. She still hadn't told Mandy about the Barbies in Bondage email she'd received that morning. She knew that Mandy would be more upset by Sara being targeted than when Mandy herself was threatened. Did it mean the sender bore a grudge against both of them? But why? Because they were a couple? Did some sick homophobe have them in their crosshairs?

Sara didn't know what to make of it or when the grudge began. Had she or Mandy offended this person recently, in the distant past, or sometime in between? Or had only one of them offended and the other was collateral damage? She still believed the sender was a woman, but who knew? Mandy had mentioned three horror movies: Stephen King wrote *It*, Gary Dauberman wrote *Annabelle,* and Don Mancini wrote *Child's Play.* They were all about demonic dolls and all written by men. Sara was no expert on horror movies. In fact, she hated them. But she had written an academic paper on why people enjoyed horror and had done the research.

She sighed and lifted her gaze to the far horizon, where lake met land and sky, and realized that Mandy had changed course and they were heading home. She could see the Troutmans' dock, welcoming lights in the great room, and decided she could put off telling Mandy the bad news until they were home alone together. She would also tell Mandy that likely these emails were a one-off and that the idiot would soon move on to hassle someone else. Statistically, cyberbullies were cowards who seldom confronted their targets in person. This was a good thing. They could hurl sticks and stones and sick images, but these would never hurt them. She would tell Mandy this, and they would move on.

❧❧❧❧❧

"Home are the sailors, home from the sea," Trout chanted as he passed the pot roast around the table.

"Good thing you made a double recipe, Dad," Ginny said as she heaped her plate.

Amanda was too hungry to comment as she helped herself to an oversize portion. As usual, the Troutman dinner table was jovial and chaotic with everyone talking at once. Thomas had recently graduated from a high chair to a child's chair, and after a few bites of food, the poor little guy was half-asleep, sliding off his seat.

Ginny stood and scooped him up. "I'm taking Tommy to bed."

"Need some help, Mom?" Lissa offered.

"Nope, I'm good," Ginny answered before disappearing into one of the bedrooms.

Amanda noticed that Lori was watching Ginny's family with a wistful look in her eyes. Was she homesick for her own family? Amanda was sure Lori had not told the Troutmans about her revenge porn mess, and Amanda and Sara had already decided to keep her secret. It was Lori's story to tell, if she chose to do so, but Amanda's mom was a great listener, and Ginny was a trusted confidante. They might be able to help her.

Next she glanced at Lissa, who was demolishing a buttered biscuit, leaving tiny crumbs in her red hair. Amanda hoped someone had warned her niece about the dangers of the internet because like Lori, Lissa was on her phone all the time.

"Are you guys spending the night here?" Lori asked Lissa.

Mom answered, "We'd love to have you stay, Lissa. We have plenty of room."

Ginny rejoined them. "We'll take you up on that offer, Diana. Tommy's dead to the world, and Trev won't be home until late tonight."

"It's settled then!" Trout exclaimed from the head of the table. "What about you, Lori? Would you like to spend the night?"

"Can I, Mandy?"

"I don't see why not."

"But my Jeep's at your place."

"No problem," Trout told Lori. "I'll drive you down to Mandy's whenever you're ready. The more the merrier, I say."

Amanda felt Sara's hand on her thigh. Sara gave her a little squeeze and a knowing glance. They would finally be alone, and Amanda was thrilled. They needed some quality time to unwind and love each other. Besides, it would be good for Lori to get to know her new family better, and Lori seemed like a different person when she was with the Troutmans. She lost the attitude, the teen slang, and seemed more like the natural young woman Amanda had met two years ago.

"Matthew, do you mind clearing away the dishes?" Mom asked when everyone had finished stuffing themselves. "I want to show the girls my new listing."

"No, you want to *show off* to the girls." Trout winked. "Diana's moved into the big-time. She's a bucks deluxe Realtor now, so she leaves the chores to her lowly husband."

Mom blew him a kiss. "Thanks, love," she said and then strode to the sunroom, which she used as an office.

"I'll help you, Trout," Sara offered. "I'll rinse, you stack the dishwasher."

"Nope, you all go with your mother. I'm fine," he said as he gathered up a stack of dirty plates and moved toward the kitchen. Amanda watched him slip Ursie a large chunk of beef, and the dog trailed along with him for more.

Chapter Seventeen

Ursie was smiling...

Amanda, Sara, Ginny, Lissa, and Lori followed Mom into the study, where she had already booted up her laptop.

"Watcha got, Diana?" Sara leaned over Mom's shoulder. "A million-dollar listing?"

"No, I've hooked a three-point-five-million-dollar listing!" Mom crowed. "It's waterfront in Cornelius, wait till you see..."

Mom initiated a video tour of a four thousand-square-foot mansion as five sets of eyes followed along in awe. The huge white stucco building with a trendy black tile roof had multiple wings cradling a pool, adjacent tennis court, and overlooking a long-range lake view. Inside, it was as over the top as Amanda expected, with vaulted ceilings, ornate trim, hardwood floors, gourmet kitchen, countless bedrooms with ensuite baths, and a dedicated theater room.

Ginny sneered. "Bet the rich dude who owns it has a trophy wife and two-point-five kids."

"It should be in Florida, not North Carolina," Amanda said.

"Well, I think it's dope, Aunt Diana. But it's extra, right?"

Mom never bad-mouthed her clients, but she said, "It is a bit much, but I'll get a huge commission, and you haven't even seen the really cool part..."

Suddenly, the upbeat music behind the video switched to the soaring Vangelis theme song from Chariots of Fire, and they were looking at the mansion from the sky.

"OMG, Grandma, did you buy a drone?"

"Rented one, and it wasn't cheap." Mom grinned. "It's the first time I've had a listing that warranted the expense. Damn, it was fun!"

"Congratulations, Diana. That's an amazing listing, and I bet it sells fast," Sara said.

Amanda had to admit it was awesome, and as she watched the flying camera slowly pan in on the dock complex, an astonishing idea burst into her brain. It was extravagant, impossible, but it was perfect. She locked it away for safe keeping.

❧ ❧ ❧ ❧

Not until they were leaving and saying goodbye did Sara realize how tired she was. The fresh air, the delicious meal, and the troubling secret she was keeping from Mandy had all conspired to sap her strength. She was glad Mandy was driving. As the four females waved to them from the bay window overlooking the driveway, Trout followed them as far as the screened porch.

"I love you, Mandy Bear," he said, drawing them into a hug. "You too, Sara Sweetie. Be good, and drive safely."

"Where's Ursie?" Mandy asked as they stepped down into the yard, leaving Trout on the porch. "Ursie always says goodbye."

"I fed her and let her out to do her business," Trout said. "She's likely wandering down the road, so keep an eye out for her as you drive away."

"Will do," Mandy promised.

As soon as Trout went inside, Sara guided Mandy around to the passenger side of the van, where they couldn't be seen, and pulled her into an embrace. "This was a wonderful day," she whispered and then kissed Mandy's ear.

"It was the best," Mandy agreed as she took Sara's face between her hands and eased her into a proper kiss.

The kiss lingered, then deepened as they held each other tighter. Sara fancied she could smell the lake in Mandy's hair and feel the heat of sunburn on her cheeks, but before the flame in the pit of her stomach could ignite into a bonfire, she pulled away. "Wait, Mandy. You're driving, and we still need to get home."

"Right, and we'll be alone. Can you believe it?" Mandy said as she gave Sara's bottom a squeeze before moving off to the driver's side and climbing into the van.

As Mandy backed out and then got on their way, Sara saw everyone still watching and waving from the window. She waved back as Mandy switched on the headlights and inched slowly down the road. They hadn't driven fifty yards before they saw a dark figure come loping toward them in the middle of the street.

"Stop! It's Ursie," Sara cried. "It looks like she's got something in her mouth."

Mandy hit the brakes. "I hope it's not a dead squirrel." She turned off the engine and set the brake but left the headlights on as they got out to investigate. Ursie was smiling, and Sara chuckled. To the uninitiated, Ursie's smile looked like she was baring her teeth and scared people to death. In truth, it was her way of welcoming strangers.

They approached the old Doberman, and both squatted to pat the dear beast.

"I'm glad it's not a squirrel," Sara said as Ursie snuggled up to her. "But what's this? A ribbon?"

"Someone put a bow around her neck?"

Sara watched in fascination as Mandy untied the elaborate thing that did look like the big, wilted petals of a bow, with its tails hanging down under Ursie's chin. Once undone, the adornment became a horror because hanging limp in Mandy's hand was a long, blue silk stocking.

Chapter Eighteen

Stalker...

Amanda dropped the stocking to the ground, while Sara stood frozen in shock. Ursie licked Amanda's face and wagged her stubby tail as Amanda explored the dog's fur and inspected her paws.

"Ursie seems okay." Amanda choked out the words, while Sara remained mute. It seemed time itself was frozen in the headlights. Two owls called out a duet, and Amanda struggled to breathe as she blinked back tears. "I should take her back to the house, so she won't chase after us."

It took every ounce of Amanda's will to rise and latch on to Ursie's collar. Her legs were rubber as she began what seemed an impossibly long journey, but fortunately, Ursie needed no coaxing. She broke loose and trotted on her own all the way to the porch steps. Sara still had not moved.

"Are you okay, honey?" Amanda tentatively reached out and touched Sara's sleeve, half-fearing too much contact would break them both.

"What the hell is happening to us?" Sara whimpered as she stared at the stocking, as if it was a poisonous snake. In slow motion, Sara picked it up and walked robotically to the van. She opened her door and tossed it onto the backseat. "Please, let's just go home."

Amanda lost track of the miles as they drove in total silence. Words seemed inadequate, but her mind raced incoherently. She kept checking the rearview mirror.

"Is anyone following us?" Sara asked.

"I don't think so."

"Did someone follow us to the lake this afternoon?"

"God, I have no idea!" Amanda moaned, but how else would their stalker know where they were going? And yes, they now officially had a stalker, not just an anonymous psycho bugging them online. Had this person followed them all the way from their condo in Davidson? If so, then the stalker knew where they lived. The idea was beyond terrifying.

"Could it be someone we know?" Amanda whispered.

Sara was stony-faced. "Maybe, since she knows where we live, knows to follow your van, and knows the location of the Troutmans' home."

Amanda considered the possibility. "This person you're describing knows *me*, not *you*. They know where *I* live, *my* van, directions to *my* family home, and sent *me* the email. So it seems to be a vendetta against me, don't you agree?"

Sara groaned and pinched the bridge of her nose, a sure sign she was getting one of her migraines. "I'm so sorry, Mandy, but it's not about you. It's about both of us. I'm so ashamed, but I've been keeping something from you..."

Over the next several miles, Sara described the Barbie email she'd received that morning. The image of dolls bound together was far more sinister than the one that came to Amanda. As Amanda listened, she longed to comfort Sara, who was obviously distressed and beating herself up with guilt, but Amanda still worried that touching her would push her over the edge.

"It's no excuse," Sara sobbed, "but I didn't tell you because I didn't want to spoil our perfect day."

Seeing Sara cry broke Amanda's resolve. She took Sara's hand, folded it into a ball, and held it against her chest. "It's no big deal, honey. I understand, but we're in this together, so please don't hold back again."

"I won't. I promise."

Sara's hand was ice cold as Amanda continued to hold it against her chest, but because she wanted to keep both hands on the wheel, she repositioned Sara's hand between her thighs, where it would warm up fast.

"Are you getting fresh with me?" Sara smiled and then swiped away her tears with her free hand.

Sex was the last thing on Amanda's mind, but she was relieved to see Sara smile. "How come you keep calling our stalker *she*? Is it a sexist thing, or do you believe it's a woman?"

Sara laughed. "Should we call this person *non-binary*, or *she/he* or *intersex*? Whatever. My gut says it's a woman."

"Really? Political correctness aside, since when did you consider gut feelings valid?"

"You're absolutely right. I've been trained to work with evidence, but in this case, it just feels like a woman."

"So be it. From now on, we'll use female pronouns until proven otherwise."

Amanda relaxed a little because the back-and-forth banter felt almost normal. But then, Sara pulled her captive hand out from between Amanda's thighs and reached into the backseat to retrieve the blue stocking.

Sara opened the glove compartment to get some

light and then studied the stocking. She pulled it out to its full length, examined the wide band of fancy lace at the top, and said, "It's not really silk, it's probably a nylon blend." She ran her hand up inside it and flexed her fingers. "It's smooth and silky, but it's a compression stocking, so it'll stay up on a woman's leg without garters."

"Who has real silk nowadays?" Amanda interrupted.

Sara shrugged. "The lace is pretty but machine-made. You can probably buy these on Amazon."

Amanda didn't care. She'd just as soon throw the obscene thing out the window. "She more likely bought them at Victoria's Secret. It's so sleazy."

Ignoring Amanda, Sara picked up her phone and Googled Amazon. "I was right. These blue stockings are made by Benefeet and cost $9.99 a pair."

"Cheap, I guess—like the creep who's stalking us."

"But Barbie dolls aren't cheap..." Sara continued scrolling. "The blonde representing you looks like a Rebecca Welton doll, and the brunette is a Teresa. Each costs fifty bucks."

Amanda grunted in acknowledgment because she knew Sara did research when she was nervous. It was her go-to activity for reducing stress. Amanda was glad that Sara was distracted but didn't give a flying fig about dolls. Also, it seemed like an investment of just over a hundred dollars to finance a stalker's reign of terror was a bargain.

Sara said, "The problem is, there's nothing unique in these props. Anyone can buy them online, so they're impossible to trace."

"It's okay, honey, we'll figure it out," Amanda

said as she drove into their condo complex. But would they? How could they? The monster had now made personal contact, which meant she could do it again. Amanda feared they wouldn't know who to avoid until it was too late.

"This is serious. I think we should go to the police," Amanda said as they fast-walked to their front door, her gaze skittering around the parking lot, where danger lurked in every shadow.

"I'm afraid you're right." Sara's hand trembled as she fumbled to get the key into the lock. They rushed inside, double-locked the door, and put on the security chain. Amanda quickly checked the window locks and closed all the drapes. "But no police tonight," Sara continued, stopping Amanda's frenzy. "Not one more word about this until morning. What do you say?"

"Yes, please." Amanda exhaled a long sigh and then led Sara straight to the bedroom.

Chapter Nineteen

Make a list...

They made love, the surest route Sara knew to oblivion. The first time was frenzied, a coupling marred by desperation, and it was disturbing. Sara the shrink knew that fear, or a life-threatening event, could trigger the phenomenon. Lovemaking was a coping mechanism to prove you were alive, safe, and for some people, perpetuating the species. Fortunately, Sara quickly forgot to analyze because Mandy's eager body and talented hands overpowered her mind. The second time was unrushed, tender, and utterly satisfying. Had there been a third time? Sara thought so, as she sipped her morning coffee. Yet she couldn't be sure because the end result had been a sweet, profound sleep. The best she'd had in days. It left her lingering in bed, enjoying the aftermath, until nine o'clock. When she untangled from Mandy and took a shower, Mandy slept straight through it.

By her second cup of coffee, Sara heard Mandy stir and then the faraway pulsing of water in the master bathroom. She heard the steel-cut oats bubbling on the stove and the gentle tinkling of the pot lid as they simmered. It was another fresh, sunny day, but Sara had no idea how to use it. There were too many variables. Would Lori be back? Would Maya and Shar call with a dinner invitation? All she knew with certainty was they had to deal with the stalker, but where to start?

She held her breath, checked her emails, and then exhaled in sheer relief because their tormentor had left no new messages. Was it over? Of course not, and Sara still believed the stalker's wrath was aimed at her, not Mandy. Yes, the person knew where they lived, where the Troutmans lived, but anyone with a little research skill could find that information.

Unfortunately, Sara's personal details were far from secure from anyone working at the clinic. Her address and emergency contact—Amanda Rittenhouse—were front and center in her employment file. Even a clever patient could access them. It wouldn't be a stretch for the stalker to figure out that Mandy was Sara's partner and then Google Mandy's details, as well.

Sara didn't have many disgruntled patients, thank heavens. Most were grateful and appreciated her counsel. But there were a few angry ones. Janice Kenny, a troubled but brilliant information technologist, was a prime example. Jan suffered from chronic depression and acute anxiety. She'd come to Sara fresh from losing her job. She was self-medicating with alcohol and sleeping pills. After a full year of biweekly counseling, and after finally finding the proper medication, Jan was back on track. She had a new IT job and even a steady boyfriend.

All that changed two months ago when Jan caught her boyfriend in bed with another man. She went ballistic. After the breakup, Jan spiraled out of control and stopped taking her meds. She raged against homosexuals, started quoting Leviticus, and telling the story of Sodom and Gomorrah. Jan's rage was so intense that Sara found it impossible to keep treating her with the proper empathy and reassigned her to a new counselor.

As far as Sara knew, Jan knew nothing about Sara's relationship with Mandy. How could she? Yet the possibility that Jan had somehow found out had been flashing a red hot warning signal in the back of Sara's mind ever since Mandy got the first email. Jan was technically capable, and the creepy dolls were just her style.

Sara was determined to follow it up.

❦❦❦❦❦

Amanda stepped from the shower and vigorously toweled her body and hair. She slathered on lotion, pulled on a Disney World T-shirt and sweatpants, and then checked her reflection in the steamed mirror. She looked rested. A night in Sara's arms was always the best medicine for whatever ailed her, though her lips were a little bruised, muscles a bit stiff. It was worth it. Plus, the house was blessedly still without Lori in residence. The delicious aroma of hot oatmeal drifted from the kitchen, the day was fresh and sunny, and suddenly, she felt able to open her email. *Thank you, Jesus!* No new message from the stalker. Was it over?

Probably not. She put on a brave face and walked to where Sara was standing at the counter, slicing strawberries and bananas. "Good morning, honey," she whispered before planting a kiss. Sara's lips were slightly swollen, very seductive, and her white terrycloth robe gaped enough to show a hint of cleavage.

"Good morning, sleepyhead," Sara said, pulling Amanda into her arms. "Thanks for last night. I needed that."

"Me too." She breathed in the scent of Sara's warm

skin, like clover in sunshine, and rested her cheek on the generous cushion of her breast. "Forget the world. Let's stay like this forever."

Sara sighed and pulled away. She slid the oatmeal off the burner. "Maybe not forever, but let's not talk about it until after breakfast."

"Agreed. But then what?"

"Then, we make a list."

True to their vow, they spoke of nothing worrisome until they'd licked away the last morsel of oatmeal and drunk all the juice. Sara said she'd reached her caffeine limit, so she excused herself and went to the study, while Amanda poured herself a second cup. When Sara returned, she had two lined notepads and handed one to Amanda.

"Are you serious?" Amanda stared at the pad.

"Look, we can't go to the police without a list of suspects. What do we tell them? That we've gotten some weird emails with Barbie dolls and blue stockings? That someone tied a blue ribbon on our dog? They'd laugh in our faces."

"Maybe they should laugh. Maybe it's a silly prank."

"Do you really believe that?" Sara wrote a name at the top of her list: Jane Doe—patient.

Of course, Amanda didn't believe it. Would a prankster bother to track a dog belonging to her stepfather? And then tie a bow on a ninety-pound Doberman? "Who's Jane Doe?"

"One of my former patients, a very troubled woman with an ax to grind. She's my top suspect, and I plan to talk to her today."

Amanda felt blindsided. She'd expected they'd spend the day together. And Sara would never reveal her patient's name nor give a single detail about her mental state. She took confidentiality very seriously, but some of Sara's patients were seriously dangerous. "I don't like this, Sara. If Jane has it in for you, should you even be talking to her? Also, I don't think you should go alone."

Sara's eyebrows shot up, and her facial muscles stiffened. Amanda knew the look. Sara was going into shrink mode, dropping a professional shield between herself and Amanda. In the beginning, Amanda had been hurt and resentful when Sara blocked her, but now she knew it wasn't personal. Or negotiable.

"I'm sorry. You're right," Sara said, surprising Amanda. "I'm no longer Jane's therapist, and it would be too confrontational to question her directly. But the woman who's counseling Jane now is a good friend, a forensic psychologist, and I'm sure she'd question Jane on my behalf."

"Your friend studies criminals?"

"Yes, she does. She's also a lecturer at UNC Charlotte and does consulting work with the police, mostly criminal profiles."

"Huh…I don't suppose you'll tell me this woman's name."

"Maybe, if you ask nicely." Sara winked. "But who's on your list?"

Amanda drew a blank. She couldn't think of anyone who would want to hurt her. Naturally, she'd pissed people off, but not to where they'd seek revenge—except for Russel. The wealthy, middle-aged lawyer had bought a number of her small sculptures and kept showing up at her shows. A "groupie," of sorts. Amanda knew he was interested in her body, not her art, and he became abusive when she said no.

He harassed her with vile texts and emails, and kept turning up at her favorite coffee shop and even the grocery store. When she outright told him she was a lesbian, he was repulsed, and the cyber messages got really ugly. But then, as she ignored him, he just stopped. Suddenly. Six months ago.

"Are you sure we shouldn't consider men?" Amanda asked, her pencil poised above her pad.

Sara blinked. "Like that piece of shit Russel Cowley?"

Amanda nodded and wrote his name at the top of her list. She'd told Sara about Russel, and at the time, Sara had wanted to intervene. Call the cops. Hire a hit man. But Amanda forbade it. When Russel disappeared, Amanda assumed Sara had forgotten all about him.

Sara said, "Actually, we have made quite a few male enemies over the years, but most of them are dead or in jail." She finished with a bitter laugh.

It was true. Over the next half hour or so, they reminisced about the bizarre adventures they had shared, encountering criminals ranging from thieves, fraudsters, drug dealers, and bent politicians to cold-blooded killers. None of those encounters were by choice. The old threats had all been neutralized. But just for fun, they added their names to the bottom of their lists. Oddly, there were very few women among them.

Amanda said, "Remember Melinda Meeks? She was a piece of work." Several years ago, during the midterm elections, when their friend Shar was running for Congress, Melinda had infiltrated the campaign. The mousy little woman had seemed harmless, but in fact, she was the daughter of a crazed evangelical preacher, hated liberal elites, despised homosexuals, and eventually murdered a dear friend. Amanda wrote her name under Russel's.

"But Melinda's in prison, isn't she?" Sara said.

"I guess...just saying." Amanda thought the listing exercise was a waste of time, but it rekindled old memories. Like a vulnerable young woman named Tammy Tillman, an ex-heroin addict whom Sara had counseled. The woman had tried to turn her life around and developed a talent for baking. Sara had recommended that they hire Tammy to make the cake for Ginny and Trev's wedding. Big mistake. The fallout took them to the Outer Banks to rescue Tammy from a drug-dealing boyfriend who proved to be a murderer. Turned out, they needed to be rescued from Tammy, who was so enthralled, so mind-controlled by the boyfriend that she helped him kidnap Amanda and Sara. In the end, Tammy had come through and saved their lives. At great cost.

Tammy was sentenced to the North Carolina Correctional Institute for Women. Sara had intervened to have her placed in a treatment program, where she received psychiatric care, but Amanda had always had a soft spot for Tammy. Always felt guilty about the harsh sentence. So without mentioning it to Sara, who carried her own burden of guilt for bringing Tammy into their circle in the first place, Amanda had kept in touch. She followed Tammy's progress through the system, knew she'd been given early parole and was currently living in her old home in Mooresville.

As Sara completed her list, Amanda gazed at the crisp blue day through the patio doors and finished her coffee. She had always wanted to reconnect with Tammy, to make sure she was okay, and Tammy's house was only twenty minutes from Amanda's studio at Trout's Place.

Did Tammy bear a grudge against them? Could she be their stalker? Amanda thought not, but she wasn't sure. Certainly the woman was unstable—or had been. She reached across the table and touched Sara's wrist. "Are you really going to work today?"

Sara rolled her head around, working out the kinks, and also gazed at the lake. "I guess I need to. Thursday is Jane's day for counseling. If I leave now, I can meet with my friend and suggest questions for Jane. I'd like to rule her out. Or in."

"So you're going?"

"Yes, sorry."

"When do we contact the police?"

"Let me try this first. Maybe we can nip it in the bud. I'd rather stay here with you, babe. Will you be okay on your own?"

It was Amanda's moment of truth. "Sure, I'll be fine. I'll head up to my studio and get some work done, maybe check on Lori. She may want to hitch a ride back with me."

Sara groaned. "Oh, God, can't we leave her there for now?"

Amanda laughed. "I'll see what I can do." The condo was their sanctuary, but lately, it had been invaded in so many unforeseen ways. Amanda wasn't devious by nature, but Sara didn't need to know about her intended side trip. She had enough on her plate already.

"It's settled then," Amanda said. "We'll rendezvous here, and I'll bring home barbecue."

Chapter Twenty

Déjà vu...

A manda and Moby Dyke drove north again on Interstate 77 toward Mooresville, like she'd done a hundred times before. Past the few remaining brown fields, scattered with leafless trees. Past the new interchanges with high-rises and suburban clutter, all under a cloudless blue winter sky. Her thoughts were floating, and she was oddly detached. Everything felt like déjà vu. Or a curtain call.

The last five days had resurrected so many ghosts from her first seven years with Sara. It started with the wedding in Asheville, with so many acquaintances re-entering their lives, then continued with the sudden appearance of Lori, who connected Amanda with her whole new Mayberry family. Soon they would reunite with Maya and Shar. They had been Sara's best friends, who soon became Amanda's best friends on that fateful visit to Cape Hatteras, where they also confronted the evil surrounding Tammy Tillman.

It seemed the major actors in her new life had all come onstage for a curtain call. They were holding hands and taking bows. Would the audience throw flowers or curveballs? Amanda didn't know. This weird conjunction of stars in random space included malevolence, as well as joyous reunion. Lori's cyberbullies, the blue silk stockings, and Ursie's smile—were they all connected? Was it wise to court a ghost like Tammy, as Amanda intended? Or should they all be ignored until the stage lights dimmed and the curtain fell?

She shook her head, took a deep breath, and blinked a few times. Without realizing it, Amanda had reached her Mooresville exit. She was at a crossroads. Should she turn west to her studio, like she'd promised Sara, or east to confront Tammy? The problem with crossroads was they required decisions, and the problem with curtain calls was they signaled an ending. Amanda thought about Grandma Vivian's engagement ring, hidden in her compact, in her makeup bag, at the back of her closet. The ring symbolized the start of a whole new play. But first the play had to be written, and the author had to make decisions to guide the plot in the desired direction.

She took another deep breath and turned east.

❧ ❧ ❧ ❧

Sara drove her Miata south on Interstate 77 toward her clinic in Charlotte, like she'd done a hundred times before. She didn't want to go there, didn't want to do this. She wanted to spend the day home alone with Mandy. It was like playing hooky in reverse. She felt odd showing up to work when she was supposed to be on vacation, like she was doing something wrong, going where she was unwelcome. Yet she fought the traffic, signaled and switched lanes, wove in and out of the uptown chaos as her mind wandered, asking the same question over and over: Why is this happening?

And why now? It seemed it had started in Asheville. Had they pushed a wrong button there? Offended some unbalanced soul at the wedding party of relative strangers? Or was it connected to Lori's internet mess? Lori's problem started from inside-out. She and her girlfriend, Lilly, had unwittingly started the pornography train to god only knew how many perverts. Sara and Mandy had moved Lori's problem from the outside in to the cops. When Mandy and Lori visited Red at the police station, they had initiated a cannonball run of deletion and retribution. Did the bad guys know who had come after them? Were they seeking revenge by unleashing the Barbie doll series? Both events involved internet terror campaigns targeting members of the same family. Was it a coincidence? Sara didn't believe in coincidences.

On the other hand, the attacks were as different as blatant to subtle, sleaze to sophistication. The mind of the blue silk stalker was on a completely different plane than the monkey brains forwarding Lori's nudies. Monkey brains didn't show up in person or decorate Dobermans. They tittered in their basements and rarely saw the light of day. No, their stalker's style was insidious innuendo, it was personal. If she'd showed up once—she'd show up again.

And it was all Sara's fault. Mandy was right. Sara didn't trust gut feelings, but this time, she did. Their stalker was some demon unleashed from Sara's past—a friend she'd disrespected, an ex-lover, or most likely, a patient. Knowing she was to blame, but not knowing who blamed her, was driving her crazy. And crazy made her mean, especially to poor Lori.

What was that about? Sara loved Lori like family and was perfectly aware that Lori idolized her. Or she used to. Yet ever since she'd arrived, Sara had behaved less like a mentor, more like a critical mother. This morning when Mandy had offered to bring Lori back to the condo, Sara had nixed the idea. Lori was a vulnerable teenager, like many she counseled, so why didn't Sara show Lori equal compassion?

Because it wasn't Sara's role. She had typecast herself as the adult in the room, the analyst who rejects gut feelings, coincidence, and any emotion not supported by reason. She liked proof and facts, but were those the same as truth? Sara did not like the person she'd become. She thought about the elegant custom engagement ring she'd commissioned for Mandy and her hope for a brand new forever life. The ring was hidden away with her underwear. She wanted to hide her brain away with her bras, panties, and other unmentionables, replacing it with an open mind.

As she abruptly changed lanes to take the exit she'd almost missed, Sara was bombarded with a cacophony of honking horns. The man she'd cut off gave her the finger. She deserved it. She was a car wreck. She would change.

But not before nailing the blue silk stalker.

Chapter Twenty-one

A lump in her throat...

When Amanda drove into the old part of Mooresville and turned right on Main Street, moving into the poorer part of town, she recalled the first time she'd visited Tammy. Sara was with her. That day, the brutal sun of July beat down on the Miata's convertible top, making the interior smell like a heated pup tent. The sports car was brand new and so was their relationship. They were in those early days of heightened awareness. They had slept together only once so that every glance or brushing touch caused an ache so potent it hurt. Did Amanda still feel it? Yes, but it was different now. The glance and brushing touch didn't hurt anymore; they gently aroused with the comfort and certainty that they were in it for the long haul. They lived together, owned the bed, and shared the past. They knew that small missteps wouldn't end them, only strengthen them.

That day, when they passed the abandoned mill and turned into mill town, where Tammy lived, the rows of decrepit wooden bungalows, once owned by the factory workers who made blue jeans, were steaming. Malodorous garbage spilled from the cans lining the cracked curbs, junk cars sat on concrete blocks, and half-naked teenagers played in a gushing water hydrant. When they stepped onto Tammy's sagging porch, a pit bull in the yard next door barked viciously and flung his teeth against a chain link fence.

Today the decrepit bungalows, trash cans, and cars on blocks were silent under the frozen sky. The teenagers were in school, the hydrant was dormant, and the dog was gone. The neighborhood seemed asleep. Or abandoned. Today Amanda was alone, with a hard lump in her throat as she hesitated to knock. The powder blue paint on the screen door was flaked and scaled, like a painful sunburn, and stuffing billowed from the cracks in the upholstered porch furniture, like dirty snow.

With her knuckles poised to knock, Amanda was stricken by the fact that for the past several years, she had enjoyed blissful freedom with Sara, while Tammy had been in prison. Did Tammy blame her and Sara? Would Tammy's pent-up rage cause her to attack with Barbie dolls? Tammy had been to the Troutmans' home the day of Ginny's wedding. She had served the magnificent cake she'd baked, met the family, and patted Ursie. She had motive and opportunity. Amanda assumed the years of incarceration had changed Tammy. Would Tammy even recognize Amanda? Would Amanda recognize her?

She steeled herself, knocked on the door, and listened for a response. She heard distant traffic moving on Main Street and the honking of Canada geese flying overhead. Eventually, she heard the faint sound of a radio coming from within, closely followed by light footsteps approaching the door, and finally the clinking of a guard chain being released.

Suddenly, the door opened, and she was face-to-face with an older Tammy Tillman. Staring through the rusted screen, Amanda saw that the petite, shaggy-haired dishwater blonde still had the figure of a young girl but the eyes of an old lady. Those piercing, pale blue eyes were wide with surprise. Or shock.

"Is that you, Mandy?" Tammy asked in her distinctive, husky voice.

"Yeah, it's me. Hello, Tammy."

"What the fuck?" Tammy opened the screen door so fast that Amanda had to jump back out of its way. "What the fuck?" she repeated. "Didn't expect to find you standing on my doorstep. Come on in."

Tammy was smiling, and she didn't have a butcher knife in her hand. Amanda smiled back and stepped over the threshold.

Tammy's furniture was still shabby, but the small house was neat and meticulously clean. As Amanda followed her to the kitchen in the back, she was surprised by how well she remembered the place. It seemed frozen in time because it had been—while Tammy was doing time. That summer day Amanda had visited, the rooms smelled of vanilla and hot baked goods. Today it smelled like tomato soup.

"I was about to have lunch," Tammy said. "Will you join me?"

Seriously? After all this time and trauma, a lunch invitation? "Are you sure? I don't want to intrude."

"If you're hungry, then eat," Tammy commanded through a crooked smile as she took out a second soup mug and set a second place at the round oak table. "I could use a PB&J sandwich, how about you?"

"Y-yeah, thanks," Amanda stuttered as she moved toward the old double farm sink under the window, out of the busy woman's way. While Tammy slathered bread with peanut butter and jelly, Amanda glanced out at the yard of weeds that had once been a garden. She tried to think of something to say. Should she mention prison or avoid the subject? What would Sara do? By the time they settled to eat and Amanda picked up a spoon, she blurted out, "What happened to the dog next door?"

Tammy tilted her head and blinked several times. "Oh, you mean Hamilton, the pit bull. I'd almost forgotten. Those folks next door were long gone by the time I moved back."

It was awkward, at least for Amanda. "Are you still baking those amazing cakes?"

A cloud of regret dimmed Tammy's eyes. "Nope. Got no time for that shit anymore. I was raised up to be a cleaning woman, so that's what I am. Destiny, right?"

Wrong. Tammy's murdered mom, Lynette, had owned a thriving cleaning service on the Outer Banks called Mer-Maids. The Tillman family was riding high until the cops found out the maids were stealing from the clients and running drugs on the side. But Tammy had escaped all that and become an entrepreneur, selling her baked delights, mostly wedding cakes, to a growing audience. It was why Sara had believed in her.

"You could start up your business again, Tammy. You were so damn good at it! I know you'd be successful."

"Ya think?" It wasn't a question, but rather a sarcastic denial. "I call this my lunch, but it's really my breakfast. I got up just a few minutes before you showed up, and I'll take a nap after you go."

Tammy explained that she worked night shifts cleaning big corporations when all the employees were gone. She got home around dawn and then sacked out. "I don't have enough energy during the day to start a business. Besides, I earn good money cleaning." She shrugged.

It seemed a terrible waste of talent. "But you used to sell your baked goods online. Couldn't you start up that way?"

"Someone stole my laptop while I was in prison, and I can't afford a new one. Now can we talk about something else?"

As Amanda searched for a new topic, she realized that without a laptop, Tammy was unlikely to be their cyber stalker. Short on cash, she wasn't buying silk stockings and Barbie dolls on Amazon. She had to say something.

"Are you seeing anyone?" she stupidly asked.

"Why? Do you want a date?" Tammy winked. "I never had anyone as fine as you in prison. Like, only the fat bull dykes wanted my skinny ass."

Amanda was shocked, blushing from the roots of her hair to her toenails. Tammy never talked like that before. "But you're straight!" she blurted.

"Damn straight!" Tammy smiled. "Sorry, I couldn't resist, and you should have seen your face! Yeah, it's always been men for me, but I don't have a very good track record, do I?"

"Guess not," Amanda agreed and finished her lunch.

"What about you? Are you still seeing Sara?"

Amanda flushed again, acutely aware of how lucky she was, compared to Tammy. "Yes, we're still together."

"I knew it!" Tammy crowed. "Love is love, right?"

"Right." Amanda helped clear the dishes from the table to the sink. Tammy washed, Amanda dried. In silence. They were strangers from completely different backgrounds who had shared a few intense weeks. Did they have anything to say to each other? When they finished the cleanup, Tammy took a seat and indicated that Amanda should sit across from her.

"It's great to see you, Mandy, but why are you here?"

Good question. It had been foolish to think that Tammy was their stalker. It was ludicrous. Had she ever really believed it? The lump in her throat was back. Digging deep, Amanda finally understood the real reason for her visit.

"I wanted to see you, Tammy. I care about you, I worry about you, and I hate how things ended between us."

Tammy's face blanched a whiter shade of pale. In that moment, she looked like a vulnerable Jodie Foster facing down Hannibal Lecter. When she spoke, her voice was so tiny that Amanda could hardly hear her. "Thanks, but I'm fine. Don't apologize because you did nothing wrong."

"But you did something right," Amanda continued, taking the younger woman's hand. The lump in her throat was gone. "You saved our lives, and I never thanked you. So thank you. I should have said it sooner."

Suddenly, Tammy seemed shy and pulled her hand away from Amanda. "It's my thirtieth birthday next month. If I bake a cake, will you and Sara help me eat it?"

Chapter Twenty-two

It's possible...

S ara's clinic was tucked away on a side street
near the massive Carolinas Medical Center,
a sprawling complex that spanned multiple city
blocks and generated the traffic that made parking a
nightmare. The clinic was situated in three suites of
a 1970s-style office campus that had seen better days.
She circled the lot, hoping someone would be foolish
enough to drive away for a lunch break, and finally
got lucky, stealing some older guy's space. Then, as
she walked up the cracked sidewalk, which in summer
was shaded with mature trees, it struck her how cold
and utilitarian the place looked. As a city employee,
with some supplementary income from a large mental
health nonprofit group, Sara understood her status
was low on the totem pole compared to psychiatrists
in private practice who made big money and hung out
in upscale offices, but she wouldn't have it any other
way. Her patients had no health insurance. They were
charity cases, sometimes homeless, often convicted
felons, addicts, or disturbed teenagers, folks deemed
hopeless, and they needed her. She made a difference,
or so she hoped.

But today she still didn't want to be here, still
didn't want to do this, but there was no turning back.
She pressed the security button mounted on the wall
beside the reinforced glass doors, waved to April, the

receptionist, and was buzzed in. The waiting room was quiet, with only two sets of anxious mothers seated with nervous kids. Sara glanced at the big red and white sign saying *Zero Violence*, with an X crossed over the word "violence," and passed two posters depicting the smiling mug shots and bios of the Doctors of the Month, of which Sara was one. She grinned at her images, flipped it the bird, and then approached the desk.

"What are you doing here today, Dr. Orlando?" April said. "I thought you were on vacation."

April looked her up and down because Sara wasn't dressed to her usual professional standard, which wasn't much: pantsuit, whatever blouse was clean, and low heels. Today she looked more like her patients in jeans, running shoes, and her old Navy peacoat.

"I'm not here officially," Sara said, "but I'd like a word with Dr. Yee. Is she available?"

If April was curious, she didn't show it. She gave one of her huge gold hoop earrings a tug and tapped her keyboard. "Dr. Yee's just finishing up in the training room, but then she has a one o'clock appointment. If you hurry, you can catch her for maybe twenty minutes."

"Thanks, April." Sara rushed into the hallway leading to the administration offices and the training room, where Sara and other doctors trained volunteers to man the "hotlines." These volunteers were the first line of defense in suicide prevention and crisis intervention. They answered phone calls from people on the edge, urged them to accept visits from the mobile dispatch units of social workers who would offer immediate in-home help, or take them to the hospital. The doctors gave the volunteers the right words to convince the callers not to hang up. It was important, exhausting work, and when Dr. Angela Yee emerged, she looked far less frazzled than Sara always felt after a session with the volunteers.

The tall, slim Asian woman was in her late forties but looked a decade younger. As usual, Angela wore a lovely dress and high heels. Perfectly applied makeup enhanced her serene face, and her silken black hair was masterfully cut to curve with her jawline. She seemed unsurprised to see Sara, but then, Angela seldom showed her emotions. She would make an excellent poker player or a no-nonsense forensic psychologist.

Angela smiled. "Sara, how can I help you?"

"May I speak to you a moment? About Janice Kenny?" Sara glanced nervously over her shoulder. She knew full well that Jan was Angela's one o'clock, and although the patients' consulting rooms were in a wing on the opposite side of the building, she didn't want Jan to see her.

In the meantime, Angela gave Sara a long, probing look. She knew the history between Sara and Jan—the homophobia, the breakdown of mutual trust, all the reasons Sara had asked Angela to take over Jan's counseling.

"You realize Janice is my next patient. Is there a problem?"

"There might be..." Sara didn't need to say anything more. She had Angela's attention. They went to Angela's quiet office, where they could be alone. Angela sat at her desk. Sara sat across from her.

"It must be serious, or you wouldn't approach me like this," Angela said.

"Yes, Mandy and I have acquired a troublesome stalker, and I want your opinion about whether or not Janice Kenny is behind it."

Angela stared, her expression unreadable. "She's my patient now, so you shouldn't be involved."

"I know, and I want you to leave me out of it, but could you ask Jan some hypothetical questions? I've made a list of subjects that could provoke a response that could give us some idea if she's capable."

Angela frowned. She picked up a pen and clicked the ballpoint in and out. "Are you asking me to profile a patient? It's highly irregular."

"I'm frightened, Angie. If Jan is doing this, she's dangerous not only to me and Mandy, but to herself." Sara knew that Angela was a by-the-book therapist, as she should be, but Sara needed help. She removed the list of indirect questions from her bag and slid it across the desk.

Angela quit clicking her pen and picked up the list. She scowled at it and said, "I guess you better tell me, but make it quick."

Sara gave it to her in a nutshell: the Barbie dolls, the blue stockings, the bondage, and the blanked-out faces. When she got to the part about Ursie, Angela's almond eyes expanded in shock.

"So your stalker has made personal contact. That changes things. You must contact the police, Sara."

"We will, I promise, after today..." Sara let the sentence trail off, implying that Sara would go to the authorities only after Angela questioned Jan. "But," Sara admitted, "I don't know why Jan would target Mandy. They've never even met."

Angela closed her eyes in concentration as Sara fidgeted in her chair. Just when the silence was becoming unbearable, Angela said, "No, Janice has met Amanda. I saw them together at the Christmas party last year when we all came with our families. Janice was doing so well then under your counseling that she'd been invited to attend." Angela's eyes popped open, and she let out a deep sigh. "I introduced her to Amanda. I told Janice that Amanda was your friend. Sorry."

Sorry? Panic clawed at Sara as the jigsaw pieces fell into place. The Christmas party was before Jan caught her boyfriend in bed with another man, before the homophobia, before Jan fired Sara. There was nothing wrong with Jan's memory. She would put Sara and Amanda together and jump to the right conclusion.

Sara forced Angela to meet her eyes. "So do you think Jan might be the stalker? Will you talk to her?"

To her credit, Angela did not look away. "To answer your first   question, yes, I think it's possible. As to your second question, yes again, I will speak to her. But I make no promises. I will not reveal the content of our conversation."

"Understood. I owe you one, Angie."

"You owe me at least three, Dr. Orlando. Now get the hell out of here, or I'll be late."

Smiling, Sara watched Angela Yee's sleek figure glide down the hallway and out of sight. She knew Angela would never tell her what transpired in her session with Jan, but Angela might give her some sort of a signal. So she decided to hang around for forty-five minutes, until the session was over. She made her way to the vending machines, fed in a dollar, and got a Diet Pepsi. She strolled back to the reception area, where she could sit against the back wall, out of sight behind the Plexiglas panels. From that vantage point, she could watch the action in the lobby and keep her eyes peeled for Jan's departure.

She came up from behind and tapped April on

the shoulder. "Mind if I sit back here awhile?"

"Did you see Dr. Yee?"

"Yes, I did. Thanks."

April winked and touched her gold hoop. "Make yourself at home, Doc."

Sara sat in an uncomfortable chair, crossed her legs, took out her phone, and sipped her Pepsi. She checked her emails but found nothing new from their stalker. Maybe, as Mandy had hoped, it was over. Sara prayed this was true. The fact that Angela had not outright denied that Jan could be their stalker spoke volumes. When Angela spoke to Jan today, would Jan sense that someone was suspicious? Would that stop her?

The minutes dragged like hours. Sara recrossed her legs in the opposite direction and finished her soda. The phone held no interest, but she kept it out on her lap so she would look busy. She imagined Mandy at work in her studio, hopefully forgetting her worries and enjoying herself. Sara loved to watch Mandy lost in her work, her slim body leaning over a piece of steel, a welding torch in her gloved hand, her face pinched in concentration behind a Plexiglas shield. Sometimes Sara wished her job was physical, with a tangible reward, like Mandy's exquisite sculpture.

Just as she was wondering why she had chosen her thankless profession, Sara sensed a commotion in the lobby. When she looked up, she saw Janice Kenny stomp across the floor with Angela Yee close behind. Both women looked downright distraught. Sara checked her phone. It was only one thirty, so their session had ended fifteen minutes early. What the hell was that about?

Sara watched Jan's body language and tried to

gauge her emotion. Jan's short arms and legs were pumping with electric tension, her dark eyes looked furious behind her thick glasses, and her frizzy brown hair was wilder than usual as she stormed from the building. Angela seemed to be struggling to regain her famous calm as she strode purposefully around the corner and into the administration wing.

Sara jumped up and headed her off. "What happened, Angie?" she cried.

But Angela held up both hands, palms out, stopping Sara where she stood. It was the first time Sara had seen the placid Dr. Yee rattled.

"Please, tell me something!" Sara begged.

Sara didn't expect an answer as Angela turned her back, her high heels clicking away on the tiled floor. But then, at the very last minute, she looked back over her shoulder, an odd look on her face, and said two words: "It's possible."

Chapter Twenty-three

We can relax now...

So are we going to Tammy's thirtieth birthday party?" Sara asked as she helped herself to another serving of barbecue.

Amanda was bone-tired after her day in Mooresville, and she suspected Sara was exhausted, as well. But thankfully, they were alone. Amanda had stopped by her parents' house after her visit with Tammy, but Lori hadn't wanted to come home with her.

"I don't know what to say. Tammy invited us, but I think it was a reflex action, you know? After I apologized for the way things ended between us, she got all flustered and blurted out the invitation."

Sara put down her fork and searched Amanda's eyes. "I don't think that's what happened. You were being kind, and kindness is the scariest emotion of all. Tammy didn't know what else to do with it."

Amanda didn't know what to do with Sara's statement, true as it might be. "Okay, oh, Wise One, what should we do? Go to the party or not?"

"Do you want to?"

Yes, Amanda realized she wanted to go but didn't appreciate being psychoanalyzed. She was too damn tired. "You decide."

"Obviously, the visit with Tammy helped you, babe. It seems like you got something off your chest. We don't have much in common with her, but I think it would be fun. Let's do it."

Amanda decided she'd made a mistake by going first—telling about her day before Sara told about hers—because Sara got to ask all the hard questions and dissect Amanda's motives. It had seemed preposterous to Sara that Amanda thought Tammy was their stalker, and it was preposterous, so Sara was right again.

"Why didn't Lori come back with you?" Sara asked as she popped a hushpuppy into her mouth.

"Lori's all in awe of Ginny now and besties with Lissa. Since it's Thursday, open mic night at Buffalo Guys, Ginny invited Lori to the club to watch her sing. Once Lori sees Ginny's awesomely sexy performance and hears her growly voice, Lori will have a new hero."

Sara laughed through a mouthful. "That's good. In the beginning, I thought Lori had a crush on me, then it was Red, now Ginny. The pressure's off."

"Do I detect a little jealousy?" Amanda teased. "How do you feel about that, Doc?"

"Oh, stop!" Sara balled up a napkin and tossed it at Amanda. "Shut up so I can tell you about my day…"

≈≈≈≈

Sara split the remaining slaw and baked beans between them and chose her words carefully. "So I met with Dr. Angela Yee before she had her session with Jane Doe, and…"

"Wait!" Mandy interrupted. "Is Dr. Yee the forensic psychologist? You wouldn't tell me her name before."

Sara laughed. "Yes, she is. I told Angie about our stalker, gave her a list of questions to ask Jane Doe, and she agreed."

"So you really didn't confront Jane yourself?"

Sara snorted and gave Mandy a goofy, cross-eyed look. She'd already told Mandy she wouldn't approach an ex-patient directly, so Mandy's question didn't deserve an answer. Instead, Sara told her the basics of what happened at the clinic. Almost everything.

Mandy listened in rapt attention, so intent that she forgot to eat her meal. "Did Dr. Yee think Jane's the one?"

"She thought it was possible. I think it might be over."

Right on cue, Mandy took out her phone and so did Sara. Sara guessed that Mandy had avoided her email all afternoon, as had Sara. They both looked. "Nothing new here," Sara said with a sigh of relief.

"Nothing here, either!" Mandy crowed. "You're a genius. You scared her away!"

Sara pushed her plate aside, opened her mouth to speak, but nothing came out. She felt a niggling doubt and didn't want to project false hope. After all, Janice Kenny might not be responsible. Perhaps Sara just wanted her to be. She always told her patients not to second-guess themselves, but Sara was notoriously unable to take her own advice.

"What?" Mandy demanded. "You don't seem too sure."

"I'm pretty sure."

"Is there something you're not telling me?"

There was, but did it matter? She decided to let Mandy decide. "Well, it turns out, you met Jane Doe last year at our Christmas party."

Mandy began blinking rapidly, a sure sign that her brain was in retrieval mode. Mandy wasn't particularly verbal, at least with strangers, but her visual memory was unparalleled. She could almost see Mandy's artist eyes shuffling through the people she'd met at the party.

She suddenly stopped blinking and said, "Was it that nervous little woman with the big glasses and frizzy brown hair?"

Mandy had hit the bull's-eye, first throw. "Yes, you're right. She's the one."

Mandy looked smug. "What's her name?"

Sara closed her lips and pulled a finger across her mouth, zipping it shut. Mandy didn't need to know Jan's name, but it was a comfort to know that if, God forbid, Mandy encountered Jan in person, she'd recognize her.

"Never mind," Mandy said. "You've solved it, honey, we can relax now." Discussion over. Mandy started clearing the dishes.

Relax was exactly what they should not do. As Sara wondered how to shake Mandy out of her complacency, Sara's cellphone rang, startling them both. She checked the caller ID. "It's okay, it's only Maya."

She was thrilled to hear her dear friend's voice. Since Maya and Shar had moved to D.C., they'd mostly communicated via texts and emails, and they had so much catching up to do. After the usual sweet talk and trash talk that had enriched their friendship for decades, Maya extended the anticipated dinner invitation. The couple wanted them to come to their house in Belmont tomorrow night. She paused the conversation to ask Mandy.

"Yes, yes, yes!" Mandy said, fist-pumping the air. "But what about Lori?"

Sara told Maya that they'd possibly be babysitting Mandy's cousin tomorrow night, and Maya said no problem. There would be plenty of food for five.

After the phone call, the evening turned cozy. They took after-dinner drinks into the great room, kicked back, leaning at opposite ends of the sofa, legs intertwined, and watched a glorious pink and blue sunset over Lake Norman. No television, no phones, just reminiscences about the good times they'd shared with Maya and Shar, speculation about what the couple would do once they'd moved back to Charlotte, and then easy silence, while she and Mandy floated with their personal thoughts.

Times like these were precious to Sara. Her mind wandered from how, at that very moment, Lori was watching Ginny perform at Buffalo Guys to how much she would hate reporting back to work Monday to the delights of taking Mandy to bed that night.

She thought about the stalker only once.

Chapter Twenty-four

The long distant past...

Amanda was dozing with her eyes closed as Sara drove to Maya and Shar's. She felt content as a kitten in the sun after a lazy Friday with Sara. They had slept late, listened to mellow music, and finished their respective novels. And thinking about kittens, Amanda recalled their old nickname for Maya and Shar: the Cat Couple. Because they had two cats, of course, but also because Maya resembled one. She was a tall, erect African American who moved with liquid, cat-like strides. Her limbs were long and strong, a panther with a glistening, short-cropped Afro. She had the cheekbones of an Egyptian princess and the amber eyes of the Sphynx. But defense lawyers dare not be fooled by Maya's full, smiling lips because when it came to her job, she was a jungle predator. As an assistant district attorney in Charlotte, she took no prisoners. She was also born and raised near Philadelphia, like Amanda, so they had that in common.

Shar was Maya's polar opposite. A Southern belle, she came from one of Charlotte's original, old money families. She was white, medium height, with curly, jaw-length brown hair, big chocolate eyes, and a bosom to rival Dolly Parton's. Her accent was warm honey, and her humor was infectious. Shar was also a rebel who broke with her conservative family, founded a women's craft and clothing shop called Goddess Gifts, and became a wicked smart entrepreneur. She was also the sitting representative in the U.S. Congress from the Ninth District, a miraculous feat for any Democrat in the ruby red state.

In the beginning, Amanda had been terrified to meet the Cat Couple, and not just because she was a dog person, but because they had been longtime best friends with Sara and her ex-partner, Judith Dellinger. For years, the two couples had been inseparable. When Jude dumped Sara, Sara was devastated and unable to trust a new relationship. Penetrating Sara's defensive armor had been an emotional uphill battle for Amanda. It hadn't helped that apparently Amanda looked almost identical to Jude, a fact that once made Amanda wonder if she was just a poor substitute for Sara's lost love.

Thankfully, the awkwardness hadn't lasted long. During their first vacation together as a foursome, the Cat Couple had embraced Amanda and made her feel welcome. Maya had said that in spite of her physical resemblance to Jude, they were nothing alike. She said Amanda was better for Sara than Jude had ever been. Amanda would never forget Shar's kind words: *You are light to Jude's dark. You are sun to Jude's moon.* Now all these years later, Amanda had been with Sara longer than Sara had been with Jude. Amanda's worries were now in the long distant past. She thought about the engagement ring, how she and Sara seemed like two connected souls, and how Amanda felt secure inside her own skin.

"Wake up, babe, we're almost there." Sara gently touched Amanda's thigh. "Did you remember to bring the wine?"

Amanda yawned and scooted upright. While

she was day dreaming, the sun had dropped low in the sky, casting long shadows in the older residential neighborhood of Belmont, where Maya and Shar lived. "Yeah, I stashed the bottle behind my seat. I hope Chianti works with the meal." Amanda also hoped their friends had rum and tonic on hand.

"That wine works with anything," Sara said. "Besides, Maya and Shar aren't picky. I can't wait to see them!"

"Yes, I hope Shar has some juicy stories about how she's been kicking MAGA butt up in D.C."

Sara laughed. "I'm sure she does."

Mature hardwoods spread their bare branches alongside enormous evergreen magnolia trees. Amanda saw classic gingerbread Victorians, 1920s bungalows, and a few blocky brick ranchers. She felt a sudden nostalgia as she recalled the many good times they'd shared at their friends' house.

"Should we mention Lori's problem or our own?" Amanda didn't want to put a damper on their evening, but a tiny prick of fear made her want some support from the outside.

They parked behind Maya's aging Subaru outside a charming Craftsman-style home. It was painted rich gray with ivory trim. It had an upstairs dormer window and a wide covered front porch with chunky square pillars. The wicker furniture had been covered for the winter. Amanda would love to have a house like this for her and Sara.

Sara said, "Let's play it by ear. They'll have a million stories to tell, so this night should be about them, not us."

"We'll play it by ear then," Amanda agreed. She collected her bag, the bottle of wine, and walked down a cobblestone pathway. They passed a frozen birdbath and a full bird feeder set into the artful tangle of the garden's landscaping. A few songbirds vied for seed, their feathers puffed against the cold. "Did they keep feeding birds while they were away?"

"I imagine so," Sara said. "Remember, Maya often flew home during the week to keep her hand in at the office and to try a few cases. So the cats moved to D.C., and the birds stayed home."

"Right." It seemed like a delicate balancing act, maintaining a long-distance relationship. Maya had unofficially moved to Washington, but she'd left a footprint in both worlds. "Will they move back here for good?" Amanda wondered.

Sara rang the doorbell. "Who knows? Shar's up for re-election next November. She says she's sick of the division and gridlock in Congress and wants to quit."

But Amanda thought it was hard to relinquish power. It was addictive, like a drug. Could the ambitious Shar really give it up?

Chapter Twenty-five

Like old times...

Maya and Shar greeted them at the door, pulling them into hugs and kisses on the lips. Waves of emotion swept through Sara, her eyes overflowing with happy tears. They had been apart too long, and she vowed to never let that happen again. As they embraced, Sara noticed that Maya had lost weight, and Shar had gained. Both women had a few extra gray hairs and wrinkles.

"Not gonna let you go!" Shar said as their large bosoms smashed together.

"Gonna squeeze me to death then?" Sara laughed, wriggling free.

Mandy was getting the same treatment from Maya. They looked like two tall flagpoles, with Mandy wrapped in the folds of Maya's gold and black caftan.

"You haven't changed a bit, Mandy," Maya said.

Mandy unfurled from Maya's hug. "Liar! You have changed, Madame District Attorney. You're way too skinny."

"And I'm way too fat, thanks to fast food," Shar said as they moved down the hallway toward the kitchen. "When Maya's home here during the week, she barely bothers to eat, but back in D.C., I eat out of white Styrofoam boxes or TV dinners."

"Well, something smells good," Sara said. The whole house was infused with the aroma of warm complex spices she couldn't identify. Shar had always done the cooking before, so Sara was expecting Southern fried chicken.

Shar said, "You can thank Maya for tonight's meal, Cajun jambalaya. She experiments with cooking when we're in D.C. together on weekends, so I've let her take over the kitchen."

Sara was amazed. It seemed like her best friends had reversed roles. What else had changed in the past three years? Their house looked the same, yet different. The two display cases on either side of the great room still held Maya's collection of ebony African sculpture in one, with Shar's collection of funky handmade teacups in the other. Large oriental carpets still covered the hardwood floors, but key pieces of furniture were missing. Then she remembered. Sara had helped Maya move those pieces to Washington in Mandy's van shortly after Shar was elected.

Sara had suppressed the details surrounding that move because it had provoked a brief crisis in both couple's relationships. Maya had been terribly upset by the prospect of living apart from Shar, and Sara had comforted her with a less-than-platonic kiss, which Mandy had witnessed. Sara's lapse prompted Mandy to run off with Gina to Asheville, and the whole affair had been a stupid misunderstanding. Intellectually, Sara had known that many happy couples had brief moments of infidelity, but not her and Mandy. Mandy had claimed to understand, but Sara was devastated. It took her months to forgive herself.

"Time for alcohol!" Shar chirped.

They all crowded into the kitchen to make their own drinks. Mandy gave Maya the wine, which would go with dinner, and Mandy found her rum and tonic.

After Maya gave the jambalaya a stir, they all settled into their favorite chairs around the stone fireplace in the great room, where gas logs supplied warmth and a cozy atmosphere. Even before the alcohol took effect, they were chatting like old times. Sara and Mandy peppered Shar with questions about her life in D.C.

"Well, I've joined the Progressive Caucus, and we've been fighting like junkyard dogs to pass gun control, environmental protections, abortion and voting rights—but the so-called Freedom Caucus won't even bring our bills to the floor for a vote. It makes me want to vomit. Or kill someone."

As Shar ranted, her fair complexion turned beet red. Had she been a pearl-clutcher, she'd have broken the strand. She explained that her first term had been better, when her party held the majority, but when the balance of power changed at the last midterms, Congress had become a legislative nightmare defined by bogus impeachments and shameless lies. Sara and Mandy knew about the dysfunction in Washington. It was repulsive, dangerous, and the main reason they had stopped watching the news.

"So..." Shar concluded after they'd all had two drinks, "I'm done. Outta there. I'm not gonna run for re-election. I'll finish my term, but after that, let the fuckers stew in their own juice."

Sara glanced at Mandy, who seemed a little shell-shocked by Shar's outburst, and Maya simply looked sad. Sara wondered, had the Washington years been worth it? The election that swept Shar and the Dems into power had been a hopeful time, but now the political landscape was dismal, for them and for the nation.

"Enough of that!" Maya clapped her hands and

stood from her chair. "Time to eat." She herded them into the dining room.

Along the way, Sara excused herself to visit the bathroom, and Mandy went with her. They washed their hands at the double sinks and talked to each other's images in the mirror.

"Are they all right?" Mandy asked.

"I think they will be once they've moved home for good."

"At least Shar has a good candidate lined up to take her place, and I think he'll win," Mandy said, digging around for a silver lining.

"Hope so." They both knew Abe Akim. He was the cousin of Lena Akim, who was Sara's brother's off-again, on-again girlfriend. Abe had been the intended candidate the year Shar stepped in, took his place, and won. He was a great guy with progressive ideas, but secretly, Sara didn't think North Carolina was ready to elect a Muslim. "Let's eat," she said.

⁂

Soft candlelight, potent wine, and the delicious blend of seafood, andouille sausage, veggies, peppers, onions, and rice in Maya's jambalaya combined for a mellow atmosphere at dinner. Amanda was relieved to drop the political in favor of the personal, in spite of the fact that the girls kept asking about her art. Amanda loved to make art but hated talking about it. Shows where she was forced to explain herself to customers were torture, but Maya and Shar were friends, so she told them about the several galleries carrying her work and finished with, "I got two big commissions from Wells Fargo, but since then, nothing special."

Maya lifted her eyebrows at Sara. "Mandy's not one to toot her own horn, is she?"

"Nope, she'd rather hide her light under a bushel." Sara patted Mandy's knee under the table. "She likes making, not marketing, don't you, babe?"

"That's why you need Goddess Gifts," Shar said before Amanda could respond. "My assistant has done a great job running the shop in my absence, but she's stocked it with cutesy stuff, like dream catchers and needlepoint kits. When I get back, I'm recruiting serious artists, potters, and sculptors, like you, Mandy. Will you think about it?"

"Sure, thanks," Amada mumbled, desperate to redirect the spotlight. "Sara's the one doing really great things. She's Doctor of the Month."

"Do tell?" Shar batted her eyelashes at Sara. "How does one get to be Doctor of the Month? Bedside manner? Counseling on the couch?"

Sara laughed. "You know I can't divulge the intimate details about my relationships with patients."

Maya wanted in on the fun. "Sara, remember what we used to say about our jobs? I lock them up, you pamper them once they're out."

It was an old joke. Maya had always been amused by Sara treating many of the same criminals Maya had prosecuted.

"But why are you on vacation, Sara?" Maya continued. "I can't imagine such a thing. You're such a workaholic, are you sick?"

Amanda glanced at Sara, wondering how she would respond. She'd been having so much fun, she'd almost forgotten their personal troubles.

"Mandy's cousin, Lori, is staying with us this week," Sara answered.

"That's right! How come she's not eating with us tonight?" Shar said.

Amanda explained that Lori had decided to spend the day with her Aunt Diana. Mom had offered to show Lori the mega-mansion she'd listed, the one where Mom hired the drone, and Lori had jumped at the chance. Amanda also suspected that her Super Realtor mom would be Lori's new hero of the day. Had Lori come with them tonight, she would have fixated on either Maya or Shar—take your pick—they were both awesome.

"I didn't know you had a cousin," Maya said.

Amanda took a deep breath and told them about her surprising new mixed-race family, and they were intrigued. So much had happened while Maya and Shar were away. Could they ever fill in all the blanks? They didn't know about the wedding and their friends in Asheville, they'd never met Red and Gina. Sometimes it seemed that precious little pockets of Amanda's life were stored in separate baskets, never to combine. It was weird.

After dinner, they returned to the great room with coffee. As soon as they got relaxed and comfortable around the gas logs, Amanda's cellphone rang and so did Sara's. Their phones started pinging from the depths of their bags, so loud the girls noticed.

"I thought you turned yours off," Sara said accusingly.

"Yeah, but I turned it back on in case Lori called. What about you, Sara? I thought you'd muted yours."

Maya and Shar likely thought they were crazy. Their gazes darted from Sara to Amanda until Maya finally said, "For God's sake, answer your stupid phones! It's not rude. We understand. Just because you're with us doesn't mean you have to cut off the world."

Amanda froze. It was odd that both phones rang at once unless it was an Amber Alert or a tornado warning, but she knew it was no such thing. She looked beseechingly at Sara, but Sara seemed out-of-body, disassociating. Swallowing her fear, Amanda fished out her phone and stared at the unfamiliar email address: babyblue69@gmail.com. Fuck! She had to look, didn't she? She opened it.

This time, the Barbies were on full frontal display, either dead or dying. Again they were naked, but for the painted-on, thigh-high blue stockings. They were hanging by the neck, side by side, from a standard wire coat hanger. The ropes and nooses were fashioned from blue stockings, their blond and brunette heads were twisted at impossible angles, and each pair of plastic hands were bound in front by small blue rubber bands. Had their blank faces not been painted out, Amanda knew that their expressions would register pure agony.

She felt faint. From the corner of her eye, she saw that Sara had also opened her email and was slumped in her chair, like a strangled Barbie without its mask. Wine rose like bile in the back of Amanda's throat. She dropped her head between her knees, heard her phone hit the floor, and then it was over.

Chapter Twenty-six

A death threat...

A hand grabbed Amanda's shoulder. Another hand rubbed her back as blood rushed into her head and her vision cleared. She was staring down between her knees, her feet planted on the hardwood floor.

"My God, Mandy, are you okay?" Shar's voice cut like a buzz saw.

Amanda sat upright and lifted her head, still dizzy. She heard Maya's voice across the room, ministering to Sara. "What happened?"

"I think you blacked out for a second," Shar said. "Sara's no better. She looks like she just saw a ghost. Was it something on your phones?"

No ghost. Their stalker was back, and Sara was in distress. Amanda struggled upright and walked on wobbly legs to where Sara was slumped in a chair. Maya was kneeling on the floor, her arms around Sara. Amanda eased Maya aside and took over, rocking Sara like a baby. She saw Sara's phone lying upright on her lap, the terrible image fading to black. "It's all right, honey." She kissed Sara's cold cheek.

"What the fuck?" Shar came up behind them with Amanda's phone in her hand, the image refreshed. "Is this some kind of sick joke?" Shar showed the picture to Maya.

Maya grabbed it and stared, her cat eyes focused,

her forehead creased. At first, her expression registered shock, then concentration, and then, inexplicably, she laughed. The raucous sound bounced off the stone fireplace and echoed around the room.

Sara pulled free of Amanda and sat bolt upright as color returned to her face. "You think it's funny?" she demanded.

Even Shar seemed stunned by Maya's reaction.

"Yes, it's hilarious, right?" Maya appealed to her skeptical audience. "This shit is meant to be a cynical parody of the new *Barbie* movie, isn't it? Whoever designed it thinks the movie is a slick chick flick and wants to crap all over it with a horror movie vibe."

Had Maya lost her mind? Everyone glared at her until Amanda stood and snatched the phone from Maya's hand. "I appreciate the art critique, but you're dead wrong. This isn't a joke..."

"It's a death threat!" Sara shouted at her longtime friend. "You may be the tough-ass prosecutor, but I'm the shrink, and I tell you this is serious. That image isn't a one-off, it's number three in a series, and you law enforcement types know it takes three deaths to make a serial killer. In this case, I hope it's only a stalker, but she's escalating."

Sensing Sara didn't want to be touched at the moment, Amanda gave her some space. She'd never heard Sara snap at her best friend that way. Her outburst left them all speechless, especially Maya, who looked like she'd been slapped in the face.

Finally, Shar said, "Sorry, guys, it sounds like we need to talk about this." She meekly retreated to her place on the sofa.

Maya was still on her feet but slumped like a marionette at the end of loose strings. Finally, some heavenly puppet master lifted her right arm, and she touched Sara's shoulder. "Forgive me, I'm sorry. Shar's right. Please tell us exactly what's going on, and maybe we can help." Maya also retreated to the sofa.

Sara looked up. "I'm sorry, too. I overreacted, and I didn't mean to freak out on you."

"We've been under a lot of stress," Amanda explained, hoping to ease the tension. "I don't know about you, but I could use another drink." The others agreed, and since Amanda was the last woman standing, she headed to the kitchen. When she returned with a tray, the tension was gone, equilibrium restored. Once all the drinks were in hand and Amanda had taken her seat, Maya and Shar promised not to interrupt, and then she and Sara started telling their story.

They began by showing them the first two blue stocking images tucked away in their junk mail, and then they described all the events of the recent past, starting with the wedding in Asheville. Amanda told the saga of Lori. Since Maya and Shar were practically family and wouldn't blab, she described Lori's revenge porn problem. Because the porn and stalking were both internet-related, Maya and Shar assumed a connection, but in the end, no one could find one.

Sara said, "The only teenager in Lori's circle who knows Mandy and me is Lori's girlfriend, Lilly. But why would Lilly blame us when it was Lori who ghosted her?"

"Dead end," Maya muttered.

Amanda didn't mention Russel Cowley, the man she'd rejected, or Tammy Tillman, whom they'd already deemed innocent. But when Sara described the background and psychoses of Jane Doe at the clinic, their friends jumped on Jane as the primary suspect.

"It's gotta be her!" Shar said.

"Not enough for a restraining order," Maya said. "No judge I know would grant one on such flimsy evidence. Besides, would Jane Doe have the imagination to create these stylized images?"

Sara said, "She's dark, she's an IT expert, it's possible."

"But what's with the blue silk stockings?" Shar wondered. "Why blue? Because it's sad or sexy? I don't get it."

"I get it!" Maya crowed. "*Bluestockings* were groups of women in eighteenth century England who held gatherings for men of letters and members of the aristocracy with similar literary interests. Over the years, the word has been applied derisively to 'elitist' women who affect literary or learned interests, pursue higher education, promote feminism, and even lesbianism. Being tagged a bluestocking then, and even now, can be an insult, meaning a woman is unfeminine and not good marriage material."

Amanda barked out a laugh. "Well, thank you very much, Professor. You think our stalker is into archaic literary history? She's after us because we're 'uppity lesbians' who don't know our place in this man's world? Seems like a stretch."

Maya laughed, too. "You're right, it's ridiculous. Besides, if your stalker is literary, she'd add words to the pictures, and that hasn't happened."

Another dead end, but fascinating. Amanda had studied the subliminal impact of line, color, and symbolism in art. The stalker's work was closest to art noire, with roots in German Expressionism, which often depicted cynical, corrupt, and tragic storylines. Again ridiculous because the stalker's style was more like pop art meets comic book. Her pictures were crazy or insane.

"Maybe you need to go further back in time," Shar suggested. "We all agree it's a woman, it's personal, but it's also sexual. What about ex-lovers, girls? Dig deep. Who did you hurt bad enough? Who's been festering all these years and wants revenge?"

Amanda glanced at Sara, and they both cracked up.

"Not me." Amanda giggled. "Before Sara, I was with Rachel Lessing. You know, that crush-on-an-older-woman thing? Rachel's down in Sarasota. She dumped me for a younger model and never looked back."

"Poor baby," Shar teased. "I wish some sophisticated older woman had broken me in. I had mad crushes on quite a few."

Maya turned to Sara, a worried look in her eyes. "What about your ex, Judith Dellinger? Your breakup was pretty intense, and Jude knows how to hold a grudge. What do you think, Sara?"

Amanda expected Sara to laugh it off, but instead, her shoulders tensed. "No, mine was the same deal as Mandy's. Jude dumped me for a poli-sci professor, and after her, Jude hooked up with a biology professor, or so you said. So yes, I was gutted, but Jude moved on. It's not her."

Amanda sensed that Sara's scar tissue wasn't as tough as she'd supposed, and she wished Maya had never mentioned Jude. Even after all these years, Jude's cruelty and insensitivity still hurt Sara. Maya should have known better. After all, it was Maya and Shar who'd been there to pick up Sara's pieces.

"Are you sure?" Maya pressed. "Jude is single again, and you never know…"

"What?" Sara growled. "Don't tell me you've been in touch with her. After the way she treated me?"

Both Maya and Shar looked guilty.

Shar intervened. "No, not in touch, really. Just holiday cards, the occasional text, and one long phone call after Jude dumped the biology teacher. You know how it is, Sara, the four of us were friends for years. We took vacations together and cried together. You can't just toss that all away. But in the end, as you know, we chose you, not her."

Amanda longed to comfort Sara because on some level, the girls' continued contact with Jude, no matter how minimal, must have felt like a betrayal. Amanda was also distressed to see that Sara's old wound still hurt. Amanda's love hadn't been enough to heal her.

The evening had become contentious. Amanda wished with all her heart that the emails had never come to vomit all over their reunion. At the same time, it was a relief to share their burden with dear friends like Maya and Shar. Amanda had needed this. Two sets of fresh eyes on the problem helped to clarify because the girls also thought their stalker was a woman, who was dangerous and escalating.

"So you will contact the police tomorrow?" Maya gently changed the subject. "I'll go with you if you like. I have a contact on the CMPD cybersecurity team."

Amanda and Sara had a CMPD contact, too. They had Red, who had steered them in the right direction in Lori's case. She could do the same for them. "Can a stalker be charged with a crime?" Amanda asked.

Maya sighed. "It's tricky. I hate to say it, but something concrete usually has to happen first. It's like murder, which can't be charged unless somebody gets killed."

Chapter Twenty-seven

The back burner...

Sara lay awake long into the night, spooning with Mandy nestled against her stomach and thighs. Mandy had been slow to sleep, as well. They were wired from the evening with Maya and Shar, which had stirred up complex memories—good and bad. Taking comfort in Mandy's gentle breathing and the warm puffs of Mandy's breath on her hand, Sara wondered why, after all these years, hearing Jude's name still upset her. It was partly because it upset Mandy, who just wanted to protect her, but it was mostly because she'd never told anyone the true horror story about their breakup.

Sara listened to the soft sigh of heat pushing through the floor vent and relived that awful day when she'd come home from work to find all her worldly possessions packed up on the porch outside their town house. She'd tried her key, but Jude had changed the locks. In a blind panic, she'd called Jude's cellphone, and the deep, dead voice that answered sounded nothing like her partner of four years.

Had Sara seen it coming? Not really. Maybe? They had grown apart, talked less and worked more, but Sara would never forget the hurtful words Jude hurled like daggers. Jude said Sara was boring, intellectually and in bed. Sara had no mind of her own, no passion, and she'd never loved Jude as much as Jude loved her.

Sara was pathetic, and Jude was sick of her. So without warning, Sara was out on the street, her heart and ego in shreds. Somehow, she'd made it to the shelter of her parents' home and holed up in the little garage apartment where she'd spent her teenage years. From there, she moved robotically through her work and social life with her emotions completely shut down. Until she met Mandy. And Mandy worked hard to bring her back to life, teaching her to trust again. She became Sara's sun, convincing her she wasn't boring, stupid, or pathetic. In Mandy's arms, she suddenly understood passion as she'd never known it before. Jude had been right: Sara had never loved Jude, not that way. Nor would Sara ever love anyone as she loved Mandy.

Knowing this relaxed Sara, allowing sleep to come as she cradled her beloved. Sara felt safe in her own skin and had for some time. As for Jude being their stalker? Certainly Jude was capable of extreme cruelty, but why would she bother after all this time? Sara suspected her ex had brutalized more victims by now. She had replaced Sara with a jock poli-sci professor at Queen's University, but she was long gone. Jude's biology teacher? Sara had never met the woman, but she felt sorry for her and prayed she hadn't suffered the same abuse as Sara.

❧❧❧❧❧

Something startled Amanda awake. Intense sunlight leaked in around the edges of their drawn drapes, and the bedside clock said 10:45. Sara was still sound asleep. Had the doorbell awakened her? Amanda listened intently, but the sound did not come again. She untangled from Sara, found Sara's bathrobe close at hand, and then padded down the foyer to look out the peephole in the front door.

Nobody there. Still, she had a nagging feeling that someone had come, then quickly gone away. She tiptoed to the kitchen and immediately saw the silhouette through the drawn drapes at the patio doors. The dark figure came to the glass and tried to look in. Shit! Amanda suppressed an urge to run for Sara, and instead thought, It's broad daylight, what the hell can they do to me? She approached cautiously, parted the drapes a crack, and then saw laughing amber eyes in a mocha face just before Lori stuck her tongue out at her.

Oh, for fuck's sake! Amanda removed the safety rod, opened the drapes, and unlocked the door. Lori blew in on a gust of cold air. She wore the same gray trench coat she'd had on when they first laid eyes on her last Sunday night. Only this morning, she didn't smell of cigarettes.

"Did you fly over our wall again, Superwoman?"

"Guess I shouldn't have rung the doorbell. Woke you up, didn't I, cuz?" Lori shucked off her coat and tossed it on a barstool. "Trout's friend dropped me off. I figured you guys would be up by now."

Amanda yawned, then ran fingers through her hair, which was sticking out in every direction. "You could have called, Lori. We were out late last night."

"Sick. Kick back or function?"

"What do you even mean? Can you please speak English?"

"Small group or major party?"

"Our two best friends. Dinner. Okay?"

"Okay. Do you have coffee?"

Amanda trudged toward the coffeemaker just as Sara shuffled in wearing Amanda's robe. She waved sleepily at Lori, seemingly unsurprised to find the girl in their kitchen. "Do we have coffee?"

"Coming up," Amanda mumbled. It seemed she was in charge, so she poured packets of instant oatmeal into three bowls and fished blueberries from the fridge. As she buttered bread and stuck it in the toaster oven, she paid little attention to Lori's nonstop chatter: Ginny's singing at the club Thursday night was dope, she should make a CD. The mansion Aunt Diana showed her was extreme. And Lissa was her new BFF.

"So you had fun?" Amanda asked as she set the table with the cereal, toast, and juice. Sara dug right in.

Lori said, "Dad's picking me up tomorrow morning, but I wish I could stay with you guys a little longer."

Amanda slid into her chair. "Don't you miss your friends?"

Lori seemed to deflate, a faraway look in her eyes. Had Amanda stuck her foot in it? In light of the revenge porn scandal, Lori likely had mixed feelings about her so-called friends. Even Sara put her spoon down to listen to Lori's response.

"Lilly called me..." Lori said at last. "At first she was really mad because she got the sheriff's letter like all the others. But when I explained how savage it was to see those posts, how it made me crazy, she started crying. She told me her useless brother AJ had lied. He posted the pictures himself, the little shit. Lilly kept on crying, saying she was sorry, so maybe I'll see her again," Lori finished sheepishly.

Amanda was astonished. "After all she did, you want to see her again?"

Lori shrugged, but her shoulders were shaking, and a mist of tears fogged her eyes.

Sara said, "It'll be all right."

"Yeah, it'll be all right," Lori repeated. "Thanks to you and Mandy. You saved my life!"

Tears poured from Lori's eyes, freezing Amanda with the power of Lori's emotion. Sara rose from her chair and held Lori in her arms, whispering words of encouragement Amanda couldn't quite hear. When the crying stopped, Sara smiled and took her seat.

"We were glad to help, Lori," Sara said. "Now finish your breakfast."

Why was it so hard to say "thank you" and "you're welcome?" Amanda wondered as she carried the dirty dishes to the sink. Lori's dramatic entrance into their lives had been disruptive, to say the least, but now that it seemed Lori would be all right, Amanda felt proud and grateful to have been part of the solution. She also felt so much closer to her cousin and couldn't wait to see Judd tomorrow. She was determined that in the future, the Taylor family would play a bigger role in her life.

"So what are we gonna do today, our last day together?" Lori brightened and clapped her hands.

Sara glanced apprehensively at Amanda, who knew what they *needed* to do, had *promised* to do, but Lori didn't figure into their plan to contact the police. Lori wasn't to know about their psycho stalker. No way. She had just survived her own internet terror, and they'd not drag her into theirs.

"Well, it's Saturday," Sara said, "so…"

So what? Sara hadn't finished her sentence. Was she implying the police didn't work on Saturday? Did Sara want to put it off? Amanda held her breath and waited for clarification.

"So what do you do in Davidson on the weekend?"

Lori persisted. "It's a college town, right? Let's go party with the coeds."

Amanda abruptly interrupted. "Sara, can we talk privately?"

Sara and Lori both blinked in surprise, but Sara dutifully excused herself from the table, and they huddled in the hall. "What are we going to do?" Amanda whispered.

"Look, she's leaving tomorrow, so can't the police wait until Monday?" Sara said, pleading with worried green eyes.

Sara was not a procrastinator. She regularly lectured her patients about the dangers of putting off hard decisions. Amanda felt obliged to give her a hard time, so she held a hand to Sara's forehead. "You don't have a fever, but you must be sick. Do you hear yourself?"

Sara sighed and rolled her eyes at the ceiling. "Yeah, I know I'm a hypocrite, but let's put our stuff on the back burner until Monday."

Amanda nodded, hoping they wouldn't live to regret it.

Chapter Twenty-eight

Maybe pigs can fly...

Because it was a perfect early November day with a cloudless sky and warm sunshine, they decided to walk the half mile into the village of Davidson. Amanda would have preferred another chance to drive the Jeep since Lori and Judd would be taking it away tomorrow, but she needed some exercise-induced endorphins to lift her mood.

It worked. The three walked briskly from the condo complex and scampered onto the walkway of the overpass bridge spanning Interstate 77. As the traffic roared far beneath them, Amanda felt like a bird, and her spirits soared. At the end of the bridge, they walked around the traffic circle past the newer, upscale shops, including Amanda's mom's real estate office, but they were saving themselves for the shops on old Main Street, so they continued on. They passed the little park where kids played on the swings and ducks played in the pond, and on to the corner anchored by the imposing Belk Visual Arts Center, where Davidson College's art majors studied. Amanda saw kids coming out with portfolios tucked under their arms and felt wistful. They looked so young and earnest. She'd never studied in a college, just picked up her skills from night school and random art courses along the way. Had she not run away from home, she would have enjoyed the full college experience.

Davidson College itself, with its pillared, classical red brick buildings and church with a big, tall steeple, spread out all along the east side of Main Street. It was set in an uncrowded campus of lawn and ancient trees, which in summer shaded the venerable old buildings. The students were out and about, enjoying the sunshine. Amanda sensed Lori shyly eyeing the eclectic, good-looking groups of kids. She was betwixt and between, old enough to empathize, a little too young to fit in, but she was interested, studying their style, attitudes, and standing a bit taller. They stopped at the College Store, where Amanda bought Lori a red Davidson ball cap, which she quickly put on. Lori peeked into The Soda Shop, which was straight out of the 1950s sitcom *Happy Days*, but Sara vetoed Lori's desire for a burger and malt since they'd just had breakfast. They moved on to The Village Store, which offered a potpourri of unique gifts, and Lori bought Jana a pair of handmade earrings featuring tiny enamel cardinals.

By then, Sara had that look in her eye. She was about to disappear into Main Street Books, which meant they'd lose her for up to an hour. The bookstore was run by two older women who worked hard to maintain their business in the digital age when most folks bought paperbacks from Amazon or jumped right to Kindle. Unless desperate for an instant-gratification read, Amanda and Sara supported the store, but Lori wasn't interested. She stood firm on the sidewalk and pointed to the Summit Coffee shop next door.

"Can we go there instead, Mandy? I'd kill for a cappuccino."

Amanda noticed two lonely tables set up outside in spite of the weather. One was occupied by two pretty college-aged women wearing shorts, sandals, and heavy fleece jackets, seemingly oblivious to the cold as they sipped hot drinks and watched the passersby. Lori smiled at the women.

Amanda just felt old. "Okay, as long as we sit inside."

"Pussy," Lori muttered as they entered through old wooden double doors and were suddenly enveloped by warmth being lazily circulated by an overhead fan. The rich aroma of brewing coffee, sugary pastries, and heated wool coats sent Amanda into sensory overload. The muted chatter of a half dozen customers echoed off the pressed tin ceiling.

"My treat," Amanda said as she led Lori to the counter. Instead of cappuccino, Lori ordered a caramel latte and a gingerbread muffin. Amanda got an Americano and a sugar cookie. They carried their goodies to a table near the front window where Lori could watch the two coeds and Amanda faced the store, so she could eye the patrons.

While Lori chatted about everything from how she wanted to show Main Street to her family to the pros and cons of going to college, Amanda's mind wandered, lulled by the heat and seduced by the cookie. About the time Lori decided to buy another muffin and returned to the counter, Amanda felt a chill when the door opened to a new customer, and Russel Cowley strolled in.

Amanda was stunned. She hadn't seen her stalker for six blessed months and believed the man had finally decided to leave her alone. She longed to disappear, hide under the table, anything to avoid him. She held her breath, her heart racing as she made herself small and kept her face down.

"Amanda Rittenhouse?" Russel's tenor voice

boomed in the crowded space. "Fancy meeting you here, doll! It's my lucky day."

He approached the table and pulled out Lori's chair. Amanda smelled the mix of sweat and aftershave pouring off him, but she didn't look up.

"It's Russel Cowley, your favorite customer. Surely you remember me?"

God, how could she forget? His dogged pursuit and obscene emails had nearly driven her 'round the bend. When she finally made herself look at him, he hadn't changed. Today he wore expensive-looking gray trousers and tasseled loafers, a pink mosaic polo shirt, and a loose blue jacket that couldn't conceal his expanding waistline. His beefy face was still red, and his gray-blond hair was freshly cut. She assumed he'd just stepped off the golf course.

"Did you wonder what happened to me? Sorry I missed some of your openings, but I've been in London. We're opening a branch of Cowley and Craig overseas. Impressive, right? I prefer the weather here, though. It's too rainy over there."

Did she give a flying fuck? She wouldn't offer him an umbrella in a shit storm. She still hadn't uttered one word. Couldn't he take a hint?

He pulled the chair out farther and prepared to sit. "Mind if I join you?"

Amanda was about to open her mouth and say something she'd regret when Lori, her guardian angel, swooped in.

"Sorry, dude, this seat is taken." Lori elbowed Russel aside, a smug smile on her face.

Russel seemed surprised and then confused as he glared at Lori. As his face got even redder, Amanda could almost hear the gears spinning in his little hamster brain as he tried to link them together.

"Beg pardon," he huffed and then glared at Amanda. "Better watch yourself, Miss Rittenhouse. That girl is jailbait!" With that, he stormed off to order.

Lori slipped into her chair, wildly amused. "*Jailbait?*" she whispered.

"Yeah, he's an old-school pervert. Thanks for saving me."

"No problemo. Don't tell me you swing both ways."

Amanda rolled her eyes at the ceiling. "We have history. Russel is one sick guy. He panted after me for weeks, no matter how rude I was. He bought my sculpture and followed me around like a groupie."

"Like a *stan*, same difference."

"Can we change places, so I don't have to look at him?"

Lori agreed, and they switched, but Amanda still felt Russel's pig eyes boring into her back. Lori kept up a steady commentary. "Like, he's sitting by the wall, watching you, throwing lots of shade. What a tool!"

"Maybe we should leave," Amanda said.

"Nope, the tool is leaving. He just put a lid on his coffee cup."

Russel passed them in hostile silence and pushed out the door. Lori seemed to have forgotten him, but Amanda watched him hang a right on the sidewalk and stomp into the parking lot. Moments later, his gray BMW turned south on Main Street, and she breathed a sigh of relief because he hadn't turned north toward their condo, so maybe he wasn't stalking her. Right. And maybe pigs can fly.

Chapter Twenty-nine

An uncomfortable coincidence...

Sara left Main Street Books with six new novels she'd been wanting to read. They would hike up the debt on next month's Visa bill, but they were worth it. As she shifted the strap of the heavy bag to her shoulder, she passed two long-legged girls in shorts who were leaving their outdoor table at the coffee shop and soon spotted Mandy and Lori seated just inside the shop's window. They saw Sara at the same moment, waved, and then quickly joined her on the sidewalk.

"Want a coffee to go, honey?" Mandy asked.

"And a muffin?" Lori said. "They're to die for."

"No, thanks, I'm good. What I'd really like is to show Lori our favorite art gallery while we're here. Okay by you, Mandy?"

"Um, okay, I guess."

Sara glanced at Mandy. What was the problem? Usually, she'd jump at a chance to visit Athena Gallery. Located in a charmingly converted 1920s bungalow on South Main Street, it was owned by Jan and Shelly, two intriguing lesbians whom Sara hoped to cultivate as friends. Jan had recently accepted several of Mandy's sculptures to show on consignment, which would complement the excellent paintings on exhibit, from mostly local artists.

"What's wrong, babe? Do you want to head home now?" Sara noticed that Mandy looked a little pale, and she was definitely distracted.

Lori giggled. "Mandy's afraid she'll run into her creepy boyfriend at the gallery. He's a groupie who collects her work."

"What?" Sara was alarmed because Mandy refused to look her in the eye.

"His name is Russel," Lori continued. "He hit on Mandy in the coffee shop and called me *jailbait*. Total loser."

"Russel Cowley's back? Oh, shit!" Much as Sara wanted to control it, anger bubbled up under her breastbone and threatened to spill out her mouth in a gush of filthy expletives. Last May, when Cowley made Mandy's life a misery, Sara had lost her cool and said she'd cut off his balls and feed them to the turkey buzzards who hung around their waterfront.

"Did I say something wrong?" Lori wondered.

"I'm so sorry, Mandy." Sara ignored Lori and touched the back of Mandy's hand. "I thought Cowley had ridden off into the sunset."

Mandy didn't respond. She was staring at the traffic inching north on Main Street in their direction. She pointed to a gray BMW. "That's Russel's car," she said, her voice barely audible.

Sara and Lori looked. It seemed the BMW had just pulled out from the parking lot at the Athena Gallery a half block away. Had he gone there looking for Mandy's work? Sara had never met the man, so she didn't recognize the driver, but as the car drew close, Lori confirmed.

"Yeah, that's him. He's pretending not to look, but he sees us. He's cruising you, Mandy. Check it."

"Ignore him!" Sara hissed as she pulled Mandy and Lori off the sidewalk into an alley beside Ben &

Jerry's. "Don't give him the satisfaction. Wait till he's out of sight." But they all kept watching his car. Sara hoped the asshole would keep heading north out of town, toward Mooresville, but instead, he turned left at the Belk Visual Arts Center heading for the interstate— or their condo.

"Yes, I want to head home now," Mandy answered the question Sara had asked five minutes ago.

The defeated look on Mandy's face made Sara's heart ache, and she knew exactly what Mandy was thinking. The morning they'd made their lists of suspects, Mandy had placed Russel Cowley at the top of hers. In spite of Sara's insistence that their stalker was a woman, that the emailed images suggested a woman's style, Mandy remained unconvinced. It was an uncomfortable coincidence that Cowley had shown up around the same time as the emails, and Sara didn't believe in coincidences. Should she consider him a suspect?

They crossed the street and walked home along the east side of Main Street for a change, past the CVS, the library, and the village green. Lori seemed at a loss, cracking jokes and no doubt wondering what the hell was wrong with her older companions.

"Can I carry your books, teacher?" Lori teased as she pulled the heavy bag off Sara's shoulder and slipped it onto her own.

"Thanks." Sara smiled. Literally and figuratively, it felt like a weight had been lifted. She and Mandy were overreacting. Cowley was no big deal. He was nothing. "I'm taking us out to dinner tonight to celebrate," she announced.

"Celebrate what?" Lori said.

"Our last night together and all the fun we've

had."

Even Mandy, who hadn't spoken for some time, perked up. "Well, it better be an exceptional restaurant."

"We'll go to North Harbor Club, only a few steps from home. The food is fabulous, the atmosphere is relaxed and classy, and we can watch the boats go in and out."

Mandy said, "Yay! I'm having the filet mignon since you're buying."

Sara jabbed Mandy with her elbow. "The most expensive item on the menu? Give me a break."

By the time they crossed the overpass bridge, the trio's mood had improved considerably. Mandy was weaving back and forth, the wind ruffling her hair like duck down in a hurricane, her arms spread out like a bird. Although weighted down by Sara's books, Lori attempted a lopsided moon walk, and there wasn't a gray BMW in sight.

They were all laughing by the time they stepped into the privacy of their tiny front porch. Sara was first to the door. She dug into her pocket for the key, but when she turned to insert it, she froze in terror.

The hook of a wire coat hanger hung on the doorknob. The strangled Barbies hung by their necks on the blue stocking ropes, their naked bodies and painted blue legs swaying in the gentle breeze. Now, along with their blanked-out white faces, a heart-shaped blob of red enamel had been broken like a blister between each pair of plastic breasts; each blob wept a trail of blood down across each pelvis and into each crotch. Everything was gooey-looking and shiny, like it had been dipped in high-gloss varnish.

Sara's scream shattered the afternoon, yet it seemed not to come from her own mouth. Fear and rage coursed down through her arms and into her hands as she grabbed the sticky horror from the door and flung it to the floor.

"No, Sara, don't touch it!" Mandy shouted, as in a dream.

Next Sara reached over and turned the dolls face-down, to hide their degradation and disgrace. She pulled the green scarf from around her neck to cover their nakedness, and then she cried.

Chapter Thirty

A vaudeville routine...

Amanda felt cold and had difficulty breathing. Was she going into shock? Lori was laughing hysterically, inappropriately, and Sara seemed to be in a trance. Sara had managed to unlock the door, so Amanda gently eased Sara aside and elbowed the door open.

Sara wandered into the hall. "Call the police now," she said in a low, detached voice.

"Don't touch it, Lori!" Amanda barked over her shoulder as she followed Sara inside.

"What was that shit? Performance art?" Lori seemed on the verge of tears, yet she kept up a nervous giggle that sounded more like hiccups. Eventually, she stopped gaping at the green scarf littering the deck like a burial mound, came inside, and closed the door behind her.

"Call the police," Sara repeated as she drifted toward the kitchen.

Amanda took out her cellphone and drew a blank. Should she dial 911, call Red, or go looking for the number for the Davidson cops? She called 911, but when the operator asked the nature of her emergency, Amanda balked, finally saying that someone had left something disgusting on her door. She was also able to recite their address and was told that someone would respond ASAP.

"What was that shit?" Lori asked again as she stumbled after Sara.

"Long story," Amanda mumbled and joined the zombie parade. They found Sara standing at the kitchen sink. She had dropped her bag and coat on the floor and was obsessively scrubbing her hands and arms, punishing her skin, as if mere water could wash away the filth and decay of the thing she had touched. Amanda approached cautiously. She draped her jacket on a chair and then placed her hands on Sara's shoulders. "Are you okay, honey?"

Sara shrugged Amanda's hands away and continued scrubbing. "Did you call?"

"Yes, they're on the way."

Lori tossed her gray trench coat on her favorite barstool and left the bag of Sara's new novels in a corner by the fridge. "I could use a beer," she said.

I could use a Valium, Amanda thought. She took a Diet Pepsi from the fridge and gave it to Lori.

"What now?" Lori demanded as she jogged from foot to foot. "Does this mean we aren't going out to dinner?"

Amanda stared hard at Lori. Yes, the girl was upset and confused, and who could blame her? Yet Amanda wanted to wring her neck. She was seventeen, almost eighteen, but behaving like a ten-year-old brat. Amanda yanked the new red Davidson ball cap off Lori's head and shoved it into her hands. "Lori, please let us handle this. Take the Pepsi to your room and stay there until we finish with the police. Okay?"

Lori's amber gaze darted back and forth, reflecting first nerves, then defiance, and finally acceptance. Adult Amanda had given teenaged Lori a direct order, and by God's grace, Lori had listened. "Okay," Lori muttered, and then headed to the guest bedroom, closing the door behind her.

Amanda then turned to Sara, who was drying her hands and arms with wads of paper towel, then stuffing them into the trash can. "Please sit down and relax," Amanda begged. It was so unlike Sara to crumble in a crisis. Amanda was worried and unnerved.

"Where are the cops?" Sara asked again.

"They'll be here soon."

Right on cue, the doorbell rang. Amanda expected Sara to beat her to it, but instead, Sara slumped into a chair and stared out at the lake. Amanda took a beat to compose herself and then marched through the foyer and opened the door.

"Well, hello again, Mandy Rittenhouse!" The small, wiry man standing there was obviously an undercover cop. He had darting gray eyes in a pale, wolf-like face. Something about him was familiar and reassuring... was it the New Jersey accent?

Yet she couldn't place him. "You got here fast," she said.

"The least I could do for an old friend." He smiled, exposing sharp canine teeth in a narrow mouth surrounded by afternoon shadow. The collar of a gaudy Hawaiian shirt folded over his black leather jacket. "You don't remember me, do you?"

"Sorry, I'm having a brain freeze."

"Understandable, considering that mess over there..." He pointed to the deck and then to a huge African American. The uniformed officer was lifting Sara's green scarf off the tangle of Barbie dolls. He wore thick latex gloves and a look of disgust on his face. "Do you recognize my partner, the giant? He's

Rodney Woods, and I'm Detective Peter Sokolsky. I'm good friends with your mom."

"Of course, Detective Sokolsky! Please come in." As Amanda ushered him inside, the memories flooded back. Sokolsky and Woods were like a vaudeville routine who worked together seamlessly. They had responded to the murder scene of Amanda's friend Brownie Bruinstein. Sokolsky had worked that case with dogged professionalism, and over the years, he had indeed crossed paths with her mom, who had a talent for blundering into encounters with criminals.

Sokolsky stepped into the foyer, removed his latex gloves, and shook Amanda's hand. "I trust you'll help me understand the background and motive behind that macabre bit of theater on your doorstep. It's not pretty, Mandy. Those two tortured dolls? Someone's gunning for you and Sara."

How could she help him understand when she was so in the dark? "Sara's in the kitchen, come in and say hello." It was a bonus that Sokolsky had met Sara and knew about their relationship.

But Sara did not say hello. She tore her attention away from the lake, stared at Sokolsky through eyes devoid of recognition, and gave him a limp little wave. Something was wrong, but Amanda pressed on and offered coffee. He accepted. As Amanda brewed enough for everybody, including Officer Woods, Sara remained mute and unresponsive. She refused coffee but watched them drink theirs, contributing nothing, even when Amanda showed Sokolsky their suspect list and the string of threatening images still stored in her junk mail.

Sokolsky frowned and tapped an annoying tattoo on the tabletop with his stubby fingertips.

"Your stalker is one sick lady, Mandy. You need to be extremely careful."

"So you think it's a woman?" Amanda asked.

"I do," he confirmed.

"Well, *I* don't!" Lori's voice interrupted.

Amanda hadn't heard her leave the room and sneak up on them. Now she wanted to not only wring Lori's neck, but also bind her hand and foot and stash her under the guest bed. As it was, she had no choice. She introduced her cousin to Sokolsky.

"I know who left that shit," Lori told the detective. "It's a creepy guy named Russel Cowley. That psycho stalked Mandy once before, and he's at it again. He showed up while we were at the coffee shop this afternoon, then drove off toward the condo." Lori finished her spiel, helped herself to coffee, and then joined them at the table.

Much to Amanda's alarm, Sokolsky was taking notes, writing down Russel's name. He said, "Cowley the lawyer? I know the guy, and I'll check it out."

∾∾∾∾

"Shut up, Lori!" Sara shouted. At least, she thought she'd shouted, and it did seem loud. She couldn't hear too well, and when she tried to lift her hands off the table, she couldn't move. She was numb from her elbows to her fingertips. Mandy's voice, Lori's voice, and that stranger at their table couldn't penetrate the cotton in her ears.

Mandy stood over her, touching her. "What's wrong, honey? Are you all right?"

"She's so pale," Lori said.

"Did she touch the dolls?" the man said.

Sara felt giddy, and she couldn't breathe. A great weight sat on her heart, and her lungs closed, like deflated balloons. Her arms itched, but she couldn't scratch. Her forehead sank lower and lower as the light dimmed.

"Call an ambulance!" Mandy screamed, and Sara's world went black.

Chapter Thirty-one

Pie in the sky...

Everything happened at once. Sokolsky made the call, while Amanda and Lori hovered over Sara, unsure how to help. Amanda was frantic, yet frozen, like a tiny projector in her brain had stalled on a nightmare frame while intense heat burned up the film. She knew some first aid. Sara's pulse was weak, and her breathing was shallow. Would moving her to the sofa do more harm than good? Torn by uncertainty, she clung to Sara's clammy hand, whispered words of encouragement, and ignored Lori's escalating freak-out. Amanda didn't know how long she sat there, praying and bargaining with a god she didn't believe in, but soon she heard sirens and commotion in the hall. Two sets of hands took hold of her shoulders and eased her away from the table.

"We'll take over from here, love," a gentle female voice said as she and a male companion began working with Sara.

The emergency responders wore what appeared to be hazmat suits, so Amanda couldn't see their faces or gauge their level of concern. The woman gave Sara oxygen, and the man checked Sara's vitals, stating that her blood pressure was dangerously low.

"She was poisoned," Amanda told them with sudden certainty. Had Sokolsky already explained that Sara had touched the dolls and likely absorbed the poison through her skin? It now seemed blatantly obvious. "Sara washed her hands, though!" Amanda cried, as if that would somehow make Sara all right.

"Yes, ma'am, the detective told us all that," the male responder said.

Did this team know what to do? It seemed so because a third person in an alien suit was bagging up Sara's coat with heavily gloved hands.

"What poison?" Lori howled as yet another responder wheeled a gurney into the kitchen.

Sokolsky followed. "Did either you or Lori touch it, Mandy?"

Amanda had to think. She'd elbowed the door but never touched the knob where the coat hanger hung. "Sara washed her hands really well before I held them," she explained, barely able to speak.

"Well, that's a blessing," Sokolsky said through clenched teeth. "The washing will hopefully save Sara's life."

Save her life? The enormity of Sara's plight hit Amada like a freight train. It knocked her onto the rails and barreled across her heart as the three medics gently unfolded Sara and placed her on the gurney. They covered her with a light blanket and then rapidly wheeled her through the foyer to the front door. Amanda was hard on their heels. "I'm going with you," she cried and grabbed onto the gurney.

"Me too." Lori was right behind.

Sokolsky said, "Hold your horses, ladies, you're not going anywhere. Let the medics do their work."

Amanda tightened her grip. "Fuck you, Sokolsky! Try to stop me!"

The detective held the door open, and the parade squeezed through. Amanda called over her shoulder,

"Lori, call your Aunt Diana. Trout will come get you and take you to the lake house. Then your dad can pick you up from there tomorrow."

"Hell no, Mandy. I'm not going home until Sara comes home."

Sokolsky blocked Lori. "Call Diana, young lady. You can't stay here. The whole condo is a crime scene, and we can't have you in the way."

Amanda managed to hang on to the gurney's railing as they all took a wide berth around the horror still lying under its green shroud on the porch. The giant officer Rodney Woods had stepped away onto the grass, his big latex-clad hands folded solemnly in front, a fearful look in his eyes. No doubt Sokolsky had warned him to let hazmat handle it. She was aware of curious neighbors congregating behind the yellow tape strung well away from their front door.

As they quickly approached the open ambulance, the female responder asked, "Are you related to the patient, dear?"

Amanda didn't hesitate. "We're getting married."

Amanda couldn't actually see the smile behind the woman's bulky mask, but it was reflected in her eyes. "Congratulations," the medic said. "That's good enough for me. Wait until we have Dr. Orlando secured, then hop on in."

Amanda breathed a sigh of relief. She'd heard horror stories about same-sex couples being denied access to their mates in hospitals. That absolutely, positively was not happening to her. "Thanks," she murmured, but the kind responder was already in the vehicle.

Amanda lost sight of Sara for a moment, until the male responder signaled for her to come. She never got close enough to Sara, however, because he put her onto a small jump seat in the rear, handed her a paper mask, strapped her in, and said, "Stay put, and don't get in our way."

Seconds later, the ambulance careened out of the complex, turned on its lights and siren, and then roared down the ramp onto the southbound lane to Charlotte.

"Wait!" she cried. "Aren't we going to Lake Norman Regional? It's only two miles north."

"No, ma'am, we're headed to Carolinas Medical Center. They have a specialized poison unit there."

She supposed this was good. Of course, it was. But it emphasized how serious Sara's condition was and sent a fresh shockwave of fear through Amanda's system. The big medical center was near Sara's clinic, but it seemed the far end of nowhere to Amanda. As they sped farther away from home, with traffic scrambling off the highway to get out of their way, Amanda clung tight to a guardrail to keep herself from bouncing around like a Ping-Pong ball. She strained to see what was happening with Sara. From her vantage point, she saw they had attached a more massive oxygen mask and inserted an intravenous port inside Sara's left elbow. When the redheaded medic started a clear drip into the port, she asked what it was.

"Saline solution. Hydration," he grumbled.

In the meantime, the woman cleansed Sara's hands and forearms before applying a clear gel. As she wrapped the areas in gauze, she explained, "Your partner absorbed the poison transdermally. The gel should help prevent infection and blisters."

Amanda squeezed her eyes shut and swallowed the bile at the back of her throat. It was unimaginable, Sara's lovely, porcelain skin attacked in this way. "What kind of poison?"

"That's the problem, isn't it?" the grumpy redhead said. "Fuck if we know. I heard the cops say they were sending that load of crap on your doorstep to the CMPD crime lab. We won't know how to treat your friend until they identify the poison, and unless we get her blood pressure up pronto, we're screwed."

Amanda was terrified, but then the kind woman laid a comforting hand on her arm. "Don't mind Jason, love. His bedside manner stinks, but he's good at his job. Dr. Orlando will come through this."

Promise? Amanda didn't ask the question because she knew promises at this point were pie in the sky. Like God. She'd never been a true believer, but at times like this, she wished she was. She gazed at Sara's beautiful, sleeping face and gave thanks to whatever powers that be that Sara did not seem in distress. She looked, yes, like an angel, which was another mythic, religious being that didn't exist. Amanda did believe in the power of love, however, and if that worked, then Sara would come through this with flying colors. But just in case, she said an earnest prayer to God. It never hurt to hedge your bets.

Chapter Thirty-two

A country girl...

By the time they reached the hospital, Amanda was geographically and emotionally lost. The ambulance veered around to the emergency entrance beside the towering buildings, but before it entered a covered tunnel, where other vehicles were offloading patients, the driver stopped. The female medic released Amanda's seat belt and opened the rear door.

"Sorry, you can't come any farther, love. We'll be taking your partner into receiving for blood tests, stabilization, and whatnot. Then she'll likely end up in the critical care wing." The medic paused to pry Amanda off her seat and then escorted her down metal stairs to the concrete driveway.

"But I didn't get a chance to say goodbye." Amanda jerked her elbow free of the woman's firm hand.

The woman lifted her mask and regarded Amanda through kind, pale blue eyes. "Dr. Orlando couldn't hear you anyway. She's sound asleep."

More like comatose. Amanda searched the woman's face and realized she was much older than Amanda had supposed. She had pure white hair and a British accent like the character Vera in their favorite BritBox series. Fortunately, the medic was not an old curmudgeon like the detective. "My partner's name is Sara," she told the woman.

"Good to know. I'll tell the team. It will help Sara feel more comfortable when she comes 'round."

"What's your name?" Suddenly, Amanda needed to know.

"Brenda, love, and yes, I'm British. I moved across the pond to be near my son. He does PR for the Carolina Panthers football club—if you can call all that shoving and bashing football."

Amanda didn't need Brenda's life story, but she couldn't help but smile. She followed Brenda to the grand entrance to the Atrium Health System's lobby, where worried-looking folks of all ages and races bustled through the doors, some with canes or wheelchairs.

Brenda said, "Go to the reception desk. They'll take your picture and give you a day pass. If I were you, I'd hole up in the café for an hour or two. Have a coffee, make your calls, and try to relax. Sara won't be given a room assignment for a good long while."

How could she relax when her mind, heart, and soul got left behind with Sara?

"You should call her family," Brenda said.

The thought hadn't even occurred, but then Amanda realized that Juan and Sofia were in Puerto Rico with Sara's grandmother, and her brother, Marc, was in Los Angeles visiting his latest girlfriend. But Sara had the Rittenhouse-Troutman clans, all their friends, and of course, Amanda. She would not be alone.

After thanking Brenda and saying goodbye, Amanda got a coffee and a doughnut. The choice was weirdly reminiscent of the items she'd purchased at Summit Coffee only hours ago, a lifetime ago. She wove her way through the press of humanity crowding the concourse and found a table for two against the wall.

The massive flood of people was disorienting; she'd become a country girl. They all looked purposeful, like they knew their mission and destination, while Amanda felt unfocused and unhinged.

Had Brenda suggested she call the family because Sara's condition was critical? She picked up her cup with trembling hands and put it right back down. The last thing she needed on an empty stomach was caffeine nerves. The EMS crew had made her turn off her phone in the ambulance, but now she took it from her bag and stared at the blank screen. When she thumbed it on, she saw numerous missed calls from Lori, but the only person on earth she wanted to talk to was Mom. How would she ever explain their bizarre situation? Without overthinking it, she connected with Atrium's Wi-Fi and hit speed dial.

Mom answered immediately. "Oh, honey, I am so sorry! Are you at the hospital now?"

Hearing the love and concern in Mom's voice pulled Amanda's trigger, and the pent-up tears flowed. "Sara's really sick, Mom. I don't know what to do!"

"I know. Lori's here with us, and she told us all about it. It's going to be okay, I promise."

There it was, the promise no one else had been willing to make, but coming from Mom's lips, Amanda was inclined to believe it. She closed her eyes, allowing her mother to comfort and reassure her. Clearly Lori had done as Amanda had asked and had Trout come get her, but as Mom recounted the facts according to Lori, it was plain that neither Lori nor Mom had a full understanding of their stalker issue. Good. They didn't need to know all the gruesome details.

"I can't believe that horrible man Russel Cowley would do such a thing!" Mom regurgitated the Lori theory. "They'll catch him, Mandy, and he will pay."

"I don't think he did it, Mom," Amanda muttered, but Mom wasn't hearing it. When Mom finished her rant about Russel, Amanda explained that they were at Carolinas Medical Center in the city and that she was in limbo waiting for an update about Sara's condition.

"Sara will pull through, she's a fighter," Mom again promised. "And we're all coming to support you."

"No, Mom, please don't! I can't even see her, and I'm positive Sara won't want visitors." Much as Amanda needed Mom's hugs, she envisioned Mom, Trout, Lori, Ginny, Trev, and Lissa all arriving like a swarm of kindly locusts.

"Lori called her daddy, and Judd's driving down a day early," Mom continued. "Ella and Jana wanted to come, too, but they have school duties that won't wait. All the Taylors adore Sara, you know that. Judd and Lori intend to stay in town until Sara's home safe."

Amanda was overwhelmed by the outpouring of love and support, but seven people descending on the hospital? She couldn't allow it. "No, Mother, I forbid it!" she snapped. "I just can't deal with you all right now. I'll call as soon as I know anything, and we'll take it from there. Please…?"

Amanda listened to her mother's pregnant silence, knowing full well how stubborn she could be. But Amanda was stubborn, too. Finally, Mom said, "I will honor your wishes, honey, and I do understand, but if I don't hear from you every hour on the hour, we will come. Do you understand? Take care of yourself," she finished. "And eat something."

Mom hung up, and Amanda obediently picked up her doughnut. She took one bite, but it tasted vile, so she put it back in its wrapper. She wiped her eyes with a paper napkin. Family was mostly a blessing, sometimes a curse, but she'd take them—warts and all. Then, for the second time in one hour, she prayed to the God she didn't believe in.

Chapter Thirty-three

Waiting...

Amanda had never been good at waiting. She tried to zone out and think of nothing, especially not Sara, enduring god-knew-what in some undisclosed location in this sterile city within a city. From her chair against the wall, Amanda saw neither day nor night nor anything at all to indicate a world existed beyond this busy concourse. She'd lost track of time and lost count of the humans rushing by, and when the foot traffic doubled, she assumed it was suppertime, and her stomach rumbled. And her phone rang, startling her from her trance.

"It's six o'clock, and you didn't call," Mom scolded. "Every hour on the hour, that was our agreement." Amanda explained that she still had no news, but Mom said, "Well, do they have your number so they can contact you? Have you approached the desk and asked for an update?"

Amanda panicked. Did they have her number? She couldn't remember. She had no idea how hospital contacts worked, but she'd probably messed up. "I'll check again," she told her mother.

"Have you eaten supper, Mandy?"

"Yeah, sure," Amanda lied.

"Well, that's a relief. I know how you are, honey, but you have to take care of yourself before you can take care of Sara, right? I love you, and we'll talk again at seven."

When Mom hung up, Amanda tried to concentrate. Yes, the reception desk had taken her cellphone number and said that someone would text her with Sara's progress, but should she have been more proactive? She dumped the coffee and doughnut into the trash, pushed her way through the tide of people flowing mostly in the opposite direction, and finally reached the reception desk.

When it was her turn, an overworked older man consulted his monitor and confirmed that they had all Amanda's details. He advised her that she should move on to the critical care wing, where Sara was expected at some unspecified time in the future. She learned that visiting hours ended at ten p.m. with few exceptions, she was allowed to eat food in the critical care lounges, and above all, "Don't pester the nurses. Don't call them, they'll call you," advice Amanda intended to ignore.

Newly emboldened, Amanda waited in line to purchase an egg salad sandwich, chips, and a Diet Pepsi. Following signs, she marched onto a glassed-in overpass leading to a different building, noticing that it was now pitch dark outside and raining. She took two different elevators and eventually stepped out into the critical care lobby. She saw restrooms, two large visitors' lounges with televisions and seats filled with tired-looking people, and the heavy double doors leading to an octagonal nurses' station.

She pushed straight through the doors, walked right up, and got yelled at by several of the dozen or so nurses behind a high counter.

"Ma'am, please, you can't come in here without a mask!"

A mask was provided, and Amanda slipped it over

her face. She approached a young woman with frizzy red hair, the only person not staring at a monitor. The woman's name tag said "Bethany." Amanda explained her situation, filled out a form identifying herself as Sara's wife, and was told to wait in a lounge. Someone would contact her as soon as Sara was brought up.

Should she believe Bethany? She seemed nice enough, but as Amanda returned to the lounges, she decided to trust but verify. She would apply her mother's every hour on the hour rule, provided Amanda could wait sixty whole minutes between visits to the nursing station.

She stuffed the hated mask into her pocket, and after a pit stop to the women's restroom, took a seat upholstered with blue and green diamonds as far from other visitors as she could get. Ignoring the home improvement channel on TV, she wolfed down her food and gulped her Pepsi. *Stay strong* was her new motto. Her first fifteen minutes passed quickly—the next fifteen, not so much.

She wanted to call Maya and Shar. She'd never properly thanked them for having them to dinner, and the couple felt almost like family. They also knew the whole truth about their stalker, and they'd be beyond horrified to hear what had happened to Sara today. They deserved to know. Sara was Maya and Shar's oldest and dearest friend. But as she imagined telling them, Amanda's tears welled up, and her strong woman mask slipped. To tell them would make it real. She couldn't do it. Not yet.

She was reaching for a paper napkin to dry her eyes when a gentle hand touched her shoulder.

"Mandy, are you okay? They told me I'd find you here."

She looked up into the pale gray eyes of Detective Peter Sokolsky. He looked more rumpled than usual with dark stubble growing on his wolf-like features, and he smelled more like sweat than his habitual, sharp aftershave. He was also soaking wet.

"It's gushing like a fire hose out there," he complained as he shucked off his suitcoat. "How's Sara?"

She sniffed back more tears. "Don't know yet."

"I'm so sorry. This is fucked up, but I bet she'll be okay."

So everybody keeps telling me.

"The dolls are at the crime lab as we speak. They'll get a result real soon, and that's a good thing..." Sokolsky faltered, seemingly out of positive news.

"So what do you want?" She hadn't intended to be so abrupt, but it was the only way she could keep her brave mask in place.

"Well, first off, thanks for sending me on a wild goose chase. The Russel Cowley lead was a waste of time."

"Lori's lead, not mine," she grumbled.

"Anyway, the good lawyer was mighty pissed. He spent the entire afternoon on the golf course with three other guys who back up his alibi. They'd already teed off before you girls got home. I had egg on my face until I laid into Cowley about stalking you. He didn't deny it."

"What did he say?"

"He said he was a jerk, and he's sorry."

"What did you say?"

"I told him if he ever did it again, I'd cut off his balls and putt them into the eighteenth hole."

Amanda laughed. It felt really good.

"Cowley won't bother you again," Sokolsky said, and then excused himself to get a free coffee from the hospitality kiosk set up in one corner. He returned, sat beside her, took a sip, and made an ugly face. "This is worse than the swill they brew at the station."

Holding the paper cup in one hand, he reached into his pocket and took out his cellphone. At that precise moment, a clap of thunder exploded just beyond the window. Sokolsky jumped and spilled coffee all over his pink and green Hawaiian shirt. "Shit on a stick!" he roared. Making another trip to the hospitality kiosk, he tossed the coffee and mopped his shirt with the complimentary napkins.

He returned to his seat and tapped at his phone, bringing up a picture he'd taken of Amanda's suspect list, with Russel Cowley's name at the top. "Okay, we can eliminate suspect number one, so who's this Tammy Tillman?"

Amanda blinked several times, remembering the morning she'd met with Tammy, the cake Tammy planned to bake, and the kind invitation she'd extended to her thirtieth birthday party. "Tammy didn't do it. Including her name was a stupid mistake."

Sokolsky enlarged the image and pointed to the name Melinda Meeks. "I remember this pathetic woman. I investigated when she murdered the district attorney. She's a homophobic psycho, but she's cooling her heels in the psych ward at the women's prison. Dead end."

Amanda gulped. "Yes, the others on my list are dead ends, too."

Sokolsky grinned. "Yeah, I checked them out. But it beats me how two upstanding citizens like you and Sara have rubbed elbows with so many unsavory felons."

What could she say? It was beyond understanding.

And then Amanda's phone rang. It was seven o'clock. "Not now, Mom," she answered. "I'm with Detective Sokolsky."

"Peter is there?" Mom practically swooned. "That's excellent, Mandy. He'll solve your case. May I speak with him?"

"Sorry, gotta go. No news about Sara, and I'll call you at eight." Amanda disconnected.

"Ah, that was my dear Diana," Sokolsky said. "I'll make a point to catch up with her as soon as this case is solved."

Amanda was glad they were both so optimistic about the outcome, but they were a mutual admiration society and therefore biased. She watched as Sokolsky brought up a photo of Sara's list.

He massaged his stubble and said, "I've been through Sara's list, and every name is a non-starter but this one. Who the hell is Jane Doe?"

Amanda took a deep breath. She'd almost forgotten that Sara had settled on Jane as her prime suspect. At the time, Amanda had been convinced, but now she suspected that Sara wanted their dilemma to be her fault. Sara had always carried a load of misplaced guilt about the potential danger some of her patients posed, as if it could spill over into their lives. "I don't know the woman's real name, but Jane Doe is an ex-patient with a grudge..." She explained the story to Sokolsky as best she could.

"Surely someone can help me identify her?" he said.

Amanda wracked her brain and came up with a name. "Dr. Angela Yee is a forensic psychologist who works in Sara's clinic. Dr. Yee is treating Jane now, and she knows our situation. Maybe she'll talk to you."

"No maybe about it." Sokolsky wrote down Yee's name. "It's after hours now, but I'll visit the clinic first thing in the morning. Is there anything else you can add to help me?"

"Nothing relative to the case, but I'm so worried. Can you please conjure up some healing vibes for Sara?"

"I'll pray for her," he said without hesitation. He stood and pulled Amanda to her feet and into his embrace.

He smelled of sweat and coffee, but the hug felt good. She didn't want him to go, but, of course, he did go—off into the night and the rain.

Chapter Thirty-four

Amorphous spirits...

The heavy double doors sighed open, and someone touched Amanda's shoulder. "Wake up, Ms. Rittenhouse. They just brought Dr. Orlando up. She's in a room now."

Amanda startled. Had she really fallen asleep? The television still droned, and the rain still poured as she looked up into green eyes and a mask surrounded by frizzy red hair. Bethany, she remembered, and her nightmare reality came rushing back.

"My shift ends at eight, but I have time to introduce you to Dr. Orlando's doctor. Come, please."

Suddenly wide awake, Amanda put on her mask and followed Bethany. The nurses' station was much busier than before, with people juggling clipboards and playing musical chairs.

"Second shift is eight to eight thirty tomorrow morning, so some folks are leaving," Bethany explained. "Dr. T will be here a while longer since some toddler decided to drink antifreeze and is on the way to emergency. Look, here he comes! You'll have time for a quick chat."

"Are you Ms. Rittenhouse?" The exceptional-looking man was gliding down the hallway, his hand outstretched. He was well over six feet tall, slim, athletic, and graceful with long fluid limbs and a monumental head—like an African king. "I am Dr.

Ngabo Twahirwa, but everyone calls me Dr. T. I am pleased to meet you."

She'd never seen skin so black. His hand was cool and dry. "You've been treating Sara?" Amanda asked, trying not to stare.

"Yes, I just brought Dr. Orlando to room 227. Will you step inside and speak with me, please?" Dr. T entered a small office tucked in behind the nurses' station. Amanda followed him. He closed the door and indicated that she should sit across from him at a desk much too small for his lanky frame. She took a seat while the doctor quickly recited his resume: born in Rwanda, educated in London, medical degree from Wake Forrest with a specialty in toxicology. That explained his formal manner and British accent.

Amanda was too worried to be impressed, but she was determined to learn everything she could about Sara's condition. She forced words past the lump in her throat. "How is she?"

Instead of directly answering her question, the doctor shook his head. "Dr. Orlando's case is quite complex or unusual, I suppose..."

"Please call her Sara," Amanda interrupted. "She would want you to."

"Yes, as you wish. Sara has been exposed to an unknown local anesthetic. She absorbed the toxin transdermally through her hands and wrists, and the poison tried to shut down her respiratory system, which caused her to collapse. We do not know if Sara touched lidocaine, Marcaine, monocaine, or any of a dozen other such toxins, of which procaine is the most dangerous. They can cause coma, convulsions, dropping blood pressure, and cardiac arrest."

Amanda felt nauseated and slightly dizzy. Not

once had the doctor looked her straight in the eye. "What are you saying?" she demanded. "Has Sara shown those symptoms?"

"No, no!" He held up both hands and gazed at her from ebony eyes. "Sara's symptoms include respiratory trauma, which we are treating with oxygen, and hypotension, which we are treating with fluid resuscitation. We are also administering a mild dose of succinylcholine as an anticonvulsant. If we knew the precise anesthetic used on her, we could adjust or eliminate the drug choice. Other than that, we are treating the affected areas of Sara's skin with antibiotic salve to reduce blistering."

Amanda closed her eyes and choked back tears. Sara's symptoms sounded serious and life-threatening. She wanted to ask the only question that mattered but couldn't get the words out. She was aware of Dr. T checking his watch, remembered the toddler who swallowed antifreeze, and knew her window of opportunity was closing. "Will Sara be all right?" She gasped.

"Oh, yes," he said offhandedly. "After surviving forone hour, victims of this type of poisoning usually fully recover."

She felt light-headed and confused. Had she heard him correctly? "If Sara's recovering, why is she still asleep?"

Dr. T's teeth were blindingly white as he smiled through plum-colored lips. "Who said she is asleep?"

❧❧❧❧

Sara was restless and needed to scratch the side of her nose, but even if she could lift her hands, which felt like baseball mitts swathed in gauze, she couldn't get under the oxygen mask covering her nose and mouth. What if she sneezed? If she cried, who would wipe her tears?

Her feet worked well enough. She wiggled her toes, then pushed at the too-hot blanket, but her efforts were futile because the bedclothes were too tight, encasing her like a mummy. The fluorescent lights were too bright, the beeping heart monitor too loud, and when the hanging bag containing her clear medicine was empty, it set off an alarm that howled until some nurse taking her sweet time took pity and came to replace it.

Sara wasn't complaining. She was alive, wasn't she? But even if she wanted to hurl obscenities at her caregivers, she couldn't because it took too much breath, and her throat hurt. Most upsetting of all was, where the hell was Mandy? Someone had told her that her "wife" was in the building, which normally would have delighted her and given her fodder for endless teasing in the future. As it was, if Mandy was here, then why couldn't she see her? Sara loved her, needed her, and wanted her more than anything on earth!

A different someone had said visiting hours ended at ten p.m., and if the big clock on the wall was to be believed, that gave them less than two hours to be together. If their visit got put off until tomorrow, could she make it through the night?

※※※※

Dr. T escorted Amanda to room 227 and said, "We were lucky, Ms. Rittenhouse. Whoever poisoned Sara did not know what they were doing because the anesthetic was diluted too much to kill. Again, I am certain that Sara will make a full recovery and be released from hospital in a few days."

"Thank you, Dr. T." She returned his lovely smile and gave thanks for stupid killers. Stupid and indiscriminate. That poison could have hurt not only Sara, but also her and seventeen-year-old Lori. She said goodbye to the doctor, who loped quickly away, like a graceful giraffe.

The door to 227 was closed, and her emotions were in turmoil. Now that she knew Sara would recover, the hours of tension fled from her body, leaving her weak, tearful, and exceedingly grateful. She paused, uncertain who to credit for the miracle—those amorphous spirits of goodwill she believed existed in the universe or the gray-bearded God she'd never believed in. It didn't matter. What mattered lay just beyond the door.

Chapter Thirty-five

Courage and resilience...

A manda muted her phone, took a deep breath, and then knocked lightly before entering the room, closing the door behind her. The space was cool, the lighting dim, and the silence complete but for the soft pulsing from some machine. There was a door leading to a bathroom, a utility cabinet, a whiteboard posted with nurse's names and shift information, a green recliner, and one visitor chair, but all Amanda saw was the hospital bed occupied by a very precious patient.

She approached quietly, her heart skipping with equal parts hope and fear, and immediately saw that Sara was awake. Behind the clear plastic dome of an oxygen mask, Sara's lips curved up in a smile; above the mask, her green eyes gazed lovingly through half-closed lids. Amanda rushed to the bed, whispering Sara's name again and again. When she reached out to take Sara's hands, she saw they were swathed in gauze, with only the fingers exposed, and stopped herself from grabbing them.

"I love you," Amanda murmured.

"Love you more," Sara's lips mouthed the words, her voice muted and hoarse.

Amanda held a finger up to her own lips. "Don't try to talk, honey. We've always managed to communicate pretty well without words, haven't we?"

Sara nodded and then surprised Amanda with a wink. Then Sara smiled seductively, slowly ran her tongue along her upper lip, and smiled again. She was flirting! Amanda was astonished by her courage and resilience. While Amanda mumbled incoherently about how sorry she was about what had happened, Sara was summoning joy and reassuring Amanda with her positivity.

Amanda pulled the chair up to the bed and sat so they were face-to-face. "You are amazing!"

Sara wore a loose hospital gown patterned with little green flowers. It was held together with strings tied behind her neck like a bib, and it crisscrossed her lovely breasts like folded wings affording little protection from the nurses' busy hands or Amanda's roving eyes. Amanda took advantage. She kissed Sara's bare shoulder and then trailed more kisses down her arm to her elbow.

Sara's lower half was tightly cocooned in the bedclothes. "Are you comfortable? Is there anything I can do?" Amanda asked. Sara frowned and then kicked at the blankets with her feet. It seemed she was too hot, so Amanda untucked the blanket and folded it into the crack between the mattress and the foot of the bed. She loosened the sheet. "Better?"

"Yes, thanks," Sara croaked and then shoved at the guardrail between them.

Amanda figured out how to lower the guardrail and eliminated the barrier. She learned how to work the bed to raise Sara's shoulders or feet. She spotted a roller tray with a water pitcher, paper cups, and a bendy straw. "Do you want a drink?"

"Yes, but I'd rather have a beer." Sara's words were actually audible that time.

Amanda laughed, got the water, and then carefully lifted Sara's mask so she could drink. While Sara's mask was up, Amanda pulled down her own mask and gently kissed Sara full on the lips.

"What the hell's going on in here?" a female voice shouted from the doorway.

Amanda panicked. She hadn't heard the nurse enter, and like a kid caught with her hand in the cookie jar, she clumsily replaced Sara's mask and repositioned her own. The nurse was middle-aged, heavy, with short gray hair and suspicious blue eyes peeking out above her mask. As she barreled toward them, she reminded Amanda of an old-time cartoon character who whacks folks with a frying pan, in this case, a bedpan. Amanda prepared to duck.

"Who are you?" the nurse demanded as she reached between them to fiddle with Sara's mask. When Amanda gave her name, the nurse said, "Oh, so you're the wife."

Amanda nodded, and Sara rolled her eyes, enjoying Amanda's discomfort. The nurse introduced herself as Velma and said she'd be Sara's caregiver until eight the following morning. She also explained that Sara had some use of her fingers and was capable of pressing the call button. "So don't go thinking you're her nurse, Ms. Rittenhouse. That's my job, you hear?"

"Understood." Amanda wanted to stay on Velma's good side because she intended to ask a very big favor. "I won't get in your way, but I'm here to help."

"Good to know," Velma said as she eased Amanda up and out of her chair. "You can start by stepping out into the hallway for a moment. Dr. Orlando needs a bedpan, and I'm sure she'd appreciate some privacy."

Amanda bit her tongue and controlled her temper

as Velma pulled a privacy curtain along a ceiling-mounted track, cutting Amanda out, but she called to Sara through the curtain, "I need to call Mom anyway to let her know you're okay. She's been worried sick. Everyone has," she finished and then stepped into the hall.

≈≋≋≋

Sara endured the indignity of the bedpan and longed to be free of the mask, the tubes, and especially Velma. The nurse meant well, but she was bossy. Sara didn't need to be reminded that she was sick, needed rest, and wasn't to overexert herself. She wasn't to pull off her bandages or remove her oxygen mask—as if she could—and she wasn't to strain her voice.

"On a scale of one to ten, how's your pain?" Velma asked.

How to answer? If she was truthful and said seven, Velma would inject some morphine into her IV and knock her out. Sara desperately wanted to stay awake for Mandy, so she held up four fingers. Velma seemed skeptical, but she agreed to return in an hour and ask again. When Velma finished checking Sara's vitals and entered the information into her phone, she finally allowed Mandy back into the room. When Sara saw Mandy's sweet face, she literally felt her heartbeat stabilize and her blood pressure stop spiking.

"Thanks, Velma," Mandy said. "And by the way, I will be spending the night here in Dr. Orlando's room."

My God, was that true? Sara was over the moon. How had Mandy managed such a coup? When Velma questioned her, Mandy said that someone named Dr. T had signed off on the idea.

"That's funny. Doctor T never said anything to me about it," Velma grumbled.

"Because he left before your shift," Mandy smugly replied.

Was Mandy lying? Sara didn't care because when Velma grudgingly agreed, all was well in Sara's world. After telling Mandy that she'd find pillows and blankets in the utility cabinet, Velma left, and Mandy pulled up her chair. She was close enough that Sara could smell her familiar scent and feel her warm breath on her arm. She wished that Mandy could climb in bed with her, but realistically, that was not to be.

Instead, she listened as Mandy brought her up to date on all that had transpired since Sara's collapse: the dead end with Russel Cowley, the hours of waiting, and the visit from Detective Sokolsky. Sara nodded her approval upon hearing that Sokolsky would visit Angela Yee at the clinic in the morning. Surely, Angela would share her information about Janice Kenny. Then Sokolsky would confront Jan, and the nightmare would end.

Sara worried that Mandy was hungry but couldn't get the words out to tell her to go eat. But she loved it when Mandy dragged the green recliner up parallel to the bed and lounged back so they were lying side by side. When Velma returned, Sara accepted the painkiller that would carry her off to dreamland because she could feel the warmth of Mandy's arm against hers as they fell asleep together.

Chapter Thirty-six

Fall back...

Amanda had served her fair share of time as a hospital patient, but she'd forgotten all the interruptions: the hourly wake-ups and bright lights when Velma checked Sara's vitals, the bedpans, and the staff chattering in the hallways. In self-defense, when the empty bag alarm went off like a screaming hyena and no one responded, Amanda learned how to shut it off herself. She'd then stagger stiff and angry to the nurses' station to demand a refill.

Sara staged her own rebellion by deciding to walk to the bathroom rather than face yet another bedpan. Amanda resisted, but Sara insisted. Did Sara's legs even work? But Sara kicked away her covers, swung her legs off the bed, and growled until Amanda helped raise her upper body. Once Sara was standing somewhat steadily on her feet, Amanda supported her with her left arm and moved the attached IV tower with her right hand. Dragging the tower along with them, avoiding the tangle of cords on the floor, they managed to get Sara seated on the toilet. Sara's eyes glowed with victory, but then Sara felt less victorious when she had to accept Amanda's help to wipe herself. By the time Sara was settled back in bed, Amanda figured they'd taken two steps forward, only one step back.

Amanda revised their progress another step back when Velma and two aides stormed into the room.

Apparently, Sara's voyage had set off major alarm bells, landing them on the "troublesome patients" shit list. Throughout the scolding, Sara remained defiant and shouted for Velma to remove her "damn oxygen mask." Everyone, including Amanda, was shocked by the volume and clarity of Sara's voice.

"Well, now!" Velma exclaimed. "It seems the good doctor has found her vocal cords." Velma then checked the patient monitor screen. "Her respiration rate is much improved."

"So can you take off the mask?" Amanda pleaded.

Velma frowned. If Velma could read Sara's stubborn monitor by the firm set of Sara's lips and her angrily narrowed eyes, then she would make the right decision. After a brief stare-down contest between patient and nurse, Velma waved the two aides away and removed the mask. In its place, she looped a nasal cannula over Sara's neck and inserted its little prongs into her nose.

"Much better." Amanda smiled.

Arms crossed, still frowning, Velma again checked Sara's respiration. "I suppose it will do," she conceded.

"Thank you." Sara sighed.

"You are welcome," Velma grumbled as she left. "And I expect no more trouble from you two tonight."

The moment the door closed behind her, Amanda whooped with joy. Sara was walking, talking, and practically breathing on her own. Amanda carefully hugged her and then gently kissed Sara's lips.

"Oh, be careful!" Sara cried when the kiss deepened.

Amanda pulled back in alarm. "What's wrong?"

"Your kiss…" Sara smiled. "It takes my breath

away."

❧❧❧❧❧

Sara couldn't believe she'd slept so soundly and so had Mandy. After their small victories—the bathroom, mask, and an exceptional kiss, it seemed the worst of their ordeal was over. She felt better. She could even lift her hands a little and wiggle her fingers. She still didn't know the person and motivation behind the malevolent poison attack, but then, after years of practicing psychiatry, she still couldn't understand the human heart. All she knew with certainty was that as long as Mandy was by her side, they would survive and hopefully thrive.

It was morning, and the rain had stopped. Weak bands of sunlight leaked through the slatted blinds on the big window at the end of the room. Yesterday when the blinds were open, she'd seen the view of a tar roof, a gigantic HVAC unit, and a tiny patch of sky. The sky had helped her cope. Now as she listened to the rubber soles of shoes squeaking on the tiles in the hallway, the drone of her machine, and the rolling breakfast carts, she realized she was hungry. When had she last eaten? Was it only yesterday? Yes, Mandy had made instant oatmeal with blueberries and toast before their walk into Davidson. Only one week ago, they'd driven home from the wedding in Asheville. Myriad unimaginable events had been compressed into one short week, and the result was disorienting, distressing, but as Sara watched Mandy sleeping beside her, contorted on the recliner in a position guaranteed to cause her cramps and stiffness, Sara felt at peace with fickle time. She closed her eyes and fell back into the twilight zone, grateful to be alive.

≈≈≈≈

"Wake up, sleepyhead!"

Amanda startled when someone shook her foot. Dragging her eyes open and trying to get her bearings, she saw the hospital room bathed in bright light, Sara sound asleep, and a young woman she'd never seen before smiling down at her. She was obviously a nurse, pretty and African American, she reminded Amanda of Jana. She seemed gentle and shy, like Jana.

"I'm Kayla. I'll be taking care of Dr. Orlando today."

When Amanda tried to sit up, she ached all over, including muscles she didn't know she had. She stretched and squinted at the big clock on the wall. "But it's only seven thirty, where's Velma? Her shift doesn't end till eight thirty."

"Yes, ma'am, it's seven thirty, but it should be eight thirty as far as Velma's concerned. I agreed she shouldn't have to work an extra hour, so I've been on duty for a half hour."

"So you came to work too early?" Amanda pointed at the clock.

The young woman began to sing the old Simon & Garfunkel song, "Hello darkness my old friend…"

"Pardon?"

"Daylight savings comes again," Kayla finished with a flourish. "We fell back at midnight. You need to get with it, girl."

"What? No way." As usual, Amanda had missed her most hated day of the year when she lost an hour of daylight. "I'll have to turn my watch back."

Kayla shrugged. "Personally, I'd much rather turn my scale back."

Amanda groaned. Everyone loved a comedian, but it was way too early. She noticed that Sara was also slowly waking up, a puzzled look on her face. Amanda brushed back a stray lock of black hair that had fallen across Sara's left eye, kissed her forehead, and said, "Welcome to Sunday, honey. It's time to fall back."

"Whatever." Sara yawned and pointed to the covered tray on Kayla's cart. "Is that my breakfast?"

"Yes, ma'am. Scrambled eggs, cream of wheat, orange juice, and coffee."

Sara's appetite was back, a very good sign, but Amanda's stomach growled when Kayla lifted the lid and delicious food smells drifted her way. "Sara probably can't eat all that, but *I* can." Amanda pulled the recliner upright and reached for the tray.

Sara slapped her hand away. "No way, Mandy, that food is all mine."

"Oh, so *you're* Mandy?" Kayla said. "You might want to head down to the lounge while the doctor has her breakfast and a bath. You got a gang of folks asking after you, and they all look mighty hungry."

Chapter Thirty-seven

Musical chairs...

A manda hadn't expected an emotional reaction, but when she left Critical Care and saw almost her entire family crowded into the second lounge, tears sprung to her eyes. She stopped in her tracks, yanked off her mask, and wiped them away with her sleeve. The whole motley crew must have risen before dawn to get there so early. As soon as they spotted her, the Troutman, Dula, and Taylor families jumped to their feet, everyone talking at once, all concerned about Sara.

Amanda explained as they hugged and kissed, keeping it simple, saying only that Sara was much better, but not out of the woods yet. Amanda wanted to spare them, especially Lissa and Lori, the gory details about the blue silk stocking terror campaign. Someday she might share, but Amanda doubted it.

Eventually, Mom and Trout sat together on one sofa, Ginny, Trev, and Lissa on another, and finally, Lori stepped forward holding her father's hand. Judd looked as tall and strong as Amanda remembered him from two years ago, but he'd shaved his head smooth as a brown egg, and his neatly trimmed beard and mustache were more white than black. He pulled her close, smothering her in his embrace.

"Thanks for everything you and Sara did for Lori," he whispered. "I don't know how we'll ever repay you."

What could she say? That they'd got by with a little help from their friends and that it took a village? It was trite but true. She nodded into Judd's shoulder, not knowing how much the others knew about Lori's trouble. So many secrets.

Mom held up a small suitcase and said, "I stopped by the condo and got you and Sara a change of clothes, Sara's handbag, and phone, too. I assume you'll be staying at the hospital for the duration."

"Let them try to kick me out!" Amanda said, jutting out her jaw. She then told them that only two visitors were allowed into Sara's room at one time. "So you'll have to take turns, and you'll have to wear stupid masks."

It was decided that Mom and Trout would go first since they'd already eaten breakfast. Next Ginny and Trev.

Trev said, "Fuck the rules. Lissa's going in with us. She's a kid, so she gets a free pass." He winked at Amanda. "Let them try to stop her!"

Lori and Judd would go last, not because they were family-once-removed, but because Judd said he had a lot of catching up to do. Amanda also suspected that father and daughter wanted to thank Sara privately for her help with Lori's scandal.

Amanda hated being separated from Sara so long and hoped the onslaught of family wouldn't tire Sara out too much. At the same time, Amanda had her own selfish needs. As soon as Mom and Trout disappeared through the double doors, she said, "Don't know about you guys, but I'm starving!"

They all headed for the cafeteria.

Kayla took Sara into the bathroom, helped her wash up, and brush her hair, so that when Sara returned to find Dr. T standing tall and erect as an ebony statue at the foot of her bed, she felt almost human. Sara remembered the doctor from before, as from a dream, as he greeted her with a thousand-kilowatt smile.

"I am most impressed by your progress, Sara. Your partner asked me to call you by your first name, is that acceptable?" Sara nodded as Kayla tucked her into the bed, and Dr. T continued, "I see you have eaten a full meal and are breathing well with only the cannula, so we can eliminate the anti-nausea medicine..." He paused to gently pinch her cheek and upper arm. "You are no longer dehydrated, so we can discontinue the saline drip, no more fluids."

"Does that mean you can unhook me from all these tubes and remove the port?" The IV in the crook of her elbow hurt and restricted her movement. She was like a puppet who longed for no strings attached.

"Yes, we can unhook you. No, we will keep the port. Unfortunately, we have not yet received your toxicology report, so until we know precisely what anesthetic was used, we may require the port for future use."

"Why is the result taking so long?" Sara demanded.

Dr. T laughed. "As it is top priority, I am sure the lab will send the report very soon. I am told it will be hand-delivered to my personal attention no later than tomorrow afternoon."

"Does that mean I have to stay in Critical Care? Kayla says I can only have two visitors at a time."

"You must stay until we analyze the report,"

he stated and then grinned at Kayla. "However, since you are a very popular lady, with two visitors already outside this door, I need not be informed if the rules are bent a little."

After a quick peek under the gauze on Sara's hands, he pronounced that her skin was healing and instructed Kayla to remove the bandages at the end of her shift. Yes! Had Sara been able to curl her fingers, she'd have given him a fist bump.

Dr. T gave a quick bow, and then he departed.

The next two hours were a whirlwind of activity inside room 227. Sara was overjoyed to see Diana and Trout. Mandy's folks were like second parents to her. Trout, with his easygoing manner and laid-back sense of humor, reminded her of her own dad, a hard-working gardener who had grown his small business into a large landscaping company. Both men wrapped Sara in a blanket of security.

But Diana was nothing like Sara's traditional housewife mom. Like Mandy, Diana was worthless in the kitchen, fiercely independent, with a rebellious streak and a true and loving heart. Diana and Mandy were more alike than Mandy cared to admit, but Diana was definitely more motherly. Sara appreciated that although Diana was desperate to know the details of their stalker case, she did not push. Sara also appreciated Diana bringing her clothes, her phone, and her purse.

Between visitors, Kayla disconnected the IV tower and rolled the hated thing to a far corner of the room. The nurse then escorted Ginny and Trev Dula into the room, and like most women, Kayla seemed awed by Trev's rugged good looks and hesitated only a moment before allowing Lissa inside, too. Lissa rushed over and grabbed both sets of Sara's fingers, causing Sara a brief jolt of pain, which she concealed, and then asked a million questions before Ginny eased Lissa away.

Ginny, who was Mandy's soulmate stepsister, with her short punk hair, tats, and nose stud, was much gentler, but focused like a laser. As she consoled Sara in her low, gravelly singer's voice, Sara knew that of all the members in Mandy's clan, Ginny would be the one she and Mandy would confide in someday, but not today.

Throughout the visit, Trev, the edgy veteran of the Afghanistan and Iraq wars, stood at ease offering smiles but few words. Over the years, Trev and Sara's brother, Marc, had become close friends, but of the two men, Sara would never truly understand Trev.

By the time the Dulas left, Sara was exhausted, yet she wanted to visit with the others, especially Judd, whom she hadn't seen for ages. Before the Taylor family entered, Kayla helped her to the bathroom and gave her a drink of water, so Sara felt ready for round three.

Lori ushered in her father, who looked even more substantial than Sara remembered. Unfortunately, the pair also let in a vampire, AKA the phlebotomy technician, a pale, black-haired woman who appeared at odd times day and night to suck Sara dry.

"So sorry," Kayla apologized as she moved Judd and Lori deeper into the room to make way for the technician. "If either of you two is squeamish, you shouldn't watch," Kayla warned.

Lori frowned at the nurse. "Do I look like a wimp? I'm Lori, and by the way, you look exactly like my little sister."

"Oh, yeah?" Kayla placed her hands on her hips.

"Then help me out, Lori. Can you give that nurse with the tray a red crayon?"

"Why should I?"

"Because she wants to draw blood."

Judd whooped at the punchline, but Lori said, "You make lame jokes like my sister, too."

After Kayla and the vampire left, Sara chatted with Judd, who kept thanking her for helping Lori, but Sara steered the conversation back to what was happening in Judd's life. He told her about the progress they were making restoring the old Taylor homestead, "Mayberry" sheriff department gossip, and news about Ella and Jana. Sara deflected Lori's questions about poisoned Barbie dolls. She didn't want to talk about it, other than to tell Lori that the Russel Cowley lead had fizzled.

"You're losing your voice, Sara," Judd said after about twenty minutes. "We pushed you too far, and I'm sorry. Don't say another word, but we'll talk again soon. The family will get out of your hair for now, but we'll all be back tomorrow and the next day, until you come home."

Sara wanted to protest, but she couldn't talk or even wave goodbye when they left. As much as she loved the family, she was tired of musical chairs and needed to rest. She wanted to fall asleep holding Mandy's hand, and as though summoned by her wish, Mandy appeared at her bedside.

"Alone at last," Sara whispered and then blew a kiss with her lips because she couldn't yet toss the kiss along with her hands.

Mandy pretended to catch the kiss, planted a real kiss on Sara's forehead, and then said, "I'm afraid we can't be alone for long, honey, because Detective

Sokolsky just texted, and he's coming to see us later this afternoon. In the meantime, you sleep, and I'll eat your lunch when they bring it."

Chapter Thirty-eight

Off the grid...

Amanda polished off Sara's lunch while Sara slept. Just watching her made Amanda sleepy because the hospital was unusually quiet during an afternoon lull. She also felt semi-content, having washed up and put on fresh undies and a T-shirt, so she reclined in a patch of warm sunlight and took out her phone. She checked her texts and emails and found nothing new from the stalker. Thank God. She fiddled with a crossword puzzle app but kept getting stuck on simple words, so eventually, she succumbed to exhaustion and closed her eyes.

"You have a visitor, Mandy," Kayla's voice intruded.

Amanda blinked at the wall clock. "Is it really four o'clock, or is it five?"

"Really four. We fell back, remember?"

"Is Detective Sokolsky here?"

"Well, he looks like a cop because he's been eating doughnuts."

"How do you know?"

"Because his eyes are glazed."

Amanda groaned and sat upright. She reluctantly awakened Sara, who came to with a sweet smile on her face. When Amanda announced their visitor, Sara's smile vanished.

Sokolsky strode in, and Kayla scuttled out. The

detective looked marginally better than he had last night. He had shaved, exchanged his coffee-stained Hawaiian shirt for a white shirt and tie, and wore a rumpled sports coat over pressed jeans. He also carried a cup of coffee, and Amanda suspected he'd spill it at some point during their interview.

"What's up?" Amanda asked.

"First things first," Sokolsky said as he walked to the big window and closed the blinds, cutting off the sunshine. Did he think that gave them more privacy, which was stupid, or was he a creature of the night and light hurt his eyes? "Give me your phones." He held out his hand.

Amanda took offense. "First things first" should be asking Sara how she was feeling. Did the man have no manners?

When neither woman responded, Sokolsky looked sheepish and said, "Oh, how are you feeling, Sara?" He pulled up the visitor chair and sat by the bed.

"Much better, thank you," Sara answered, her voice still hoarse. "Why do you want our phones?"

"From now on, the police will monitor all your calls, emails, and texts in case the stalker contacts you again. Has she contacted you?"

"Not me," Amanda said and then looked through the suitcase Mom brought and found Sara's phone. Since Sara's hands didn't work, Amanda checked her correspondence. "The stalker hasn't contacted Sara, either. That's a good thing, right?"

"Not necessarily." Sokolsky snorted. "She knows she's crossed the line from harassment to criminality. If we catch her, she's facing jail time. She's taking a breather from the internet."

Amanda and Sara glanced at each other.

Hopefully, Sokolsky had some new information he'd not yet shared. "But if you take our phones, how will we stay in touch with the outside world?" Amanda asked.

Sokolsky fished into his pocket and brought out a boxy, outdated flip phone and handed it to Amanda. "This is a burner phone with no internet nor any other bells and whistles. My number's already programmed. You can make untraceable calls."

"But all my contacts are on my phone," Amanda objected. "I don't carry all those numbers around in my head."

Sokolsky handed her a small notepad and pen. "Do it the old-fashioned way, jot down important contacts and leave the rest. Do it fast, while we're talking because I want to get your phones to our retrieval geeks to research your histories and maybe track this psycho."

For a panicked moment, Amanda feared Sokolsky might see the salacious photos of Lori on their phones, which was none of his damn business, but then she remembered that neither of them had copied those images, so Lori's secret was safe. Before relinquishing her phone, she made a note of the burner's number and texted it to Maya, asking her to pick up when she saw the unfamiliar number because Amanda would be calling Maya later that evening. After madly scribbling the contact details for their close friends and family, she said, "When do we get our phones back?"

"You'll get them back when we're done with them."

❧❧❧❧

Sara didn't care about the phones, she cared

about her patients at the clinic less than one mile from where she now lay. Mandy had explained that Sokolsky intended to visit Dr. Angela Yee regarding Janice Kenny, known as Jane Doe, and Sara was desperate to learn the outcome.

"Did you speak with Dr. Yee?" she interrupted.

Sokolsky quit arguing with Mandy and turned to face Sara. He paused and cleared his throat. "Yes, I did. Not to sound sexist, but Dr. Yee is one fine-looking woman. She's also stubborn as a bloodstain when it comes to patient privacy."

Sara contained her hilarity. Even if Angela weren't happily married, Sokolsky had a snowball's chance in hell of dating her and zero chance getting her to break patient confidentiality. "How did it go?"

Sokolsky frowned. "Like pulling teeth, but after hearing what happened to you, Sara, Dr. Yee was more forthcoming. She's very sorry, by the way, and told me to give you her love and not to worry about work. She'll reschedule all your appointments until you're well enough to return."

"But what about Jane Doe?" Sara pressed.

"Bottom line?" Sokolsky groaned. "I never got Jane's real name, but Dr. Yee tried to contact the woman. She called her home, her workplace, and even Jane's emergency contacts while I killed time pacing and eating junk food from the vending machines. No luck. Jane was a no-show at her job, no one's seen her, not even her mama. She's done a runner. She's off the grid, and in my opinion, she's guilty as hell."

Sara felt Mandy's hand on her arm as they digested the disturbing information. Little flashes of light played across her eyes, the precursor of a migraine headache. She had a pretty good idea where Jan was hiding, but how much could she ethically reveal?

She blinked, an unsuccessful attempt to banish the flashes. "Jane has a favorite aunt who lives on High Rock Lake near the town of Lexington. It's peaceful, private, and she   loves it there."

Sokolsky took out his notebook and a pen. "Aunt's name?"

Sara gulped. "Sorry, you'll have to get a subpoena for that information and take it to Dr. Yee."

Sokolsky tossed his notebook onto the floor. "Damn it, Sara, I'm just trying to keep you safe! If you know the aunt's name, you should tell me. If you refuse, I'm one step ahead of you. I've already requested a subpoena, and as soon as the ink's dry, I will serve your friend, Dr. Yee. By tomorrow morning, I'll be at High Rock Lake to arrest Jane's sick ass." He took a deep breath. "By the way, do you know anything about the poison used?"

"Nope, still waiting for the results," Sara said.

"Are we done here?" Amanda intervened.

"Yes, ma'am, we're done." Sokolsky picked up the notebook and shoved it into his pocket, along with their phones. "I'll be in touch, ladies," he said more gently as he stood to leave. "Get well, and stay safe."

"Thanks," they both muttered as he closed the door behind him.

Mandy sighed and kissed Sara's cheek. "What do you think?"

"I think I need a Maxalt pill. You'll find some in my purse."

"Migraine? I'm so sorry, honey." Mandy fetched the pill from Sara's purse. "Are we allowed to self-medicate in here?"

"Fuck it," Sara said as she swallowed a pill with

Mandy's help. "Regarding Jane Doe? Her disappearance is certainly suspicious, but the plot seems too complicated, not her style. Honestly, I just don't know." Sara closed her eyes. "I do know we need to call Maya and Shar. Can you do it, babe?"

Chapter Thirty-nine

A manila file folder...

When they woke up Monday morning, after a surprisingly good sleep, Velma was back. The older nurse was bossier and stricter than Kayla, but at least she didn't crack endless punny jokes. Amanda didn't know whether to attribute their solid sleep to the probability that Sokolsky would soon arrest their stalker or to sheer exhaustion.

Amanda had called Mom, asking her to please not allow the family to visit because Sara needed to rest. Mom was disappointed but understanding. She had grilled Amanda about her new, unrecognizable burner number and wanted details about Sokolsky's visit, but Amanda kept their secrets, saying only that Mom's favorite cop was about to solve their case. Unfortunately, Mom had called back, explaining that of all the family members, only Judd and Lori had insisted on visiting later that afternoon. Because Sara was healing so well, Judd intended to take Lori back home to Mount Airy on Tuesday morning, and they wanted to say their final goodbyes.

"I'm actually going to miss Lori," Sara said as an aide rolled a breakfast cart up to her bed, positioning the tray above Sara's lap.

"Yeah, Lori's a pain in the you-know-what, but it's been fun getting to know her," Amanda said as she greedily eyed Sara's scrambled eggs and toast. Amanda would also miss Lori's Jeep and her Gen Z vibe. "Do you need some help eating that?"

Sara lifted her heavy hands onto the edge of the tray and clumsily wiggled her fingers. "Help *me*? Or do *you* want to eat it?" Sara smirked. "My fingers may look like raw sausages, but they kinda work. I'll try to use this fork, but even if I can't, all this food is going into *my* mouth, babe."

"Got it." Kayla had removed Sara's bandages at the end of her shift and applied antibiotic ointment. Her hands looked swollen and sore but much better than Amanda had anticipated. Sara was definitely on the mend. "I'll pop down to the cafeteria and grab something," Amanda promised as Sara ate with some assistance.

"I wonder when we'll hear from Dr. T," Sara said through a mouthful. "They should have my results by now."

"Someone's supposed to hand-deliver them from the crime lab today, then hopefully, they'll take your port out, and you'll be done with Critical Care."

"Yeah, with Velma back on the beat, I can only see two visitors at a time, but I'll be damned if I'll let her kick you out when Maya and Shar get here."

"She wouldn't dare," Amanda said as the aide arrived to remove Sara's tray. At the same time, Amanda sensed a traffic jam at the entrance to room 227, and as the aide maneuvered her way out, Maya and Shar eased their way in.

Shar rushed to the bed, her fair complexion flushed. "My God, what the hell happened?"

Maya was right behind her, as poised and graceful as ever, but her cat-like amber eyes were moist, and her long fingers trembled around a mixed bouquet of flowers. "Sara, love, we just saw you on Friday night, and now you're in the hospital?"

Shar gave Amanda a funky handmade pottery vase, glazed hot pink and decorated with yellow smiley faces. "This is from Goddess Gifts."

"The flowers are from the hospital gift shop. Sorry, it was the best I could do on short notice," Maya apologized. She thrust the bouquet at Amanda. "Can you put some water in the vase, please? Hopefully, they'll cheer up this dreary place."

While Sara thanked them and Amanda did Maya's bidding, Amanda noticed the girls staring at Sara's hands. Shar seemed like an angry avenger, but Maya was about to cry.

"So what happened?" Shar repeated as she perched her plump body on the edge of Sara's bed.

Sara sighed. "I was stupid. I made the mistake of playing with the two lynched Barbie dolls hung on the door to our condo."

Both women gasped and clumsily tried to hug Sara. When Amanda called them last night, she'd omitted the gruesome details, so the facts would come as a shock to their dear friends. Amanda placed the vase on the windowsill. Because Shar was on the bed and Maya was now openly crying in the recliner, Amanda took the visitor chair and dragged it to the foot of the bed as Sara tried to explain, her voice still hoarse. Amanda also kept on the lookout for Velma, who would undoubtedly try to remove one of them.

"You got poison on your hands?" Shar's brown eyes blazed.

"The stalker escalated, as we feared," Maya said as she rubbed Sara's arm. "I am so, so sorry! Lord, I'd love to prosecute this monster and put her behind bars or send her to the loony bin for life."

Retelling the story seemed to be taking a toll on Sara, who was becoming progressively paler. It felt good to share with Maya and Shar since they were the only ones who knew the truth about their ordeal, but Amanda didn't want Sara upset.

"On a positive note," Amanda interrupted, "the cops are all over this attack, and a detective named Sokolsky's about to arrest that ex-patient of Sara's we told you about."

"The woman who caught her fiancé in bed with another man and became a homophobe?" Maya asked.

After Sara confirmed, their guests seemed to relax and started offering theories about Jane Doe's motive: Sara psychoanalyzed, Maya discussed likely prosecutions, and Shar ran angry fingers through her wild brown hair and suggested several gory ways to punish Jane that had nothing to do with law and order.

Amanda tuned out because Sara seemed more relaxed. She stared out the window to the tar roof, where a lone pigeon strode around the puddles looking for crumbs. All too soon, Amanda heard Velma's familiar knock on the door, and the older nurse rushed in with blood in her eye.

"I can count to three, girls," Velma said, "and there's one too many in this room. Someone has to leave."

Then, much to Amanda's surprise, two more visitors pushed into the room. Judd, tall and commanding, tipped an imaginary hat and smiled. "C'mon, nurse, what's the harm? Looks to me like everyone's well-behaved, and Sara seems to be enjoying herself. Give us a break."

Amanda held her breath. As charming as Judd

could be, it might help the cause more if he was wearing his sheriff's uniform and toting a big ole gun on his belt.

"Chill, we're all family, right?" Lori put her hands on her hips and struck a sassy pose as she stared curiously at Maya and Shar.

Velma split the difference. "Okay, three can stay, two must go."

"Let Sara choose," Judd suggested.

"I choose Judd," Sara said. "Sorry, Mandy, but I know you're hungry, so why don't you and Lori grab some lunch in the cafeteria, while I introduce your handsome cousin to our friends?"

Lori groaned, but Amanda liked the idea. She really was starving, so she dragged Lori into the corridor, out the double doors, took off her mask, and quickly led Lori into an elevator. "The cafeteria has a meatloaf special today," she said, hoping to entice the girl.

"Gross," Lori said as they got off at the ground floor and moved toward the concourse. "Was that the lesbian couple you guys had dinner with Friday night?"

"Yep. You'll get a chance to visit with them after your dad."

As they rounded a bend leading to the cafeteria, Lori suddenly grabbed Amanda's arm. "Wait! Check it out! Do you recognize that woman?" Lori pointed at a striking woman strolling into the lobby from the street. She had long brunette hair pulled into a tight ponytail and a slim, yet voluptuous figure.

"Nope." Amanda kept moving.

"Mandy, it's Dr. Nicole Moss from the police crime lab. Red introduced us, don't you remember?"

Amanda's frazzled mind changed gears as she

stopped to look. Dr. Moss, the name did ring a bell. More importantly, it was the CMPD crime lab that was in charge of analyzing the poison used on Sara. She recalled that Dr. Moss was one of their top chemists, and this woman was clutching a manila file folder to her breast. Was it possible?

"Okay, let's say hi," Amanda said, but Lori was already fast-walking to catch up with Moss.

"Hey, remember me?" Lori blocked Moss, and when Amanda joined them, Lori said, "I'm Lori, and that's Amanda. Red introduced us in your office last week."

Moss removed her trendy, blue-framed glasses and stared at them, but Amanda saw no trace of recognition in her milky azure eyes. Amanda definitely remembered those eyes. "Lori's right, Dr. Moss. Red had given you a pair of women's panties to test, and we tagged along."

As Moss looked back and forth between them, she clutched the file tighter and frankly, seemed spooked. "Yes, I suppose. What do you want?"

Red had warned them that Moss could be abrupt and rude, it was her nature. But Amanda was determined to ask. "Pardon me, but Dr. T is expecting a result to be hand-delivered from your lab regarding a poisonous anesthetic used on my partner, Dr. Sara Orlando. Is that the result you're carrying?"

Moss frowned and seemed to be considering her options. Amanda could be way off base, but her question seemed to have struck a nerve. Would Moss confide in them?

"This report is confidential," Moss said at last, pinning Amanda with her weird eyes before putting the glasses back on her nose. "However, I was instructed to deliver it to Dr. Twahirwa, so it might be Dr. Orlando's result."

"Dope, right, Mandy?" Lori thrilled. "Sara's gonna bounce. She'll be home by tomorrow. Hey, Dr. Moss, can we hang with you while you take that file to Dr. T?"

Lori was pushy as hell, but while Moss blinked furiously, Amanda realized that she was actually considering Lori's proposal. "Let's not crowd Dr. Moss, Lori. Why don't you save me a seat in the cafeteria, and I'll go with her? I'll join you for lunch in a few minutes, and by then, maybe we'll have some good news to take to Sara."

Lori wasn't happy, but she backed off. "Whatever," she muttered. "I'll order you the meatloaf."

Moss stepped into an elevator, and Amanda followed her. "Do you know the way to Dr. T's office?" Amanda asked.

"Of course," Moss huffed.

"Great, because I don't. We'll go together," Amanda said as Moss pushed the UP button.

Chapter Forty

What's the big deal...?

Sara enjoyed the interaction between Judd and her two best friends. Both women seemed fascinated by this charming and unexpected addition to Mandy's family as Judd entertained them with the colorful, action-packed saga of how they'd all come to meet in "Mayberry." Maya and Judd laughed and traded stories from the sheriff's point of view versus the prosecutor's point of view, while Shar flirted like the Southern belle she was and had Judd in stitches with her accounts of embarrassing antics in the halls of Congress. Sara appreciated the fact that none of her guests talked about the stalker or Lori's revenge porn problems. It seemed they were deliberately steering clear of unpleasant topics, allowing Sara to lie back and relax.

She closed her eyes and let the good-natured banter wash over her as the sunshine warmed her face. Would Maya and Shar ever see Judd again? She doubted it, but it didn't matter because now that they were all aware of one another, even this brief interaction would be permanently woven into the complex tapestry of their friendships. Simply knowing of one another's existence deepened the understanding of what made each individual tick. What was she getting at? Sara didn't know because her mind was rambling, so that when an aide arrived with her lunch tray, it seemed like she had just had breakfast.

"Are you awake, Sara?" Maya tapped her arm. "Are you hungry, or should we let the county sheriff eat this?"

Sara had also lost track of the conversation, but before she could consider the idea of food, a sixth person entered the room, and all eyes swiveled in his direction. Imposing in any setting, the towering presence of Dr. T crowded the space to the point of claustrophobia. The aide departed, Judd stood to shake hands, while Maya and Shar stared at the tall Rwandan, who carried a clipboard and wore a dazzling white grin.

"Are we having a party?" Dr. T asked.

Sara's brain was still wandering as she paired Maya and Dr. T as an imaginary couple. They looked stunning together with their long, lean elegance and chiseled features, like they hailed from the same exotic tribe. Although he was also African American, Judd must have originated from an entirely different corner of the continent. When the men shook hands, they looked like an American black bear greeting a graceful gazelle.

"Sara, did you hear me?" the doctor said. "I have your test results."

Sara tried to focus, pushing upright on her pillow. "Well, glory hallelujah! What have we got?"

Dr. T glanced at the visitors. "Perhaps we should have some privacy, Dr. Orlando?"

Judd said, "I'll wait in the hall," and then he left the room.

Maya and Shar rose, but Sara waved them back to their chairs. "These friends can stay. They know the score."

Dr. T nodded, stood formal and erect, and then

read from his notes. "The substance you touched was procaine, a local anesthesia used for cardiac irregularities. It is rated number five in toxicity, which can be fatal, and it often causes dizziness, collapse, coma, convulsions, and even cardiac arrest. The procaine was mixed at approximately half strength into a carbopol base..." He cleared his throat and seemed confused by the text. "The substance was liberally applied to the dolls and the blue stocking strings—what that means, I do not know—but it came into contact with your hands and wrists. It says you washed those areas soon after contact, which allowed for a better outcome."

Sara felt sick to her stomach as she recalled that the horrible assemblage was glossy, like it was freshly varnished, and sticky to touch. Dr. T's words also seemed to shock her friends because Maya's mocha face paled, and Shar expelled a strangled gasp. "Bottom line?" Sara urged.

"Well, you will recover completely and soon." He smiled and lowered the clipboard. "Your hands have not blistered and will likely return to normal in one week, and you may leave the hospital tomorrow. This is good, is it not?"

"Very, very good!" Sara leaned back into her pillow. "Thank you, Dr. T."

"Sweet Jesus, Mary, and Joseph!" Shar muttered and crossed herself, although Sara knew Shar was no Catholic.

Maya groaned. "What kind of monster would do such a thing?"

The toxicologist stepped back several paces, unable to answer the unanswerable. "So I will leave you ladies now. Please enjoy your celebration," he said before gliding out the door.

Maya kissed Sara's cheek. "I knew all along that you'd be all right." Sara knew she was lying.

"Goddess be praised!" Shar hugged Sara, nearly smothering her in a big, bosomy embrace. And although Sara didn't believe in any of the deities mentioned in the girls' responses, she did feel blessed and couldn't wait to tell Mandy.

When she sensed more commotion at the door, Sara saw the lunch aide return, closely followed by Judd and a very angry-looking Lori, who was gripping a white Styrofoam takeout box.

The aide said, "Are you going to eat this, ma'am, or should I take it away?"

"Take it, please. I'm not hungry."

When the aide began rolling the cart, Judd said, "Hold your horses. Am I allowed to eat Sara's food? I hate to see it go to waste."

Lori tossed her Styrofoam box on the windowsill, shoved between Judd and the aide, and said, "Where the hell is Mandy?"

The aide left empty-handed, while the others gaped at the distraught teenager. Sara said, "Mandy's with you, isn't she? Weren't you having lunch together?"

"Yeah, but she stood me up. I saved her a seat, got a turkey sandwich and fries, waited a half hour, and Mandy never showed. I figured she came back here once she learned the test results."

Sara didn't get it. "Yes, Dr. T brought the results, but Mandy wasn't with him. Did you split up, Lori?"

"Shit, didn't Mandy tell you?" Lori was getting more agitated by the minute. "We saw that doctor from the CMPD crime lab walk into the hospital with a file, and since we knew the results were being hand-delivered, we approached her."

"What doctor?" Sara felt a tug of anxiety under her breastbone. Judd and the girls also seemed on edge.

"We asked the doctor if she had Sara's results, and she said she was taking them to Dr. T, so Mandy went with her to get the news firsthand."

"Dr. T didn't mention seeing Mandy..." The tug of anxiety became a hard knot in Sara's chest. "Mandy probably went back to the cafeteria, and right this minute, she's wondering where you've gone."

"Who is this doctor from the CMPD?" Maya demanded, her voice tense.

"We met her the day Mandy and I went down to the police station," Lori said. "Red introduced us."

Maya and Shar glanced at each other, Sara wondered what in the world was going on, and Shar finally said, "Do you know this doctor's name?"

"Yeah, sure, Dr. Nicole Moss. She's some sort of hotshot chemist, and she's a lesbian." Lori smirked.

"Oh, my God!" Maya moaned. "This can't be happening! Lori, did you happen to tell Dr. Moss that Mandy and Sara are a couple?"

Lori scrunched up her face. "Yep, I did. Red told us that Nicole was deep in the closet. The woman was such a tight-ass that I wanted to goose her, you know? So I outed you guys, Sara. Mandy was pissed at the time, so I'm sorry."

"You are an idiot, Lori," Judd scolded.

"What's the big deal?" Lori whined.

Sara had never heard of this doctor, but from Maya's and Shar's reactions, something was way off. "What's wrong?" she said, feeling the onset of a panic attack.

While Shar paced, Maya said, "It's a long story, but Dr. Moss might be dangerous. She is seriously disturbed, and we share some weird history. Lori, you need to locate Mandy as soon as possible. Please go back and check the cafeteria, we have to find her."

Judd was already at the door. "How can I help?"

"They got onto an elevator together," Lori said in a tiny voice. "They were going to Dr. T's office, but I don't know where that is!"

Sara's panic attack intensified. She groped for the cannula still loped on the headboard, fitted it around her neck, and stuck the prongs into her nose. The oxygen hit hyped her up even more. She felt Shar's fingers nervously kneading her arm, they were ice cold.

"I don't know the full story," Judd bellowed as he dragged his jittery daughter to the door, "but Lori and I will scout around a little, and I'll get hospital security into the hunt sooner, rather than later. Don't worry, Sara. We'll find her."

"Who is Nicole Moss?" Sara pleaded once the women were alone.

"Fuck, Sara," Maya cursed. "We need to talk."

Chapter Forty-one

A bad soap opera...

Amanda stepped into the elevator with Dr. Moss, knowing she was crashing a party where she was neither invited nor welcome. She wasn't family and had no legal right to attend the meeting between Moss and Dr. T, but that was too damn bad because she had to know Sara's results. As the elevator lifted, Amanda gripped the handrail, while Moss hugged the far corner, with the file still pressed to her breast as she refused to meet Amanda's eyes. A sheen of perspiration glistened on the doctor's upper lip, and her mouth was compressed in a hard, thin line. She was pissed or nervous or maybe just shy. Amanda respected that. After all, Amanda was hardly a social butterfly, especially at art openings with strangers. Yet Amanda wasn't antisocial, as Moss seemed to be.

"I'm sorry to butt in like this, Dr. Moss, but if you remember, Sara Orlando is my partner, so her welfare is important to me."

"Yes, I remember," Moss said tonelessly and shifted foot to foot in her sensible pumps.

When they stopped on the fourth floor, Moss exited, and Amanda followed her down a hallway of closed office doors, but instead of entering any of the rooms, Moss continued to the end of the wing and stepped into another elevator labeled "Private-Staff Only." Amanda followed her into the second elevator, which was stripped-down and utilitarian, like for carrying freight or bodies to the morgue. Amanda figured they were taking a short cut and was relieved when Moss pushed another UP button because she imagined morgues were always located in basements.

"Whoa, I am so lost," Amanda said. "This hospital is as confusing as the police station was the day Red brought us down to your lab. I'm glad you're my guide, otherwise I'd never find my way back to room 227."

"Is Sara in room 227?" It was the first time Moss had exhibited interest.

For some reason, Amanda regretted sharing that information, so she avoided the question and said, "How high up does this hospital go? Dr. T must have the penthouse!" Funny, right? But Moss didn't crack a smile, so Amanda tried a different tack. "It must be exciting working for CMPD. Have you been there long?"

"Less than a year, but that's too damn long." Moss growled. "I used to teach at Queen's University and didn't have to put up with all the cops' bureaucratic bullshit."

Moss seemed bitter, and Amanda wondered why she had left the university. She suspected it wasn't a pretty story. Maya often complained about the mounds of paperwork required by the city of Charlotte, but maybe Moss disliked the crime lab for other, darker reasons. "I'm sure you see a lot of ugly stuff working in the lab, like those disgusting poison Barbie dolls you analyzed for Sara's case. What kind of depraved monster would do such a thing?"

Moss still had not looked at Amanda, but she was now sweating profusely and seemed agitated. "There are all kinds of monsters in this world," Moss affirmed as the elevator jerked to a stop.

It seemed they had come to the end of the line. Moss pressed a button, and the elevator opened to a small concrete block room with a dirty cement floor and an exit door leading to the roof. Definitely not the penthouse.

"Where are we?" Amanda gasped.

"There is a lovely view from the roof," Moss said. "Come, let me show you…"

Amanda's stomach clenched with fear; she hated heights. "I'm not going out there!"

"Oh, c'mon, you'll enjoy it." Moss looked directly at Amanda with her cold, milky eyes and smiled. "Here, have a look at this." Moss thrust Sara's file at her.

Amanda took it automatically, torn between fear and curiosity. While Moss opened her purse, Amanda opened the file. Inside, she found a travel brochure advertising weekend getaways to Cancun. "This isn't Sara's results!" she yelped.

"No, but it sounds like a fun vacation, doesn't it? Now, Amanda, let's go to the roof."

When Amanda looked up, Moss was holding a small revolver, pointed directly at Amanda's chest.

❧ ❧ ❧ ❧ ❧

Sara gazed at Maya and Shar. "Why do we need to talk? And who the hell is Nicole Moss?"

Her friends were now perched on her bed, on either side of Sara's knees, with Shar's hand on Sara's arm and Maya's on Sara's thigh. They seemed shell-shocked, unable to speak. Their distress was at odds with the benign sunshine flooding the quiet room and warming the food in Lori's takeout box on the windowsill.

"Say something, you're scaring me!" Sara pleaded.

Maya took a deep breath. "I know this sounds bizarre, but Nicole is Jude's biology teacher, the woman Jude dumped after the poli-sci professor."

Sara thought *bizarre* didn't begin to cover it. The information was almost impossible to process, like a scene from a drama in which Sara no longer had a role. "So what?"

"So," Shar rolled her eyes at the ceiling, "it's a mess. Remember how we told you we hadn't stayed in contact with Jude, except for Christmas cards and the one long phone call when Jude broke up with the biology teacher?"

Of course, Sara remembered. She'd felt at the time that any continuing contact between Maya, Shar, and Jude was like a betrayal. But she was over it.

Shar continued, "I don't need to remind you how much Jude hurt you, and I hate to open those old wounds, but if you think Jude treated you badly, I believe she was even more brutal to Nicole. At first we only heard Jude's side of the story. Jude said Nicole was a boring, clingy, pathetic excuse of a woman who made Jude's life a misery, so she tossed them out on the street, like what happened to you."

"Tossed *them* out?" Sara demanded.

"It was awful, Sara," Maya said. "It seems Nicole had been married to a man years ago, and she came to Jude with her twelve-year-old son. Before Jude, Nicole had divorced the man and married a woman, and she and her son lived with that woman for ten years until Jude came along, swept Nicole off her feet, and shattered Nicole's second marriage."

"Like a bad soap opera," Sara commented bitterly.

"Jude the home-wrecker, sounds about right."

"It gets worse," Shar said. "We never believed Jude's version of events, so we did a little research. After the split, Nicole had a breakdown, attempted suicide, lost her job at Queen's University, and her poor kid ended up living with his maternal grandparents."

Maya said, "I heard some gossip via the district attorney grapevine that Nicole had recently been hired by the CMPD. She is brilliant as both a chemist and a biologist, and we were happy for her."

"That's all very sad," Sara interrupted, "but I've never even heard the woman's name before, so what's it got to do with Mandy and me?"

Maya looked down at her lap, a guilty look on her face. "It's only a theory, but according to the grapevine, Nicole might blame you, Sara, for all her troubles. During her meltdown, she went around telling anyone who would listen that you dumped Jude and broke Jude's heart. That Jude still loved you, and that's why she hurt Nicole so badly."

For several seconds, Sara was unable to speak. The preposterous scenario was the complete opposite of what actually happened. She knew all about projection, a defense mechanism when people consciously or unconsciously attribute their own thoughts, feelings, and bad behaviors onto another person, and Jude was an expert projectionist. She had a mean streak a mile wide, but would Jude actually deflect blame on Sara for all the wrongs Jude herself had inflicted upon Nicole? If so, Nicole Moss would have every reason to hate Sara, and by extension, hate the love she now shared with Mandy.

"I can't believe it." Sara moaned. "It's too much. Are you sure?"

Shar said, "Like Maya said, it's just a theory, but it's possible. When did you and Mandy get the first threatening email?"

Sara closed her eyes, breathed oxygen through her nose prongs, and tried to concentrate. So much had happened, it was hard to remember what happened yesterday, let alone last week. Scrolling backward to Lori's surprise appearance, she finally recalled that the stalker's reign of terror began late last Tuesday, the same day Mandy and Lori visited the police station.

"Tuesday, that's right," Sara said aloud. "Mandy's exact words were *I met an uptight lesbian doctor.* Later that night, Mandy got the first email, and we tried to laugh it off as a joke, but then I found the same image in my inbox the next morning."

"So it started right after Mandy met Nicole," Shar confirmed.

"Yes, but how did she get our email addresses so fast? How did she know where we live or even more unreal, how did she know where Mandy's parents live? Did she follow us to the lake and put that horrible stocking around Ursie's neck? I don't believe it!"

Maya said, "Believe it. Nicole is brilliant, and how hard could it be these days with the internet? I know for a fact that Mandy's email is public on her artist website, and Nicole likely tracked you down through some sort of physicians' directory since you're both doctors. Real estate transactions are also in the public domain, so she could have easily tracked down your address or followed you."

"Please stop!" Sara lifted her heavy hands in protest and gulped more oxygen. If she were still on a heart monitor, it would be spiking for sure. Although there were holes in the theory, like the fact that Mandy's mom was the owner of record of the condo, Sara had no trouble believing that someone like Nicole Moss could fly over those hurdles. Plus, she was a chemist with access to poisons and the ability to mix up all kinds of nasty brews. Her beloved Mandy was in trouble, and beached on a hospital bed like a fish out of water, there wasn't a damn thing Sara could do to help. So she cried.

Shar rubbed her arm, and Maya patted her thigh, trying to comfort her with assurances that Mandy would be all right, but Mandy was missing. She was in the company of a deranged stalker in a huge hospital with a thousand hiding places. "What in God's name can we do?" Sara wailed.

"Nicole has never been violent, only to herself," Maya said.

"Oh, yeah?" Sara howled. "She poisoned me. I'm in the hospital. Is that not violent enough for you?"

Chapter Forty-two

A bird who will never fly...

Moss pushed the pressure bar and opened the exit door. Although paralyzed by fear, the simple action time-warped Amanda back to a similar door she'd encountered at Metrolina Expo during the first weeks of her relationship with Sara. That door had opened from Amanda's exhibition space to an alley. For safety reasons, the door was required to always open from the inside but then automatically lock to the outside. Many times, Amanda had locked herself out and now suspected the same thing would happen again if Moss forced her onto the hospital roof, where she'd be stranded and cut off from help.

"Let's go," Moss said. With the pistol aimed steady at Amanda's heart, Moss motioned with her free hand that they should move outside.

The gun was another emotional trigger. It was a Raven MP-25, identical to one Amanda had once owned and then discarded. The magazine held six bullets, plus one in the chamber, and while it wouldn't punch holes through steel walls, it was very accurate and would get the job done. Amanda knew how to shoot it and how to disarm it. She also knew how it felt to get shot, and as her muscle memory kicked in, she cradled her side, where the bullet had lodged between her ribs. She recalled the stunning pain and couldn't move if she tried.

"C'mon, I won't hurt you," Moss commanded.

Amanda's feet were leaden. "Why are you doing this?" she whimpered. "You don't even know me."

"Sure I do." Moss barked out a harsh laugh and shoved Amanda stumbling out onto the roof. Moss followed, and the door locked behind them, stranding them.

They stared at each other, Moss panting and Amanda in shock. It was surreal. The tar roof glistened with puddles and was littered with cigarette butts. Absurdly, Amanda pictured hospital employees sneaking up here for a smoke, but they would have the good sense to prop the door from closing with the wooden packing crate they undoubtedly sat on for their breaks. As it was, she and Moss were alone without a single pigeon to keep them company.

"Come see the pretty view," Moss said.

No way would Amanda approach the edge. She was seriously acrophobic and haunted by another flashback: a farewell exhibition for Carl in Asheville, a crowded party on another tar roof with a flimsy wooden railing. Carl had been pushed off that roof, barely surviving. Did Moss plan to push Amanda, too? Was it true that episodes like this from your past life flash before your eyes just before you die?

Scared as she was, if Amanda was going to die, she damn well wanted to know the reason. "Why are you doing this?" she repeated.

"You look so much like her," Moss said, a dreamy look in her eyes. "No wonder Sara the slut was attracted."

What on earth did Sara have to do with this? "Who do I look like?"

"Like Jude, of course, the woman Sara destroyed."

Amanda gulped a lungful of cold air to clear her head. Moss was referring to Judith Dellinger, Sara's ex, the woman who almost destroyed Sara.

"It's hard to hate you, Amanda, since you look so much like the love of my life, but together you and Sara are an abomination. You have everything I can never have." Moss moved closer to the edge as she ranted, but her gun remained steadily aimed at Amanda. The roof was surrounded by a waist-high brick wall, wide enough to sit on, if one had a death wish.

Moss continued, "When Sara the slut dumped Jude, she ruined Jude's life and mine. She hurt Jude so bad, Jude could never love me properly, not like she'd loved Sara."

The twisted story was beginning to make sense because Amanda now realized that Moss was the woman everyone called "Jude's biology teacher." Moss had obviously been let down hard, just like Sara, but somehow Moss had gotten it ass-backward.

"You're wrong," Amanda said. "Jude dumped Sara, not the other way around. If Jude told you otherwise, she's a liar."

"You're the liar!" Moss's face turned purple as she spit out the words. She stomped up and slapped Amanda hard across the face.

The blow hurt, and although Amanda's skin burned, she swallowed her scream. Moss was furious, breathing hard, and her milky eyes were dark with rage. Clearly, it was dangerous to contradict the woman. What would Sara do? She was the shrink, the master of de-escalation, so Amanda tried to conjure Sara's spirit, her wisdom.

Sara, she realized, would listen and try to empathize. Holding her panic at bay, she said, "I'm so sorry."

"Sorry?" Moss roared. "You'll be real sorry when Sara dumps you, and she will, you know. That she-devil has ice in her veins." Moss's left fingers clamped onto Amanda's arm like a claw as she dragged her to the wall, to the edge.

Amanda's heart raced as she tried not to look down. It seemed they were at the top rear of the hospital because instead of a busy city street below, Amanda saw overgrown fields running up a hillside to the forested edge of an older suburban neighborhood, a place where a body could fall and go unnoticed until some kid's dog found it.

Amanda had said she was sorry, but sympathy wasn't the key, so she opted for silence and listened as Moss spun out an increasing incomprehensible story about madness, suicide, and surprisingly, a teenaged son. Mostly, her theme was loss, and under different circumstances, Amanda might have felt sorry for her.

But right now, she felt only fear, anger, and revulsion. Beyond a shadow of doubt, Moss was their stalker, and anger won out. "You say you have a son, Dr. Moss. Remember Lori, the girl who came with me to your office? She's only seventeen, and she was with Sara and me when we found your poisonous gift on our doorknob. Any one of us could have touched it. Did you want to put a child in the hospital?"

For the first time, Amanda saw a cloud of uncertainty drift across Moss's eyes. She became slightly less rigid, but her right index finger remained tight on the trigger.

Moss said, "It was a watered-down solution on those dolls, not strong enough to kill anybody."

"I'm sure you don't want to hurt anybody. You're

a doctor, right?"

Moss laughed, but it wasn't a happy sound. Much to Amanda's distress, Moss leveraged herself up onto the wall and sat with her back to the suburban neighborhood. She patted the shelf of wall beside her. "Hop up and join me, Amanda."

Amanda felt dizzy and slightly faint. Of the two evils, she'd rather take a bullet to the brain than fall from a great height. "No," she flatly refused.

"Ha, my son is just like you, scared shitless of heights," Moss said. "Never mind, we can chat where we are."

Amanda couldn't get a handle on the woman; her emotions were erratic and her mood was swinging like a hammock in a hurricane. "I know you don't believe me about Sara getting dumped, but I was Jude's victim, too."

Moss eyed her with curiosity. "What, like collateral damage?"

It was the first time, other than mentioning her son, that Amanda had glimpsed humanity in the monster. She screwed up her courage and tried again. "Sara was a wreck when Jude broke up with her. She was messed up and hurt beyond trusting. I should know because it took me months to get through the scar tissue around her heart."

"*Jude* hurt *you*?"

"Look at me, Nicole. Can't you see it? Yes, Jude hurt me!" Amanda shouted and then started to cry. The unwanted tears coursed down her cheeks, and she couldn't stop them. "Don't you get it? Your pain isn't Sara's fault or my fault or even your fault. If you want to blame someone, blame fucking Jude!"

Amanda squeezed her eyes tight and prepared to

die. She had poked the bear with the truth, and now she had to suffer the consequences. She waited and waited, but all she heard was a crow squawking from a distant tree and Moss's heavy breathing. When eventually she dared to look, Moss was trembling and crying.

Trembling and trigger fingers didn't mix. "Please, put the gun down," Amanda whimpered. "It'll be all right."

Moss's eyes were rimmed with red. She opened and closed her mouth several times and then said, "I'm sorry. I'm sick."

"It'll be all right. Please, put the gun down."

Amanda waited and waited. Slowly, Moss lowered her gun arm and placed the pistol beside her on the ledge. At the same time, Moss carefully lifted one leg, and then the other across the wall, until she was looking outward, toward the overgrown fields below.

"No!" Amanda screamed when Moss raised both arms, like a bird who will never fly, and bowed her head. Amanda lunged forward, closing the distance between them, and threw her arms around Moss's waist. For one suspended moment, as their balance teetered outward and Amanda's head spun, it seemed they would both go over. Then, holding on tighter, Amanda leaned backward into freefall. She braced her sneakers against the inner wall and shoved with all her might, until the equilibrium shifted, and she fell onto the roof with Moss's considerable weight falling   on top of her. Had her ribs cracked? She didn't know, didn't care. She was winded, laughing hysterically, with Moss sobbing in her arms.

It was over.

Chapter Forty-three

Mixed feelings...

T hat afternoon, room 227 was like Grand Central Station, according to Maya and Shar, the only ones who had spent significant time in New York City. The Cat Couple was still there, after all the others left, and they vowed to stay until visiting hours ended at ten. Even Velma, who had started her shift at eight p.m., wouldn't dare try to evict Amanda, who was there for the duration.

Amanda secretly hoped the girls would leave sooner because Sara was exhausted from worry. Amanda was bone-tired after the episode on the roof, and she'd told no one how badly her ribs ached. She knew they weren't broken or cracked, but she'd have a major bruise, which Sara would discover eventually, but not tonight.

"I still don't know how you got off that roof," Sara said. "Sokolsky had taken our phones, and that stupid burner he gave us was here on my bed stand."

"Believe it or not, Moss let me use hers, so I called Lori. Lori told her dad, Judd told security, and they rescued us pretty fast." In fact, Amanda had been stunned when Moss handed her the cellphone; the gesture was second only to the moment when Moss gave up her gun. Since she couldn't call Sara, luckily, she had recalled Lori's number from staring at it so often during the revenge porn incident.

"So did Lori and Judd meet the infamous Nicole Moss during the arrest?" Maya asked.

"Nope. As it stands, I'm the only one in this room who has actually met Jude's biology teacher," Amanda said. "And I hope to never meet her again."

Sara broke into tears for the umpteenth time since Amanda's safe return. "I'm so sorry, babe. I can't imagine how awful it was for you." Maya and Shar echoed Sara's sentiments and gazed mournfully at Amanda.

If they only knew! If Amanda had her way, only Sara would ever learn the whole truth. The life-threatening confrontation had been horrendous, and Amanda knew she'd have nightmares for weeks to come, but the arrest had been even worse. After they toppled back onto the roof, Moss had broken completely. It seemed she had recognized Jude's lies. Coupled with the months of depression, loss, and the consequences of her own criminal behaviors, Jude's betrayal was the last straw. Moss's future looked bleak beyond comprehension. It was painful to witness, and Amanda took no joy in it.

Shar said, "I assume you guys will press charges?"

"Absolutely!" Sara answered angrily. "After what she put us through, especially Mandy? I hope they throw away the key!"

"Mandy, how do you feel about prosecuting Moss?" Maya asked.

Heat crawled up Amanda's neck as she struggled to formulate a response. Yes, she wanted Moss punished, but not in the way they supposed. They had not witnessed Moss's complete disintegration, how her hand trembled when she handed over the gun, and then held her wrists together in anticipation of handcuffs, and all the while kept repeating the same mantra directly to Amanda: "I'm sick. I'm sorry. Forgive me."

"I'm not sure how I feel about a prosecution," Amanda told Maya. "I have mixed feelings." During the arrest, Amanda had said nothing to implicate Moss because Moss did it on her own. She had confessed to the email terror campaign, the poisoning, and to threatening Amanda at gunpoint. Amanda suspected Moss would plead guilty, but if they put her on a witness stand, Amanda would be truthful, but again, take no pleasure in it.

Amanda was relieved when Maya laughed and abruptly changed the subject:

"Hey, did you see the look on Sokolsky's face? He was embarrassed and pissed as hell. I bet he wished he made that collar himself."

"No doubt," Amanda agreed. Sokolsky had barged in while Lori and Judd were still there. He'd been more rumpled, rude, and agitated than usual as he described confronting Sara's former patient Jane Doe at her aunt's lake house only to discover Jane's airtight alibi. Jane had been out of town when the poisoned dolls arrived on their doorstep, leaving Sokolsky with egg on his face. "He'll get over it." Amanda giggled. "At least we got our phones back."

"But I'll have a lot of explaining to do when I go back to the clinic." Sara moaned.

In the lull that ensued, as Amanda explored her feelings regarding Moss's fate, Shar walked to the big window and closed the drapes to the night that had fallen one hour too early. Amanda was relieved to not see the roof beyond the window glass. She hoped to never see such a roof again.

"It was fun meeting Judd and Lori," Shar said.

"Judd's a great guy, but I could tell he wished he was wearing his sheriff's hat today. It made him crazy not being an official part of the search, rescue, and takedown. He obviously adores you guys."

Maya chuckled. "And Lori's full of herself, right? She's spunky, passionate, impulsive, and headstrong—all the things you're supposed to be when you're a teenager. She reminds me of me at her age."

"Ha, ha. *You* were a good girl, Maya Hunter," Shar teased. "You got good grades, good manners, and never acted out. Your mama told me so."

"And I suppose *you* were a wild-eyed rebel, Sharon Williams?" Maya pushed back. "You were the squeaky-clean, cheerleader, cotillion debutante, sorority girl, and don't go telling our friends any different!"

Amanda felt a headache coming on, and by the way Sara was squeezing her eyes open and shut, Amanda suspected she was getting an eye migraine. "Look, guys, as much as I love you, I think we both need some peace and quiet."

"I can take a hint." Maya winked. "We'll get out of your hair ASAP, but first, you are going home tomorrow, right, Sara?"

"Right. They're cutting me loose."

Amanda added, "But there'll be a welcoming party waiting at our condo. Judd and Lori will be gone by then, but the rest of the family will be there with flowers, balloons, and casseroles."

"But you wish they wouldn't be?" Shar smiled. "I get it. You want to be alone to regroup, and Goddess knows, you deserve it."

"Yes, we do," Sara quietly agreed. "Are you going back to D.C.?"

"I'm afraid so," Shar said. "We'll hang out in

Washington until the holiday recess and be home for Thanksgiving. Can you join us for turkey day?"

Sara glanced at Amanda. "Love to, but I doubt it. My folks will be back from Puerto Rico, then there's Mandy's family..."

"Say no more." Maya held up a graceful hand. "But we'll make a firm date for dinner, soon as you're ready."

Minutes later, after hugs, kisses, and well-wishes all around, Maya and Shar left, leaving the wounded warriors alone in a vacuum of sweet silence.

❧ ❧ ❧ ❧

Sara took the migraine pill Mandy gave her and felt blessed, spacey relief. They shared a turkey sandwich from Sara's dinner tray and simply gazed at each other until Kayla came to say goodbye. She caught them holding hands.

"Sara, your hands look much better." Kayla stared at their entwined fingers.

"They feel better. When will I be able to play the piano?"

"You'll be able to play real well in about two weeks," Kayla said.

"Cool, thanks! I always wanted to play a musical instrument."

Sara watched in smug delight as Mandy's jaw dropped and Kayla gulped, beaten at her own game.

"That's lame, Sara." Kayla pouted. "Like, it's an old dad joke."

"Like, you're right." Sara grinned. "I'm gonna miss you, kid."

"I'll miss you, too, but don't make me mad

because I'm running out of patients."

Three hours later, when the lights were low and the hospital was quiet, Sara scooted over in her narrow bed and lifted the covers. She stroked Mandy's mussed hair off her forehead. "Do you think we can both fit in this bed?"

Mandy opened her sleepy eyes. "What about Velma?"

"They promised no more bed checks tonight. We'll be alone, babe. What do you say?"

Mandy climbed stiffly out of the recliner and sat on the edge of the bed. Sara knew she was hurting, physically and emotionally, and they'd said very little to each other about the day's trauma. Sara figured they didn't need to talk, not now. It would all come out in good time, when they were both ready.

Mandy took off her sneakers and jeans, left them in a pile on the floor, and then eased herself into the bed beside Sara.

"Your feet are cold," Sara whispered.

"Yeah, well, you're hot," Mandy murmured as she stretched her long length against Sara, while looping one arm around and under Sara's breasts, hanging on to keep from falling off the edge.

It felt sublime and deliriously right to fit together so naturally. Sara clumsily tucked the sheet around Mandy, securing her as best she could, and then slowly let out the breath she'd been holding throughout the long, impossible week.

Their bodies melted together and relaxed. She felt Mandy's heartbeats and warm puffs of Mandy's breath on her shoulder. She realized Mandy was conflicted about Moss and how she should be punished, but Sara was conflicted, too. Did you punish an addict for relapsing to drugs? Or a mentally ill patient for acting crazy? Sara blamed Jude and always would. Jude should come with a warning: hazardous to your health. But all that was for another day, a conversation for when they were less raw. Now all they needed was healing love, and as Sara drifted into sleep, she felt something she had not felt in days...

Safe.

Chapter Forty-four

Thanksgiving...

Thanksgiving dawned sunny and warm, very different from the cold, gray holidays Amanda remembered from her childhood in Pennsylvania. She and Sara would be feasting at the lake house today, gobbling turkey and the works. Tomorrow they would eat at the Orlandos' since Sara's folks had returned from Puerto Rico. They'd have *pernil*, roasted pork shoulder, and *arroz con gandules*, rice with pigeon peas. It would take more than a walk in the park to erase all those calories, but for Amanda, the walk would be the main course. She had been planning it for days. She was fully prepared. It was now—or never.

The glorious weather inspired Mom and Trout to eat at the big rickety picnic table on the deck overlooking the lake, and the whole gang was assembled. Trout, the only teetotaler in the group, made the toast counting their blessings and ending with "We have so much to be thankful for," words aimed directly at Amanda and Sara.

"Hear, hear!" Mom cheered, joined by Ginny, Trev, and Lissa.

Amanda and Sara locked gazes as they clinked their wine glasses together. "Thankful" didn't begin to cover it. Sara had left the hospital only sixteen days ago, and so much had happened since then. Sara's hands were fully healed, although she was not miraculously able to play the piano. They were both back at work, Amanda in her studio and Sara at the clinic, where nobody blamed her for inconveniencing Jane Doe, not even Dr. Angela Yee. They had shared a birthday cake with Tammy Tillman, made a firm dinner date with Maya and Shar for the following week, and Amanda's nightmares were occurring less frequently.

Dr. Nicole Moss had pleaded guilty, as expected. She had lost her job, lost her license to carry, and was serving a six-month mandatory sentence at a secure psychiatric facility. Sara and Yee had put in a good word for Moss at her commitment hearing, predicting that the brilliant doctor could be rehabilitated with meds, intense counseling, and supervised visits from her son. All in all, it was a good outcome, one Amanda and Sara could live with.

"I wish Lori and Judd were here with us," Lissa said.

"Me too, pumpkin." Trout ruffled his granddaughter's curly red hair. "Maybe the whole Taylor clan can join us next year."

Friends and family were the biggest reason to be thankful, Amanda thought. During their week of horror, so many people from her and Sara's past life had come onstage to support them in countless different ways. Characters from Asheville, Hatteras, Charlotte, and "Mayberry," not to mention new friends like Red and Gina, had united for a grand curtain call, reminding Amanda of the rich history she and Sara already shared.

But there was so much more history to be made, so as soon as the meal was over and the dishes had been cleared, Amanda patted her full tummy and said, "I need some exercise. Sara and I are gonna take off for an hour or two for a walk in Lake Norman State Park."

"We are?" Sara did a double-take.

"Yes, we are." Amanda glared at the family, daring anyone to object or ask to tag along. No one did. "We'll be back in time for dessert," she added before hustling Sara out the door.

≈≈≈≈

Sara sat back and allowed Mandy to drive her Miata since Mandy knew the way and this was her gig. As they drove north on Perth Road, through rolling countryside and crossing several bridges over Lake Norman, she realized how much the road had changed since they'd last come this way. Water still sparkled, and a few pristine forests remained on either side of the winding road, but there were many new housing developments she'd never seen before.

"This is where it all began for Mom and Trout—this park," Mandy said as they made a left onto State Park Road. "Mom's very first client in North Carolina was murdered here and dropped off his dock into the lake. Mom met Trout at his funeral."

"Charming," Sara commented wryly. "Not the most romantic start for a relationship."

"Yeah, but you know Mom, the amateur sleuth. Poking her nose in where it didn't belong won her the man of her dreams."

"You are too much like her, Mandy."

"Not any more. I'm done with playing detective."

Sara smiled and believed her. They'd had enough bad excitement to last a lifetime. As they entered the huge park, passing through stands of towering pines, ignoring the turn-offs to the campsites and the ranger

station, she wasn't surprised when Mandy crossed a
bridge, turned toward the boat launching site, and then
parked along the road where they could pick up the
hiking trails.

This wasn't the way Sara had envisioned the day
unfolding. She had pictured a quiet moment together
in the gazebo on Trout's waterfront, but no problem,
she was flexible and prepared. It was now—or never.

❧ ❧ ❧ ❧

As they walked up the rugged path leading
through a dense forest, Amanda's palms were sweating,
and she was uncommonly nervous. In a good way. She
hoped her timing would be perfect and that they'd
reach the summit overlooking the lake at precisely the
right moment. She was hyper aware of Sara trudging a
few paces behind her, huffing and puffing. Amanda's
own heart was racing, and her stomach was doing flip-
flops and not because it was overstuffed with turkey.

They were both panting, so when Sara beckoned
for a rest stop, Amanda obliged, and they sat on two
big rocks.

"Did you check out the postcards Carl and Ron
sent from Paris?" Sara asked.

"Yeah, the Eiffel Tower and Moulin Rouge. Kinda
cheesy, don't you think? I thought they'd be the Paris
Opera and Louvre sort of tourists."

Sara laughed. "Oh, yeah? How would you like to
spend your honeymoon, babe? Having fun or soaking
up culture?"

Mandy stared up at the treetops. "I'd like to go to
Puerto Rico. I've never seen your family's island."

The notion seemed to surprise Sara and move

her because her eyes got moist, and she reached for Amanda's hand. "C'mon, we better get moving if we want to reach the top and get home in time for dessert."

Amanda glanced at her watch as they reached the final bend, sweeping through the underbrush that terminated in a rock shelf overlooking a wide sweep of Lake Norman. They had discovered this amazing view several years ago, purely by chance, and considered it their secret place. Of course, it wasn't secret, judging by the litter of cigarette butts and an empty plastic water bottle some fool had left behind, but it was still special.

It was four fifteen, about forty-five minutes until sunset, that golden, magical time when shadows were long, with plenty of light still left in the sky. This twist of land faced west, and sure enough, the pale, pearly hues of pink and violet that tinted the horizon were also mirrored in the lake. It was beautiful and perfect.

Amanda took a deep breath, leaned over, and picked up the offending water bottle and stashed it away in her bag. Then, instead of standing, she dropped to one knee, dug into her pocket, and brought out Grandma Vivian's engagement ring. Her hand trembled as she gazed up into Sara's shocked eyes.

Amanda held out the ring. "Will you marry me, Sara?"

It seemed time stood still. Through the nervous buzzing in her ears, she heard waves lapping the shore and birds chirping in the forest. Her heart stood still, as well.

"Maybe..." Sara whispered as she dug into her pocket and brought out a second ring. She dropped to both knees, facing Amanda. "I will marry you if you marry me."

Amanda was speechless. The ring was obviously

custom-made, an eternity design. Where had it come from? "Yes, I will marry you." She gasped, holding out her left hand.

They slipped rings onto each other's fingers at precisely the same moment, both now in tears. Amanda was delirious with happiness. She hadn't expected it to play out this way, with Sara stealing some of her thunder, the way she'd stolen her heart.

After Amanda's ears cleared, she heard, along with the waves and the birds, a weird buzzing directly overhead. They looked up and saw a drone hovering less than a hundred feet above their heads, moving in for a close-up, spying on their private proposals.

Sara laughed and wiped her eyes with her sleeve. "It must be filming real estate for an ad. But it's Thanksgiving, don't these people have a life?"

Amanda took her fiancée's hand and pulled her upright, so they were both standing. She grinned and waved at the drone. "It's filming us, Sara. I hired it. I'm glad we both said *yes* because this moment will be recorded for posterity."

Sara went from shock to a hysterical fit of the giggles. "What do you mean *posterity*? Do you want us to have kids?"

"Not necessarily, but I wouldn't mind having a dog."

Author's note

Twenty-five years ago, my partner Susan and I sat on the old screened porch of the lake cottage we had just purchased and discussed a mystery series I wanted to write about a Realtor, Diana Rittenhouse, who moves to North Carolina from Philadelphia (just like we did). Diana would explore her new state, get into all kinds of trouble, and wonder how she would ever fit in (just like we did, minus the trouble).

Five novels later, the series was taken over by Diana's lesbian daughter, Amanda, who found her own adventures and wondered how she would fit in, and like her mother, hoped to find love.

It was a bittersweet moment when I wrote the last word of *Blue Silk Stalkings*, the sixth and final book in the Amanda series. (A total of eleven novels in all). In the five Diana books, the last word was always "dog," so it seemed fitting that "dog" should be the very last word from Amanda's mouth, bringing the saga full circle.

Now, all these years later, Susan and I are married (they finally made it legal), we have enjoyed a succession of six different dogs, and North Carolina feels like home. I will miss all the characters in the series, who seem like family and have played a big role in my life, but don't be surprised to see them make cameo appearances in my new Red Calendar series, a police procedural.

As always, thanks to my faithful readers. You

have the starring role and make my writing complete. I love hearing from you and appreciate your feedback and reviews. You can see all my work at katemerrillbooks. com. Or contact me at katemerrillbooks@gmail.com.

Happy reading,
Love, Kate

Other Books by Kate Merrill

Romance
Northern Lights (as Christie Cole)
Flames of Summer
Beloved Enemy (as Elizabeth Whitaker)
Framed

Diana Rittenhouse Mystery Series
A Lethal Listing
Blood Brothers
Crimes of Commission
Dooley Is Dead
Buyer Beware

Amanda Rittenhouse Mystery Series
Murder at Metrolina
Homicide in Hatteras
Murder at Midterm
Assault in Asheville
The Mayberry Murders
Blue Silk Stalkings

Red Calendar Mystery Series
The True Love Club

Miss Addie's Gift: Portrait of an American Folk Artist

Too Many Damn Yankees in Queen Charlotte's Court
A Collection of Short Stories

Kate, a longtime art gallery owner and passionate writer,

lives with her family on a lake in North Carolina. When she is not writing or creating driftwood sculpture, she enjoys swimming, boating, and playing with her cats.